Indian Wood

A MYSTERY OF THE LOST COLONY

OF ROANOKE ISLAND

RICHARD FOLSOM

ISBN: 1-4196-9219-4
ISBN-13: 9781419692192

Visit www.booksurge.com to order additional copies.

In Memoriam

Dr. Herbert Paschal

A fine history professor

Indian Wood

Indian Wood

Part One

Old Dixie

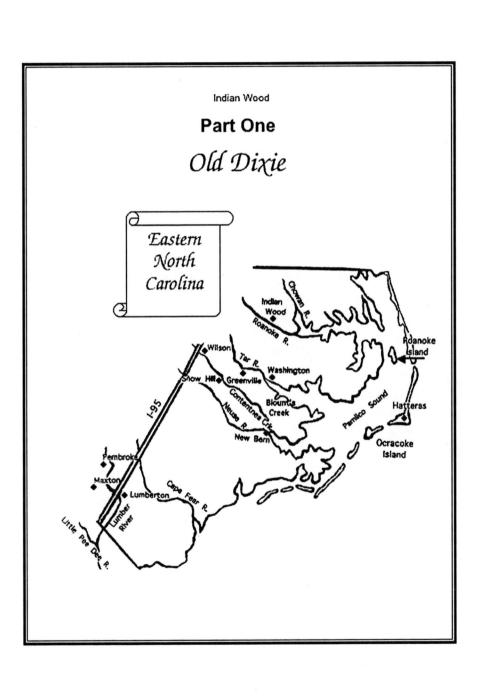

Eastern North Carolina

THE RALLY

Maxton, NC   January 18, 1958

"I'm Carl Lee Bowden, with *The Fayetteville Times*."

"Luther Surles, *Charlotte Observer*," the other reporter answered, and the two young men shook hands under a cold sheet of clouds hiding the moon and stars.

"You ever cover a Klan rally before?"

Luther's dark blue eyes drifted over the harvested cornfield. He listened to the sound of burlap being nailed to a large wooden cross in preparation for the evening cross burning. "A couple, I guess, how about you?"

"This is my first one. And to tell you the truth, it's a little scary the way they carry guns right out in the open." His voice trailed off, as one of the Klansmen walked by with a large pistol strapped to his side.

Luther motioned Carl over to the side of a green and white Chevy Bel Air parked in the middle of the field. "Only saw a few guns at the last rally I covered, but this one's different. It's supposed to be a showdown between the Klan and the *Lumbee Indians*."

Carl looked curiously at his new friend. "I thought the Klan only burned crosses to scare negroes."

Luther's head fell to the side, his long narrow face barely visible in the moonless night. "You must be from out of state, Carl?"

"Georgia," he responded. "And there's plenty of Klan activity there. I just never heard of them bothering Indians."

"But you don't have any Lumbee Indians in Georgia. That's the difference." Before Carl could ask another question, Luther turned away to the sounds in the field.

"Douse her good with kerosene, boys, and get her upright," one of the Klan leaders yelled to his men. "And the rest of you fetch yer robes and them flags."

Carl pulled on Luther's arm to turn him back around, "I don't understand. Why does the Klan want to have a rally to scare the Lumbees?"

"Miscegenation," whispered Luther, "mixing of the races. Haven't you heard that the Lumbees claim to be descendants of the *Lost Colonists of Roanoke Island?*"

Carl's face suddenly lit up. "Yeh, sure, I've heard that. So these are the people, the Lumbee Indians."

Luther nodded gently and smiled. 'Don't tell me *The Times* sent you out here with that little flash bulb camera and didn't give you any background information?"

Carl grinned innocently. "They gave me some, but to tell you the truth, Luther, I'm new. Just got out of Chapel Hill last semester, and this is my first real job. Whoever they had scheduled to cover this story got sick at the last minute, so they called me. I mean, why not, I've got to learn sometime."

Luther smiled at the lanky twenty-one year old, just a few years younger than himself, then slapped him on the shoulder. "That's right, why not?" Then he turned his head cautiously and watched as the Klansmen continued preparations for the rally.

"Out of the ways, boys," a voice called out as a late model sedan backed slowly between broken-down corn stalks to an area where the men were tacking burlap on a wooden cross. A middle-aged driver got out and pulled the trunk lid up, exposing a small greasy electrical generator. While he poured gasoline into the funnel, an old flat board Ford pulled into the center of the field. Two men lifted a small podium and portable P.A. system to the back of the truck for the guest speaker. 'Catfish' Cole, a segregationist preacher and Grand Dragon of the South Carolina Klan, was in Robeson County to deliver one of his firebrand sermons.

Carl's thoughts drifted to the connection between the Lumbee Indians and the Lost Colony. "Luther," he whispered to get his new friend's attention. "Is there any proof the Lumbees are descended from the Lost Colonists?"

Without taking his eyes off the activity in the field, Luther replied. "Mostly anecdotal; I mean it's nothing you would call hard evidence."

"Like what?" Carl asked, hoping to learn more of their history.

"Wait a minute," teased Luther. "You'll get all the background for my story if I tell you what I've found out."

Carl grinned innocently, "I'm sorry, I'm not trying to steal your information. It's just that I'm really interested. But you don't have to tell me, I understand."

Luther leaned back easily against the car and smiled as he watched Carl's breath turn to mist and disappear in the darkness. "Well, it's not really a secret, Carl. Any Lumbee in these parts could tell you the whole story, especially old man Bryant at *The Lumberton Herald*." He looked back out toward the field and continued. "They say it's part of their oral tradition, that it's been passed down for nearly four hundred years."

"No kidding," Carl responded with boyish enthusiasm. "What does it say?"

"Seems to have started back in the 1580's when a fella named Walter Raleigh got some of his friends together and sent a group of settlers to North Carolina's Outer Banks, Roanoke Island, in particular. About the time they got there, in 1587, a war was about to break out between England and Spain. So, Queen Elizabeth wouldn't let any ships leave to re-supply the colony. By the time the war was over, and a ship got back to Roanoke, in 1590, the colony had disappeared. Not a man, woman or child was ever heard from again, and that's the mystery of the Lost Colony."

Carl grinned innocently as he asked the same old question that everyone else had for hundreds of years. "What do they think happened to them?"

Luther reached inside his coat and pulled out a wrinkled pack of Camels. He offered a cigarette to Carl that was politely declined, then pulled one out and tapped the end on the back of his hand to firm up the tobacco. "There have been a lot of theories, but the only one that seems to make any sense is that they moved inland to live with the Indians. Eventually, they intermarried and were absorbed into the Indian culture."

"Is there any kind of historical record..." but before Carl could finish the question Luther responded.

"Not yet, I mean nothing so far to connect the Lumbees to the Lost Colonists." He paused while he pulled out a small pack of matches with one hand and tucked the cigarettes away with the other. Then he pulled a paper match away from its holder and scratched it along a grainy surface until a small flame erupted. Pressing the fire against the burly end of the tobacco he drew deeply, and the tip began to glow in the darkness. Luther reached up with his left hand, caught the cigarette between two fingers and exhaled, then watched as the smoke curled softly from his nostrils.

"The Lumbees claim it was their ancestors, the Croatans from the Outer Banks of North Carolina, that befriended the English when they came to start their colony. And later, when the colonists were starving and dying at Roanoke, it was their ancestors that took them in, married with them and absorbed them into their tribe."

"What part of the Outer Banks?" Carl asked.

"You heard of a place called Buxton out at Cape Hatteras?" Carl nodded his head as Luther continued. "Well, Hattorask is the old Indian name for that part of the Outer Banks."

"But shouldn't there be some kind of evidence?" Carl asked.

Luther drew lightly on his cigarette and stared out into the field. "Like I said, just some anecdotal stuff."

"Like what?" pleaded Carl.

Luther stood quietly for a moment watching the Klansmen mill about in the field. It seemed odd that only fifty or so had shown up for the rally when it had been reported that hundreds would descend on Robeson County this Saturday night. Again, he drew deeply on the cigarette and turned back toward Carl. "A couple of things; one story about a surveying party that floated down a creek in the 1730s and found 'a wild and lawless people' living in the swamps of Robeson County." Then he looked at Carl with a grin and paused as if collecting his thoughts.

"Oh yeh, and another thing about the first U.S. census in 1790. Seems they found a whole bunch of Lost Colony names among some people living in the swamps along the Lumber River, that had blue eyes and could speak the Queen's English." Then he looked at Carl with curious eyes. "Sound like a coincidence to you?"

Carl watched as Luther puffed on the last bit of his Camel then asked, "But where did those people living in the swamps come from?"

Luther tossed the butt down on the cold ground and squashed it into the dirt. "They say some of the coastal Indians of North and South Carolina used the swamps of the upper Pee Dee River to get away from the diseases and constant fighting with the white settlers, and even warring with their own neighbors. And escaped Negro slaves from around Charleston would follow the Little Pee Dee River up to where Drowning Creek enters and take refuge in the swamps. So, the surveyor may have been right, probably was a 'mixed breed of people' he found there in the 1730s."

"But what about the English influence, how did it get into the swamps?"

"Now that's another part of the mystery, Carl, and if you ever find an answer to that question, there are a lot of people who would like to know."

Carl pulled up beside Luther, leaning back on the new Chevy, conjuring up images of Indians drowning in swift black water and surveyors fleeing for their lives. "Okay, let's say that maybe the Lumbees are somehow descended from at least some of the Lost Colonists. Then why did they relocate over 200 miles from Roanoke Island to live in the swamps of Robeson County?"

Luther grinned back at him, "Now that's another part of the mystery, and if you ever find out the answer," but before he finished Carl interrupted.

"There are a lot of people who would like to know," he said mockingly.

"Most of all the Lumbees," Luther added seriously. "They're a people without a history. There's no Mayflower in their background, and no family tree to tie them all together. All they have is their oral traditions that have been passed down through generations of retelling. And now maybe you can understand why they're so fired up that the Klan would come here and try to deny them the single thread of history which might link them to their English and Indian ancestors."

Carl leaned gently against the car, considering the impact of the Klan rally on the Lumbees. It was one thing to insult them by staging a cross burning in their community, but to deny them their heritage may be too much to bear. And neither man heard the icy footsteps that came up behind them.

"Git chor ass off muh car, boy!"

Carl turned quickly and was stunned by the sight of a tall demon bathed in white, with eyes glaring from beneath a mask that rose to a point above his head. He glanced quickly toward Luther who was also caught off guard by the Klansman.

"I'm talkin' to you, Boy. I gotta wife and child in that car yer leanin' on, and I don't want no strangers hangin' round, ya hear?"

Glancing down through the windshield Carl could see a young woman sitting quietly in the front seat, and to her side a shock of red hair peering over the dash. It struck him as odd that a Klansman would bring his family to a cross burning, much less one that could easily be marred by violence. He turned away from the small innocent eyes to face the demon. "I'm sorry, we didn't see them."

Then from under the robe a sawed-off shotgun appeared, swinging in front of Carl's face and landing in the crook of the Klansman's arm. "Now you two git and we won't say n'more about this."

The reporters responded by quickly walking away. "Cocky bastard," whispered Carl. "Does the Klan hate everyone?"

"Why no, son," teased Luther. "As long as your skin's white, and you act right, you can be one of the good ole' boys, too," and they laughed quietly together.

"But to be truthful, Carl, the Klan's been getting their way in this state for some years now. So long as they don't kill anyone the law has sort of been looking the other way. And that kind of latent permission breeds power. They think that everything they do is for the good of the country, and that no one is going to stop them."

"Not even the law?" Carl asked.

"Don't you know the law's got legal ways of closing its eyes," Luther responded with a cynical grin.

Before Luther could say anymore, a voice rose from the field where the men had been soaking the cross with kerosene. "You got that generator hooked up yet, Willard?"

Just ahead of them a man rose from behind the trunk lid of the black car. "'Bout another minute here and we'll be ready to go."

A few steps away the symbol of prejudice and fear began to slowly rise and tower over the frozen cornrows. As the wooden cross fell into the posthole and was secured upright, the Klansmen who had been milling about suddenly came to life. Their voices rose with Hollywood war hoops to mock the Lumbee Indians. Guns that had been carried low were now raised, and a boisterous atmosphere took over the field.

While the transformation was taking place, all the reporters withdrew to the outside fringe, awaiting the start of the rally. A voice screamed above the others, "Doggone it, Willard, get the sumbitch goin'! Catfish is gonna be here any minute!"

Willard found the starter rope and wound it tightly around the coil. With a loud grunt he pulled hard, but the generator sputtered as if choking on the greasy gasoline. He eased his leather hunting cap back on his head, pulled up the right sleeve of his jacket and began to wind the rope around the starter again. With another loud grunt he ripped the cord away, and the generator began to rumble to life.

A bare light bulb dangled by a long cord over one arm of the cross. As the generator increased power it flickered to life, exposing the burlap wrapped symbol in a ghostly glare. An American flag, Confederate flag and 'KKK' banner were posted like sentinels on either side of the podium on back of the truck. Cheers and war hoops rose up to accompany the eerie light that bathed the field.

Carl put a fresh bulb in his flash unit, held his camera above the heads of the other reporters in front of him and shot as much as he could from that position. Then he stooped down to put in a new bulb when Luther suddenly grabbed his arm.

"Listen, do you hear that rumbling sound?"

Carl paused a moment to sort the fake war hoops of the Klansmen from the other reporter's question. "It's the generator, isn't it?"

Luther's head turned slightly as if to catch a sound on the wind. "I don't think so, Carl. It's coming from out there."

Some of the other reporters heard the low rumbling sounds coming from Hayes Pond Road and turned their attention in that direction. "Sounds like motors, lots of them," Carl added.

The noise in the center of the field began to die away as the Klansmen became aware of the caravan of vehicles moving slowly along the roadway beside them. Finally the procession came to a halt, and there was silence as doors began to open and men fell out in small groups. Then the terrifying sound of breeches being opened and the soft clinking of shells being chambered rolled up and down the line of vehicles.

A numb panic swept the cornrows as the reporters and Klansmen realized what was happening. A ragged militia of two hundred Lumbee Indians stood along the shoulder of the highway, ready to defend the honor of their tribe.

"Good Lord," came a voice from among the reporters. "Will you look at that?"

Somewhere along the roadway a voice shouted, and the line of men crossed the roadside ditch. They began taking slow deliberate strides through the field. Knee-high corn stalks from last fall's harvest crackled underfoot as they came within twenty yards of the rally area. Then the ends of the line began to move slowly around to encircle the reporters and Klansmen.

"Bobby," shouted one of the Klan leaders. "You run tell Catfish to stay put," and the young man ran off to warn the Grand Dragon.

Three Lumbee men stepped away from their ranks. With grim faces, they walked through the reporters, right up to the burlap-wrapped cross, with a bare light bulb swinging in the cold January breeze. They stood for a moment, face-to-face with the Klansmen. Then a shoving argument broke out, and one of the Indians raised his weapon till it pointed toward the glaring light. He pulled the pump lever back to release a shell into the chamber, and as the clinking metal arm rose back into position, a voice yelled out from among the Klansmen, "Lookout, he's gonna shoot!"

Fire erupted from the barrel of the shotgun and a load of birdshot ripped through the glass bulb, casting the field in darkness. For a frozen moment the only sound to be heard was the sputtering rumble of the generator. Realizing what was about to happen, Luther and Carl dropped onto the cold hard ground. Then in unison, hundreds of weapons carried by the Lumbees opened fire.

A deafening roar took over the field as strobe-like muzzle flashes lit up the night. Carl looked to his left to find Luther kneeling against the front of a car. Then he raised his head slightly to survey the madness in the field. Through smoke-filled flashing light he could see men running in every direction, falling over themselves as they stripped away long flowing robes. Some of the Klansmen dove into the woods behind the cross while others ran wildly toward the Maxton highway. And those who had reached that point were cranking their cars and speeding off into the darkness.

Amid the flashing roar of gunfire, Carl expected to see many wounded Klansmen and Indians, but to his amazement, no one appeared injured. As he continued to observe the Lumbees he suddenly realized the wisdom of their strategy. They were not firing at anyone, but up into the cold dark air. They had not come to kill the Klansmen, but to scare and intimidate them as few had ever done before.

State patrol cars and Robeson County Sheriff vehicles quickly arrived on the scene. A whiff of tear gas drifted over the field as officers collected the hidden Klansmen and hurriedly escorted them back to their own cars and trucks.

Carl stood and surveyed the scene. Occasional shots continued to ring out as the Indians began celebrating their victory. One of them struck a match to the kerosene soaked rags hanging on the cross, and flames began licking up the sides until it became a torch. In just a few minutes, the flaming cross was transformed from a symbol of Klan hatred into one of Lumbee triumph.

In the flickering light everyone could see the complete success of the Indians' plan. Klan banners and robes lay scattered about the field, including the flags that had flanked the podium. An older Lumbee wearing a 'VFW' hat picked up the American flag that had fallen off the back of the flatbed. He carefully placed it upright in the ground, and 'Old Glory' began waving in the breeze. But the confederate war flag was treated with less respect.

After cutting the flag away from its pole, several of the younger men threw ole' Dixie to the ground and began dancing on what had become to them a symbol of hatred and fear. Their anger spent, they dangled it over the end of a pole then held it up to the burning cross until it, too, burst into flame. Two other men ran across the field with the red and white Klan banner flowing over their shoulders. It was their trophy, a souvenir of victory.

Luther looked over toward Carl who was still shaking dirt from his clothing. "What the hell just happened?"

"Damn near got shot and run over," Carl replied excitedly. Then he smiled from ear to ear. "Can you believe this? They ran the Klan right out of here."

Luther grinned back as they turned to watch the Lumbees. Two men threw the looped end of a long heavy rope over the top of the flaming cross. They pulled quick and hard trying to topple the Klan symbol, but it seemed too deeply rooted in the soil. Other Indians came to help, while others encouraged them by chanting and cheering, but the flaming-cross resisted.

Just as it seemed the rope would burn through, a crackling sound was heard and the post finally split from the bottom. The men who had pulled so vigorously fell into a laughing heap and watched as the flames were nearly snuffed out by the impact.

Carl stared in amazement at the jagged piece of wood left upright in the ground, like a monument to the Indian victory. And now that it was over, it seemed a matter of arrogance on the part of the Klan to have held such a rally. 'Didn't they know there wasn't any proof whether the Lumbee oral history was even true?' Carl asked himself. 'But still,' he thought, 'there was much to admire about these Indians.'

'Where did they come from?' he asked himself as he popped another flash bulb into his camera. 'And if they are who they claim to be, then how did they get here?'

He didn't realize, in that moment, these would become the pivotal questions of his professional career. Carl could only smile curiously, as he

considered that he might be walking among some of the living descendants
of the Lost Colonists of Roanoke Island.

Indian Wood

Part Two

The Library

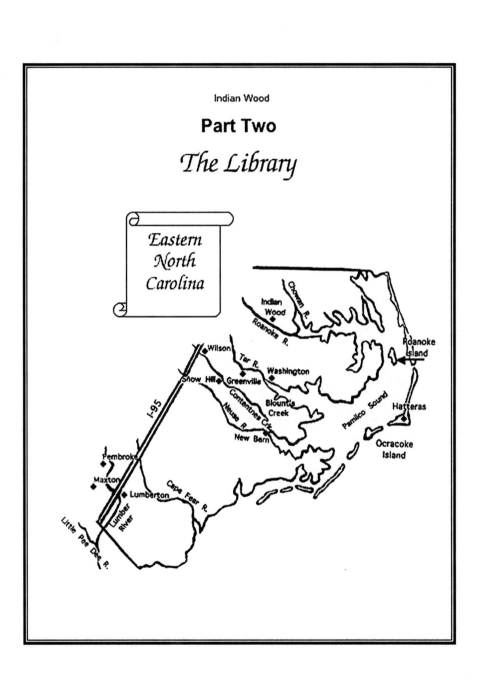

Eastern
North
Carolina

Indian Wood

Chowan R.

Roanoke R.

Roanoke Island

Wilson

Tar R.

Washington

Snow Hill

Greenville

I-95

Contentnea Cr.

Blounts Creek

Neuse R.

Pamlico Sound

Hatteras

New Bern

Ocracoke Island

Pembroke

Maxton

Lumberton

Cape Fear R.

Lumber River

Little Pee Dee R.

THE NORTH CAROLINA COLLECTION

A late afternoon breeze blew gently through the great oaks surrounding the green of East Carolina University. Small groups of students, laid out on blankets, caught the last warm rays of sunlight, as tree shadows drifted farther out over the grass and into volleyball games still being played.

Dr. Carl Lee Bowden, with black leather brief in tow, walked up the sidewalk toward a span of four Greek columns. He paused briefly at the old Joyner library entrance to enjoy the Sunday afternoon view of coeds snuggled up to young men, eyes fixed on each other as if they were alone in the world. Then he turned and stared at the short staircase leading up to the concourse entrance to the library. Thirty years before, while working on his master's degree, he sat on those same steps with fellow students discussing relevant topics of the day.

He turned for one last view of the mall and recalled long ago summer concerts. In those innocent days, even major artists would come to small college towns and play acoustic sets on grassy venues to adoring, starry-eyed college students. He thought of the young women he had escorted from the dorms that lined the north side of the green, to late night walks under the great oaks and the search for secluded areas on any part of the campus to consummate the affairs of firm young bodies.

So many friends and relationships of so long ago, how could one of them not have blossomed from romance into marriage? Then he reassured himself it was the imperatives of research that had come between him and the women in his life. Even though he knew they said it was his commitment to the frivolities of bachelorhood that kept him single all these years.

He set the heavily worn black leather briefcase at his feet and stretched his arms into the air, flexing a lean six-foot frame rigid for a moment. Then he concluded the pre- research ritual with a cavernous yawn that closed into a curious smile. He was thinking of his current love interest, a secret affair with a graduate student that had started with a common interest in the history of Roanoke Island and the Lost Colonists.

Roberta Locklear, a gentle Social Studies teacher from Cumberland County, was on sabbatical to complete her master's degree in history. She was tall, with dark brown hair and golden brown skin, and for a woman in her early forties offered a mature beauty and radiant smile to any man who caught her fancy. And for reasons Carl could not yet fathom, she had also never married.

The passion that erupted between them in the stacks of the library was spontaneous and intoxicating. Carl had discovered in Roberta an eidolon of joy, an elixir of intrigue that excited him with the memory of every moment they spent together. And for the first time, the history professor admitted that he needed a woman more than he needed to conduct research in any library.

But the relationship could not be discovered. Carl could be fired and his pending retirement jeopardized. And Roberta could lose her graduate assistant position in the history department. Even so, the possibility of discovery seemed to make the passion of their affair grow even stronger.

He leaned down and pulled up the scuffed leather case by its two looped handles. It was the same bag his oldest and best friend had given him on the day he graduated from UNC Chapel Hill with his doctorate. Luther Surles, a newspaper publisher in Washington, NC, pushed the briefcase toward him and said, "Here you go, Dr. Bowden." Luther was the first person to address him with his professoriate title. It was also the last time he ever did so. And even though they were close friends, Carl had not been able to tell Luther of the passionate woman that had entered his life.

Carl breezed through the concourse plaza and stepped inside the library. He continued along the main corridor toward the elevator that would take him up to the North Carolina Collection on the third floor. There he would take another elevator up to the *Special Collections* area of historical books, documents and artifacts. It was on the fourth floor, under the great rotunda, where much of his research and publishing efforts had often originated.

He glanced to his left at a familiar kiosk along the sidewall where a desk, lamp, and outlet for his laptop computer awaited him. In these kiosks serious scholars would often take up residence for days at a time. They pored over books and documents, searching for clues to mysteries secreted within intriguing pages only dedicated researchers could dare enjoy.

Carl pulled back the mahogany desk chair, sat down and laid his briefcase upright against the inside wall of the kiosk. From among the many items inside he pulled out one of his favorite books, a tattered old reprint of an 1857 volume, The History of North Carolina, Volume One, by Francis Hawks. The text focused on the period between the first voyage to Roanoke Island in 1584, and the fifth, and last voyage, in 1590. All the Roanoke Voyages were on behalf of Sir Walter Raleigh and his London investment company, seeking to plant the first English colony in the new world.

He enjoyed the manner in which Hawks had faithfully captured Thomas Hariot's beautiful Elizabethan prose in his rewriting of the Hakluyt narrative, A Brief and True Report of the New Found Land of Virginia. He was also pleased that Roberta had discovered the old book in an antiques shop in Raleigh and purchased it for him as a birthday present. It was filled with margin notations, written by scholars more than a hundred years before, and now it also contained some of his personal notes.

To Carl, Elizabethan English, as it was penned by those who had lived and spoken the tongue of William Shakespeare, was a pleasure to read. He thumbed through the pages, stopping to glance at the drawings of Secotan Indian villages by John White. The illustrator and amateur naturalist had been with Hariot at the military fort in 1585, and would be named governor of the company of men and women later known as the Lost Colony of Roanoke Island. But this was not the focus of Carl's efforts in the library this evening, and he reached further inside the old brief case.

Good storytelling and the gift of gab had always been two of Carl's natural talents. As a child he had used his vivid imagination to embellish historical events during 'Show and Tell' opportunities in front of his classmates. As a very young newspaper reporter he won an award for his first feature story on the night the Lumbee Indians ran the Ku Klux Klan out of Robeson County. Then later, as a high school teacher, he created and refined his 'storytelling as teaching' technique. And now at the university it made him one of the most sought-out professors on campus. Even non-history majors would choose his courses as electives just to experience the story telling charisma of Dr. Carl Lee Bowden.

It was an art form, to be able to convey the facts of history as a series of engaging stories, vignettes that held the attention of students as Carl punctuated the dates and locations of the story into their hearts and minds. And at the end of each story he would summarize the facts he expected them to remember, while students copied the information they would soon see again as part of an essay test. Those who listened, took notes and were able to render an effective retelling of the story were certain to score high and receive an excellent grade at course end. Those who missed too many classes or could not effectively recall the stories and facts often lost their way in the course and received poor grades. But the campus word on Dr. Bowden was come to class, enjoy his stories and the grades would take care of themselves.

Carl set the Hawks volume on the desk then looked back inside his briefcase for the growing ream of papers that would eventually become his novel. It pleased him every time he looked at the title, Arcadia of the New World. Inside those storied chapters he would describe the coastal native Americans as they were when the English Captains, Amadas and Barlowe, arrived in 1584 to scout the land of Arcadia and find a suitable site for Raleigh's new colony.

He closed his eyes and smiled to himself, recalling Oshanoa, one of the leading characters in his novel. In every way she was the perfect image of Roberta Locklear. Carl could not recall the moment she had become his muse. It seemed only a short time after agreeing to be an advisor for her thesis work on the Lost Colony that he was inspired to collect his own stories of what the indigenous Indian culture may have been like along the coastal rivers and sounds of North Carolina before the arrival of the English. And then a voice wafted like an echo on the wind, drawing him away from thoughts of Roberta, Oshanoa, and the feral forests of coastal North Carolina.

"Carl, are you okay?"

He opened his eyes, turned his head slightly and saw Ludie Worthington, the reference librarian for 'Special Collections' standing beside him. He smiled warmly, winked and said, "I was just day dreaming, Ludie, thinking about my new project."

"Uh huh," she responded knowingly. "Academic or carnal?" And she grinned mischievously at the professor. "I know you, Carl. You can't fool me. Remember when I first came to the library and you would sit over here and stare at my ass, every time I left the desk?" Then she laughed to herself. "And I thought you were just the cutest little professor on campus."

Carl leaned away from the librarian, looking her up and down and grinning appreciatively. She was a former college basketball player; thin, shapely and graceful, with a master's in Library Science and a doctorate in Special Collections, "You've still got it, Ludie."

"I know, Carl," she teased. "I want to keep the engine running in case I ever want to take her out for a spin, know what I mean?" Then she leaned in affectionately, "You sure enjoyed your test drive."

"Many test drives," he reminded her. "But you were the one who turned me down for the Biology professor."

Ludie shrugged her shoulders, "Yeh, I know, but ever since I was in high school, I've played both sides of the fence. And I always thought I would settle down with a man and have a normal relationship, but when Sherry invited me to her house for dinner," and she paused.

"I understand," Carl said. "And you two have been together for what, ten years?"

"Eleven," she corrected him. "And you don't seem to be suffering from a lack of female companionship. But this new one, Carl, she's really something. I mean that time I came into my office and found you two, her on the desk and you about to," then she paused. "Well, you have to at least suspect something is going on, Carl."

He smiled sheepishly, knowing Ludie was the one person on campus that he could confide in. "She may be the one, Ludie. I don't know. But it could be a disaster for us if anyone found out. I could be sanctioned, even fired, and she could be thrown out of the graduate program. I hope you understand how delicate this is."

She smiled at her once intimate friend. "I understand, Carl. You stood by me when the Library Director expressed concerns about Sherry and me coming out as a couple, and for that I would never turn on you." Then she grinned, "Sorry bastard. He never knew that at one time I had a thing for his wiry old ass," and she laughed to herself. "Oh," she added teasingly, "next time you use my office for a liaison with the brown haired lady, how about straightening up the papers on my desk when you're done?"

Then the smile faded and she got back to the business that had brought her over to the kiosk. "Here's a hard copy of the microfilmed master's thesis you wanted. I think you're going to like this. Paskil's thesis seems to support your theory about the Tuscarora Connection."

Carl's eyes widened in appreciation, "Really," he exclaimed as he took the small stack of papers from her hands and started thumbing through them.

"I hope you don't mind, Carl, but I've highlighted a few areas of interest, especially that part about the massacre at Indian Wood."

"So there was a massacre?"

"Well, according to Paskil there was, in 1712, but it was against the wrong group of Tuscarora Indians. And it wasn't the North Carolina colonists who were responsible," she added.

"Who then?"

Ludie gave him a curious look, then teasingly responded like a reference librarian. "Carl, I found the old microfilm, copied it for you and even read and highlighted some of it. Now why don't you read it for yourself like a good little student."

Carl held the papers, knowing that the answer to one of the great mysteries he had been trying to solve may at last be in his hands. He set them down on the desk, stood up and reached for his friend, hugging her softly in his arms. "Thank you, Ludie. You're the best reference librarian, ever, and I owe you big for this one."

She hugged him back then pulled gently away. "Good luck with Paskil's thesis. I hope it has the answers you're looking for. And now I have to go home. Sherry and I are meeting friends for dinner." Then she asked, "Where is Roberta? She usually comes with you."

"Oh, she's at home, down in Robeson County, visiting her mother in Pembroke. She should be back tomorrow."

"Good for her, I need to get home to see my folks more often." Then she added, "Enjoy the read, Carl; I'll see you later," and she turned to walk through the doors of the North Carolina Collection, unaware that she would never see him again.

THE PHONE CALL

Carl watched Ludie exit the door and it automatically locked behind her. Only the library staff and approved research faculty were authorized to have keycards to enter the Special Collections area after hours. As far as Carl knew, he was alone under the rotunda on the fourth floor.

He sat down at the desk, opened the small sheaf of papers that had been copied from microfilm and read the caption on the first page, '*A Master's Research Thesis Prepared by Wesley Paskil, May 16, 1956.*' Then he read the title below, *The Last Days of the Tuscarora in North Carolina After the Indian Wars of 1711–15.*

Carl took an anticipatory breath as he thumbed through the pages, pausing only to glance at the lines highlighted by Ludie on her first review. He flipped page after page, looking for key words and phrases, until right before him was a section title in yellow highlights. Then he read the words he had long been searching for, 'The Massacre at Indian Wood.'

He read the entire chapter, carefully absorbing each word and understanding why the hypothesis had created such a furor when it was first presented in the 1950s. Today it seemed rational and possible, but in that restricted academic environment it had run counter to the prevailing wisdom among state-funded researchers that early English colonists and their allies may have participated in a thriving Indian slave trade. And while the paper was eventually accepted by Paskil's advisory committee, its controversial conclusions were excluded from the normal publication venues afforded young researchers who showed exceptional promise. Wesley Paskil's thesis had been buried in the vaults of papers that had been reduced to microfilm, a dinosaur of data storage technology.

Carl's heart stirred as he read about the massacre and its aftermath. Many of the *Northern Tuscarora* warriors, living along the Roanoke River, the same ones who had refused to attack the North Carolina colonists and participate with the *Southern Tuscarora* in the first war, had been killed defending their families in the unprovoked attack. And the surviving warriors, along with their wives and children were…

Carl's heart skipped a beat. There it was before him in print. For over thirty years he had been searching for the 'Tuscarora Connection.' 'And Paskil never even realized what he had uncovered,' Carl thought to himself. 'But how could he? He didn't have the other pieces of the puzzle.'

He suddenly pushed the chair back from the desk, reached for his leather bag and ran into Ludie's small office. 'I've got to call Roberta,' he thought to himself. 'She has to know. It's everything she will need.' He fumbled with several papers until he found the one with her mother's phone number in Pembroke. He dialed carefully and waited eagerly for someone to answer the phone.

"Hello," a voice said over the din of background noises from the family gathering.

"Hello," he said quickly. "This is Dr. Carl Bowden, a history professor at East Carolina University in Greenville, and I need to speak with Roberta Locklear. It's urgent. Please, I need to speak with her quickly."

"Hold on," the voice responded. "I'll go and get her."

Carl paced inside Ludie's office, as far as the corded phone would allow, with the small aluminum container of the microfilm thesis in hand, waiting for Roberta to get to the phone. And then he heard her voice.

"Hello. Carl, is that you?"

"Roberta, can you hear me, can you hear me really well?"

"Yes, Carl, I can hear you very well, now please tell me what's the matter. Are you okay?"

Carl took a deep breath before answering, his voice quivering slightly with emotion. "I've found it, Roberta, the Tuscarora Connection, the link between the Lost Colonists of Roanoke Island and the Lumbee Indians of Robeson County. I have it right here in my hand."

Roberta was stunned and could not speak. Though she was excited by Carl's discovery, she was also disheartened that he called it the Tuscarora Connection. "Are you sure, Carl? Are you absolutely certain it was the Tuscarora and not the Secotan Indians? I mean we've always thought," but before she could say anymore he continued.

"No, Roberta, the connection is through the Tuscarora at a place called Indian Wood. It's all right here in the Paskil thesis. Ludie found it, she's the one who found it." There was no response from Roberta, but Carl's excitement could not be contained. "I can't wait for you to come back. We must get you in on this as soon as possible, so that it can be the basis for your thesis work."

Roberta's face was tense with excitement, and also pain. Carl could not possibly understand what it meant to her that it was the Tuscarora and not the Secotan Indians. After all, he only knew about her life as a social studies teacher and graduate student, but none of the conflict and turmoil of her earlier years.

"It's very interesting, Carl, and I can't wait to get back to see the paper," but there was a sadness in her voice that Carl could not understand.

"Is everything okay there? Is your mother all right?"

Roberta took a deep breath, composed her thoughts and smiled to herself. "Yes, she's fine, Carl, everything is fine here, and your findings are very exciting. I can't wait to get back and see it. But more importantly, I can't wait to get back to see you."

The sweet voice and words sounded more like Roberta, and Carl smiled warmly inside, grinning into the phone. "I almost don't know what to do with myself. Guess I'll stay here in the stacks for a little while and keep reading."

"Carl, don't stay there all night. I know how you can be when you discover something interesting. You just don't know when to stop and take a break."

"I know, Roberta, but it's what I do. Research and teaching have been my life," and then he paused, "until a few months ago." He could almost feel her smile at the other end of the line.

"I feel the same way," she assured him. "I'll be back in time to meet you for lunch, and we can discuss all of this in detail." Then she paused, almost saying those three magic words that seemed to well up in her throat every time she departed from Carl. But it was too soon, and she simply sighed, "Good-night, Carl."

Roberta heard the phone click as Carl hung up, and just before she pulled the receiver down from her ear she heard another click on the line. 'What was that?' she asked herself. She thought it sounded like someone else hanging up, and after a few seconds realized that the second click had occurred after Carl's, so the sound must have come from inside the house. 'Someone was listening to my phone call,' she thought to herself.

She turned around and looked down the hallway toward her mother's bedroom door. It was open, but the light in the room was off. She walked slowly toward the door, reached inside, found the light switch with her left hand and turned on the overhead light. No one was in the room, but the phone on the nightstand beside the bed was definitely out of place. 'Someone had been listening,' she realized.

"There you are, darling."

Roberta was startled and turned to find that her older cousin, Ramona Oxendine, had come up behind her. "I've been looking for you," then she took her by the hand and led her away from the mystery inside the bedroom. As Roberta walked into the kitchen to join the others, she couldn't help wondering who among them would want to listen in to her phone call with Carl, and more importantly, why?

GOOD-NIGHT, DR. BOWDEN

The hours passed quickly as Carl reviewed Paskil's manuscript, developing a better understanding of the events surrounding the gathering of Tuscarora at a place called Indian Wood. As he read, it chilled him to realize the peaceful and unsuspecting upper Tuscarora in North Carolina had been set upon by the remainder of Colonel John Barnwell's Yamassee Indian force and their local Indian allies. It was a massacre of any who resisted, and as was growing more common among the warring tribes of the region, hundreds of survivors had been swept away into captivity, to be later sold into slavery.

Carl wanted to know why. Why did Barnwell and his forces suddenly turn on the Northern Tuscarora? But more importantly, did the officer from Charles Town, South Carolina, have any idea that among the Indians taken into captivity were some of the living descendants of the Lost Colonists of Roanoke Island?

After sitting for hours with his back hunched forward, eyes glued to the printout of an old master's thesis, and his mind completely absorbed in the material before him, Carl barely heard the door open as someone entered the North Carolina Collection. He turned his head hopefully, wondering if Roberta might have decided to leave home early and join him in the library, but peering around the side of the kiosk he saw no one. 'Probably just another late night researcher,' he thought to himself. 'Maybe they forgot something and went back out,' and seeing no one he sat up straight in his chair.

There was one item in the bibliography of Paskil's paper that had been circled, Indian Wars in North Carolina, 1663–1763. A Library of Congress catalog number had been written beside it, along with a page number. 'Someone must have considered this important,' Carl thought as he recalled the small booklet re-printed in 1963 to celebrate the 300th anniversary of the granting of the Carolina Charter. He and other scholars had poured through the well-documented text, conducting research for their own projects, and from the back of Paskil's thesis he tore off the last page containing the bibliography.

'Time for a walk about,' Carl thought to himself, as he pushed his chair away from the small desk and stood up. Before leaving to locate the pamphlet he pulled his balled fists up toward his neck and rolled his elbows around in the air to stretch the muscles in his back and shoulders. Then, feeling a bit loosened and relaxed, he walked to the double doors behind his kiosk and pressed in the numbers to the combination lock.

The small room behind these doors contained some of the most valuable books and artifacts in the North Carolina Collection. Carl felt honored to have been given the combination, one of only a few professors on campus allowed unencumbered access to the sanctuary of knowledge. Inside, he flipped a switch that offered only dim overhead light, just enough to view the resources in the room, but not enough to damage any of the old books and documents stored there.

He squinted at the bindings of numerous titles in one case along the wall, with his right hand and index finger pointing gently toward each book as he searched for a particular volume. Finally his finger reached forward over the top of a thin beige pamphlet and he pulled it out, gently opening and thumbing through the pages. 'It's been a long time since I've looked at this,' he thought to himself.

He turned to page 26 and smiled at the underlined passages. Decades before, as a graduate student, he had noted in pencil areas he considered important, marking the span and detail of historical facts. As he continued reading, he focused on an underlined passage. It was the September1711 decision by North Carolina Governor Hyde, requesting aid from the governors of Virginia and South Carolina. The Southern Tuscarora had attacked and nearly cleared the Pamlico River of colonists. Hundreds had died in only a few days, and hundreds more were trapped in stockaded homes, their only sanctuary from the warring Indians.

It had long been a policy by European nations to use Indians to fight against other Indians. White traders, to induce the Indians to help them, would withhold manufactured goods from Europe that native-Americans had become increasingly dependent upon, as they gave up essential elements of their traditional ways of life. The Colonial governments also encouraged traders to pay for the scalps of the undesirable Indians as proof they had been eliminated.

Those not killed by mercenary Indians were taken captive and traded for rum, guns, powder and ball. The captives were then taken to Charleston, sold and put on empty slave ships returning to the Caribbean, and sold again as part of a thriving Indian slave trade. Either way, colonial governments were satisfied to eliminate the threat of warring tribes against the colonies. And it was the prospect of scalps and slaves that Governor Hyde offered as a lure to bring up the Yamassee warriors of South Carolina to fight against the Southern Tuscarora.

During the first war of 1711–12, Colonel John Barnwell patched together a small force, consisting of three-dozen white settlers and hundreds of Indians, primarily the Yamassee from the Savannah River area. Also included were some Catawba, Cheraw, Wateree, and Cape Fear, as well as other Indians from the smaller tribes in Southeastern North Carolina. As the Tuscarora were defeated in village after village, and the prisoners and plunder accumulated, many of Barnwell's Indian allies took their captives and plunder and deserted the army. But others remained, especially the Yamasse, in hopes of greater treasure and captives.

In the Spring of 1712, Colonel Barnwell and his force attacked King Hancock's fort on Contentnea Creek, a few miles above where it joined the Neuse River. A ten-day siege resulted in success, and the fort surrendered. The white captives were released and the plundered property given up. But Governor Hyde was not satisfied that a treaty had been enacted without a total military defeat of the warring Tuscarora. Barnwell was subjected to criticism and scorn throughout the colony, and his Yamasse Indian followers were left without food, or the scalps and slaves they had been promised. So, they enacted a plan to resolve the issue.

The Yamassee began to ravage throughout the Tuscarora territory, gathering plunder, captives and scalps. Many of the Southern Tuscarora were defenseless. They moved to join the villages of their Northern relatives who had not participated in the war. But now they, too, were subjected to attack by the Yamassee.

The North Carolina governor, in an effort to stop the fighting and have the Yamassee return to South Carolina, agreed to a gathering of Tuscarora at a place called Indian Wood. It was a large inland village just north of the Roanoke River. But an unspeakable treachery took place there.

Instead of ordering the militia of the colony to protect the Tuscarora at Indian Wood, Governor Hyde conveniently forgot the date, and much of the Tuscarora Indian nation in North Carolina was left exposed to a planned attack by the well-armed Yamassee and their remaining Indian allies.

Carl took a small breath and sighed into the worn pages of the Tercentenary Commission booklet. There was nothing mentioned in that historical pamphlet about the massacre at Indian Wood. The story had only been exposed in Wesley Paskil's 1956 master's thesis, and it had been quickly buried and lost inside the microfilm vaults of the college library. He took another deep breath and lifted his head, just as the dim light in the room suddenly went out and the doors to the inner sanctuary clicked shut.

Carl could see nothing in the blackness that filled the room. 'Had someone inadvertently turned off the light and closed the door, not realizing he was inside; or did someone enter the room with him?' A chill swept through his body as he tried to recall the room from memory, and that there was only one light switch next to the double doors.

'If it were an accident,' he thought to himself, ' he could simply call out, or move slowly to the double doors and turn on the light. But if there was someone else in the room, how could he get to the doors and escape?'

His heart raced and a paranoia driven panic filled him as he crept forward. He wanted to run, grab the handle and escape to the safety of his kiosk, but he forced himself to take one small silent step at a time. 'If he could not see in the darkness, then the other person couldn't see either,' he reassured himself.

His fingers tapped silently along the bookcase, guiding him safely toward his destination. And just as he thought he might be at the paneled doors he bumped into something. He listened in horror as it fell to the floor, and a desperate eagerness overtook him as he raced in the darkness toward the finish line.

He crashed into the left door panel and in that moment instinctively reached up to his right side and flipped on the light. The room was again bathed in a dim yellow glow. He turned cautiously around. He was alone, and sighed with relief.

He had forgotten about the rare maps on display in the room. They were framed in gold embroidered woods under non-glare glass and set up on easels. 'It must have been the custodian,' he reassured himself. 'Perhaps he had seen the open door, then reached in and turned off the light without realizing I was inside.'

"Thank God the tempered glass didn't break and ruin the precious old map," he whispered as he walked over and set the easel upright and carefully placed the frame on the stand. When it was correctly set, he picked up the 1963 pamphlet and single sheet that he had torn from the back of Paskil's thesis. And once again he reached for the light switch, turned it off and opened the paneled door to go out under the rotunda.

He took one step forward and was immediately stopped by someone who stood before him, pointing at his head with something in hand. Carl at first strained his eyes to focus on the person's face, but with a great shock suddenly realized that only inches from his face was the barrel of a pistol. It did not matter to him that it was a nickel-plated .38 caliber Smith and Wesson revolver. The only thing that mattered was the flash of light he saw in the barrel, and the great explosion he barely heard. The bullet struck above his left eye. His head rocked back and his body crashed to the floor, sixty-four years of memories and research disappearing in a searing heat that burned deeply into his brain.

The intruder stared for a moment as blood pooled around the back of the professor's head. Then he stepped over to the small kiosk to collect the only known copy of the Paskil thesis and the small aluminum container that held the microfilm. He heard the sound of an elevator coming up from the third floor. 'Someone responding to the sound of gunfire,' he thought to himself.

He glanced back at the professor lying between the double doors and considered that only half his deadly work was done for the evening. There was still the matter of the reference librarian. As he stepped toward the safety of the hall door and the inside staircase that would take him all the way to the ground floor and a loading dock exit, he suddenly whirled about and whispered into the dim light surrounding the stacks of bookcases.

"Good-night, Dr. Bowden." Then he disappeared into the stairwell.

THE INVESTIGATION

The phone rang and startled Luther Surles from a sound sleep. He lifted his head and looked at the bright green display, 11:50 PM. 'Hell, I've only been asleep an hour,' he thought to himself. He rolled over toward the nightstand, across the empty space in the queen-sized bed where his second wife once slept. He stretched for the phone, hoping it was not the pressroom calling about another breakdown.

"Hello," he whispered groggily into the phone.

"Luther, sorry to wake you. This is Jimmy Bonner. I've got a homicide here at the university you need to know about. Your history professor friend, Dr. Bowden, was murdered in the library sometime around ten o'clock tonight."

The news stunned Luther and he held the receiver tightly in his right hand. 'Carl, dead,' he thought to himself, 'murdered.' "But how, Jimmy, and why? Who would want to hurt a good ole' boy like Carl? He never harmed anyone. Never even said anything bad about anyone, hardly ever cussed, quit smoking years ago," and then he paused.

The university police major grunted, "Not only did I think you'd want to know, but seeing as how this took place on campus, I have jurisdiction for the moment. And this being a state university, the SBI boys are coming in from Raleigh; should be here in a few hours. So, I thought if you want to come over, take a look around before they get here," and he paused again. "I mean, with all your experience, Luther, you're a better investigator than most cops."

Major Bonner was an old friend of Luther's. His gridiron exploits at Washington High School had often graced the sports pages of the local paper in the years before he left with a scholarship to play football at NC State. But after two anterior cruciate ligament tears, his hopes for a football career were over. He considered staying at State, majoring in Physical Education and becoming a coach, but eventually returned home to study Law Enforcement and Criminal Justice at East Carolina.

As a police officer in Greenville, Bonner had often been an inside source for Luther's much smaller paper in Washington. And Luther had always been grateful, generously donating time and money to local programs that Jimmy suggested. When the opportunity presented itself to leave his sergeant's position at the Greenville Police Department and go to the university police force as a Lieutenant, Jimmy sought out the advice of his old friend in Washington. And now, five years later he was Chief, head of the campus police force.

Luther was shaking his head in disbelief, the phone rocking gently against his ear. He almost couldn't get the words out, but swallowed hard and replied, "Thank you, Jimmy. I'll get dressed and come right over. You say you're in the library?"

"Fourth floor, under the rotunda, Special Collections area. It's all part of the North Carolina Collection. We think the last person to see him alive may have been the reference librarian, Dr. Ludie Worthington, just before she left around six o'clock this evening. We'll be talking to her in a little while, just as soon as we get things straight around here. You might want to come on over, Luther, before the SBI gets here."

The publisher of the small daily paper drew in a deep breath before he could reply, "I'm coming, Jimmy. Carl and I go back over forty years." Then he added, "This just doesn't make any sense. I'll be there in less than an hour."

"Okay, Luther, see you then."

* * *

The last thing on Luther's mind, as he raced eighty plus miles an hour along the four-lane to Greenville, was that a highway patrol officer might be out at such a late hour. But there he was, blue light flashing, closing steadily on Luther's classic British Green Jaguar coupe. Luther held his pace until the patrol car was within a quarter mile, then pulled over and stopped. He leaned out his side window and waved a white handkerchief in his left hand.

The officer pulled slowly up beside the Jaguar and recognized him. The blue light cut off and the shotgun window went down, "Luther, what in the hell are you doing driving like a wild man, and at this time of night? I thought somebody had stolen your car."

Luther recognized the officer from the Beaufort County District Office. "Scott Henderson, thank God it's you," he said with relief and immediately told him that Carl had been murdered at the library.

"Heard about it on the scanner, just a little while ago. Say he was an old friend?"

"That's right, and I need to get there as soon as possible. Can you help me?"

The officer nodded his head, "Sure can, Luther. Just follow me. You're gonna get the blue light special all the way to the Tenth Street campus entrance." Then he smiled at the frantic man across from him, "Reckon that thing can top a hundred?"

For the first time since he had left home in the darkness, a smile crossed his face, "Let's find out, Scotty."

The blue light and siren came on as the highway patrol car roared away. Luther followed in hot pursuit, occasionally glancing down at the tach and speedometer as the needles crept toward their maximum positions. He had never gone over 110 MPH, not even when he raced down Germany's Autobahn in a rented Porsche 911. And barely a mile from the Greenville bypass stoplight, he glanced down to see the speedometer pegged at 120. 'Unbelievable,' he whispered to himself as he slowed down to make a left turn toward the Tar River Bridge.

Scotty turned off his flashing light and siren as they approached the campus entrance, next to an older white house that had been remodeled into the ECU Police Headquarters. Then he drove down another block to the Krispy Kréme where he could meet with other officers and discuss events of the evening. Luther turned right on Wendell Smiley Drive and pulled slowly up to the entrance to Joyner Library.

There were red and blue lights flashing everywhere with ECU Police Department vehicles and Greenville PD cars parked along both sides of the entrance. An ambulance, that was no longer needed, was backed up to the steps of the library. 'Was Carl in there?' he asked himself. 'Do they already have him in one of those plastic body bags?'

He pulled over on the right side of the driveway, slowly got out of his car, and walked toward the library in the chilly midnight air. A banner of yellow crime scene tape held back the janitorial staff and curious students that had gathered outside. Luther presented his press credentials to one of the ECU police officers and was immediately escorted to the fourth floor to meet with Major Bonner.

"So this is who we've been waiting for," a young GPD officer said in a shrill voice, "A newspaper reporter."

"Luther, this is Lieutenant Ward, and he's really impatient to have his men get started here. But I told him we have to wait until the SBI arrives, and that I wanted you to have a look at some of the evidence."

"Contaminate the crime scene is what's about to happen here," added the lieutenant.

An older detective in a long dark raincoat stepped up to Luther, "I'm Detective Harris. We've met a couple of times before." Then he looked over at the small wiry police officer. "Mr. Surles is damn good at gathering facts and information. Years ago, when he was an investigative reporter with The Daily Reflector, I worked with him on a couple of cases, and I can vouch for his competence around a crime scene."

The lieutenant looked over at Luther, "Well, all right then. Let's get this show on the road. We've got to see if these two cases are tied together."

Luther shot a quick glance over to the ECU Police Major, "Another case?"

Jimmy nodded, "Yep. You know the librarian I mentioned earlier?"

Luther nodded his head, "Yeh, Ludie Worthington. I know her. You said she was working here tonight and was the last person to see Carl."

Jimmy's head fell slightly as he continued. "Yeh, well, Detective Harris called her house, just after I got off the phone with you, and nobody answered. So they sent a unit over to try and get her to the door, but got no response. They went around back and found the door had been jimmied. Because it was a possible crime scene, a 'B & E,' or worse, the officers checked out every room, and found them in bed, together."

"Ludie and Sherry?"

"Yeh," Jimmy responded. "You knew they were," and he paused.

"Gay," Luther added, "lesbians, lovers."

"Yeh, right," he said softly, "And that's probably why they were in bed together."

Luther knew about Ludie and Sherry, and was impatient to hear the rest of the story, "And?"

"Head shots, Luther, both of them, just like Carl. And it looks like the same caliber weapon."

Luther felt suddenly light headed, 'Three professors murdered in one night, and for what? What could they have done? What did they know that was so horrible that someone would kill them?'

"Get the picture, now, Mr. Surles," said the lieutenant. "We got ourselves a multiple homicide crime spree here, and it appears that one crime scene is related to the other. So come on now, can we get started?"

It was more than Luther could absorb, and the wind seemed to slip from his sails. "Carl, Ludie and Sherry, all dead," he repeated to himself.

"You need a minute, Luther? You okay?" Jimmy asked.

"No, the lieutenant's right," he replied weakly. "Whoever did this may still be around, and the sooner we get started the sooner we can catch up to them." Then he looked up at the ECU police Major, "Can I see Carl?"

"Yeh, he's right over here, in the doorway. Once the medical guys pronounced him, I got everybody out of there. Looks like he was shot in the forehead at very close range with a low grain bullet, probably a wad cutter, a target round. There was barely an exit wound; just enough to make it a little dicey back there. Sure you want to see him?"

"I have to, Jimmy. It's part of the crime scene, and there may be something left that can help us with the investigation."

"Okay, Luther, he's right over here."

As Luther stretched white rubber gloves over his fingers and hands, snapping them tightly at the wrists, he was filled with dread as he approached the body of his life-long friend. He felt a wrenching in his heart and air sucking from his lungs as he caught first sight of Carl's legs sticking out through the double wooden doors.

Whether laid out in a casket or crumpled up as the victim of some heinous crime, the feeling is much the same. It was a concern for just how frail is the human condition, then shock that wells up into tiny little sobs that can escalate into uncontrollable weeping, and Luther was trying to suppress the emotions. 'Please, not now,' he willed himself. And with a special resolve he leaned down over Carl's body and began a very personal investigation.

* * *

Carl's eyes were open. Was he staring up at the ceiling or into heaven? Luther hoped for the latter. The small hole above his left eye bled little, but the one at the back of his skull seeped continuously, with blood clotting in his hair and pooling into a small crimson circle on the carpet around his head.

There was a booklet on the floor, *Indian Wars in North Carolina, 1663–1763*. Luther leaned over, picked it up and thumbed slowly through the pages, realizing there must be something inside that was of interest to Carl, but wondering if it was the kind of information that could get a man killed?

"What do you think this is?" Jimmy asked as he slowly pulled out a sheet of paper partly hidden under Carl's body. He looked at it for a moment and then handed it to Luther. "Looks like a list of books."

Luther studied it for a moment. "More like a bibliography, and look at this." He pointed with his finger to the title of the booklet that had been found on the floor beside Carl. It had been circled. "Carl must have gone into this room to locate this booklet."

Luther stood, stepped carefully over Carl's body and went into the room filled with old books and maps, but there was little to see. He walked back to the double doors and stood for a moment, thinking to himself. "Looks like Carl was leaving the room and someone met him here at the door."

"Point blank, right in the face. Not much skill required for that."

"Just the same, have forensics check for fingerprints on the pages of this book."

"So the shooter must have been about the same height as Carl?"

"Or maybe he leaned down, or she stood on her tiptoes, hard to tell from here."

Jimmy smiled as he realized Luther was suggesting it was far too early to draw conclusions about anything.

Luther noticed that a man had walked over to the ECU police major, "Mind if we get some close-up photos of those papers you found?"

Jimmy nodded, then Luther handed the booklet and bibliography sheet to the photographer. "As soon as possible I would like a copy of this sheet, and to take this booklet with me so that I can study it in detail."

"Sounds good, Mr. Surles, but you may need to clear it with the lieutenant and the SBI boys. They're downstairs, just arrived a few minutes ago. Looks like these two cases are going to be related," and he shrugged his shoulders. "Never heard of three college professors getting killed like this before. Bet this thing makes the national news," then he turned and walked away.

Luther looked over at the ECU police major. "Jimmy, if they will let me, I know I can help with this investigation. And please tell the lieutenant, Detective Harris and the SBI investigators that if I discover anything relevant to either case, I will share my findings with them immediately."

"Thanks, Luther. I know Harris, and probably the SBI, will appreciate your help, but I'm not so sure about that lieutenant," he said with half a smile.

Luther nodded his head and smiled weakly, "Let's go take a look at the desk where Carl was working."

It was only a few steps to the kiosk, and there against the wall was the last place Carl Lee Bowden had sat as he engaged in one of his favorite pursuits. The chair was pushed back from the desk and turned at a forty-five degree angle, and on the floor, leaned against the leg of the desk, was the black briefcase that Luther had given Carl so many years before.

The feelings returned, suddenly welling up in his throat, and he began to blink his eyes, trying to stem the salty water brimming up and over and down his cheeks. Luther pulled a handkerchief from his back pocket, the one he had waved at the highway patrol officer only an hour before. He wiped both eyes and his cheeks, took a deep breath and blew it out of his mouth, then looked at Jimmy. "I'm sorry, but that briefcase is the one I gave him and," but he could say no more.

"It's okay, Luther. I understand. You need some time alone here, at the desk?"

"Have they got photos of this area?"

"Sure, plenty. I'll go out and speak to Harris and the SBI investigators, let them know we'll make copies of everything and turn the originals over to them, except for the items you might want, but I've got to get everything in the inventory."

Luther took another deep breath, exhaled and felt better for the moment. "Thanks, Jimmy. I'll be here at the desk if you need me."

He stood for a moment surveying the world that Carl loved so much, and with another deep breath quelled the sadness within him and sat down in Carl's chair. He picked up the tattered black copy of the 1857 Hawks volume. He thumbed through the pages and saw that many had notations in the margins, most in old faded ink, but a few were as bright as if they had just been inscribed there. 'The new ones must be Carl's,' he thought to himself. 'This is another book I need to read in detail,' and he placed the volume back on the desk.

Except for a .9mm mechanical pencil and a generic ballpoint pen, there was little on the desk. He turned his attention to the briefcase on the floor. Almost out of habit, he reached for the laptop computer, but then saw a white plastic covered three-ring binder beside it and reached for that instead. He was surprised at what he found inside, a novel in progress, historical fiction by Dr. Carl L. Bowden.

Luther's mouth fell open as he studied the title page under the clear plastic cover, "Arcadia of the New World," he whispered to himself. Then he turned it over and found a map of the North Carolina coastline, the land of Arcadia as it may have appeared in 1587. He studied the old Indian names, picking out locations he easily recognized along the Outer Banks. There was *Wococon* for Ocracoke Inlet, *Croatoa Island* for Hatteras, and other names he did not know, *Port Ferdinando* and *Trinity Harbor*. Luther was grinning as he turned back to the front and pulled the hard cover open. Just behind the title page, typed in italic script, was a short description of what Carl was trying to accomplish.

"In 1524, the Italian explorer, Verrazano, sailed along the coast of what is now North Carolina's Outer Banks and called it the the land of Arcadia. In 1584, just prior to the arrival of the English colonists, in a series of sea adventures known as the Roanoke Voyages, there was a thriving Algonquian Indian nation already established in villages along the rivers and sounds of the coastal areas. They were allied together in the Secotan Confederation. This is a story of what the Secota Indian culture was like just before it clashed with the values, beliefs, weapons and diseases of the English colonists."

Dr. Carl L. Bowden

'Fiction,' Luther mused to himself. 'He always talked about one day compiling his class lectures into some kind of book, but I've never known him to work on anything but his research. Wonder what inspired him to start this and not share it with me?'

He studied Carl's working outline of chapter titles for a moment, beginning with 'The Captain's Tale, London, Fall of 1583.' Then he looked down the list of Indian names in the other chapter titles; *Aquascogoc, Neuisocs, Oshanoa, Secotans, Croatoa* and *Dasamonquepec*. He flipped the notebook over and tried to locate them on Carl's 1587 map. As he pored over the names that had been carefully placed in the book cover graphic, he noticed a small notation in Carl's own hand. On the west end of the *Moratoc River*, he saw two penciled words.

'*Indian Wood*,' he thought to himself, 'a location that had been added to the map after it was initially printed. Guess Carl planned to include it later. I wonder what it means?' Luther's eyes were weary from fatigue and tears that had welled up when recalling special memories of Carl. The words on the pages blurred together, and as he shook his head slightly to refocus, he realized he could read no more. He would have to go home, rest, and start again later in the day.

"Here you are, Luther." Jimmy Bonner had quietly walked up behind him as he studied the map. "Here's a copy of the bibliography we found on the floor." Then he added in a matter of fact tone. "Harris talked to the SBI team, and they're okay with you assisting with the investigation as long as you don't talk to the press before you clear it with them," and then he grinned at the irony, because Luther was the press. "They're dusting the book for prints, should be done in a few minutes."

Luther nodded as he reached for the copy of the sheet found under Carl's body. Staple holes in the upper left corner indicated it had been torn away from something, perhaps a larger body of work to which it had been attached. 'Wonder where that is,' Luther asked himself. 'Guess it must be at Carl's house; probably find it later,' and he thanked Jimmy again for calling and allowing him to help with the investigation.

"Find anything useful on the laptop?"

Luther sighed, "I haven't even started there. Unless he's changed the password since the last time he was down at the house, I should be able to get in, but it may take hours to go through everything. Do you think they would mind if I take it with me, so I can review it later when I'm wide awake and alert?"

After a cursory review and inventory of what was on the desk, Major Bonner, Lieutenant Ward, and the SBI agents agreed that Luther could take the briefcase, laptop, and notebook with him for review, as long as he would submit a detailed report of his findings. Luther gratefully agreed, then placed the materials inside the old black leather case, worn and frayed from over twenty years of being hauled around and tossed on desks, floors and inside vehicles.

Before he left the library Luther walked back over to the double doors
to visit Carl, before they put him in a black bag and hauled him away to the
coroner's office. A thick yellow ribbon of tape had been placed around the
body, and Carl seemed so lonely, lying there outlined on the floor. Luther
kneeled down beside his old friend and whispered quietly in his ear. "I will
not stop until I find out who did this, Carl. I swear upon forty-five years of
friendship, no matter how long it takes, I will finish this."

Tears welled and brimmed in the corners of his eyes then rolled
gently down his cheeks. He pulled the damp handkerchief from his pocket
once again and wiped most of the tears away. Then he stood up and, without
shame, walked through the line of officers and medical staff who quietly
parted for him to exit.

THE SECRETARY

Luther wanted to sleep, but tumbled anxiously in his bed until sunrise. He was trying to rid himself of a terrible dream that he would share with Carl over a late morning coffee, but then another wave of tears flooded his eyes and he missed his dear old friend. Finally, warm rays of yellow light rose above the waterline and raced through his bedroom windows. They reflected off an antique brass lamp on the dresser and cast a colorless rainbow across the ceiling.

He kicked back the covers, rolled out of bed and heard joints pop and creak with distress as he stood, then stretched and walked gingerly into the kitchen. 'Love that coffee maker,' he thought to himself as he considered the last purchase his wife, Veronica, had made before she left.

It was a stainless steel unit, with a timer that could be set the night before, so that one could wake to the smell of freshly brewed coffee. He slipped a large pottery cup under the self-serve carafe on top of the unit, pressed the handle and smiled as the dark liquid poured down into his cup. 'Even the sound of coffee is wonderful,' he thought as he reached for the French Vanilla creamer to which he was now addicted. "And thank you for this, too," he whispered, as he recalled the first time Veronica had purchased the flavored cream, and for a moment the anticipation of a wonderful cup of coffee on the back porch distracted him from the events of the previous night.

'His office, his house, funeral arrangements, there is so much that needs to be done,' he thought, as he stared out the window into Blount's Bay. 'And Carl's only living relative, a cousin in Fayetteville, was in such poor health herself, that he knew she would appreciate anything he could do.' He took a deep breath, accepted what must be done, then slipped quietly out to a rocking chair on the porch to enjoy at least the beginning of this Monday morning.

He had called in to the night press operator letting him know that he would not be in, and that someone would take his place for the time being. Then he called another old friend, Harry Hughes, the editor of the small daily paper and let him know what had happened. Harry had been with *The Washington Daily News* since the early seventies and probably knew more about its operation than Luther, or even his father who had taken over the paper just after the 'great war' in Europe, and died only a few years before.

'It's good to be the publisher,' Luther thought to himself, realizing he could not possibly take time to help with the investigation if he were the managing editor or a department head. He had inherited the paper, and even though offers had come in from media groups seeking to consolidate their regional influence he wanted to continue the tradition of a family-owned newspaper, one of only a handful left in North Carolina.

A fisherman, casting steadily to the bank on the far side of the creek, suddenly shouted with excitement, even though he was alone. His rod bent heavily toward the water, and the man had to move to the back of the boat as his prey, probably a big rockfish, headed for deeper water. The small aluminum boat seemed to be pulled by the big fish, and the man fought him steadily, letting him run then reeling him back until the next attempt to get away.

Luther saw it was his neighbor, George, a retired business professor who had taught at the local community college for nearly thirty years. These days he spent his mornings trying to catch anything that passed through the 'deep-V' channel at the mouth of Blount's Creek. Luther stood and watched as George pulled hard, and then suddenly it was over. The 10 lb test line he preferred to use was no match for the big rockfish that occasionally passed through the channel.

"Hot damn!" George screamed for anyone to hear, and then he looked up to see Luther standing on the elevated deck of his house. "Did you see that one, Luther?"

"Looked like a big one, George," and Luther lifted his cup as a tribute to the battle and the one that got away. The fisherman waved and sat down in his small aluminum boat to tie on a new rig, a chartreuse-green grub with a red head and a piece of shrimp on the barb of the hook.

Luther looked out into Blount's Bay and watched as the water shimmered with bait balls. Sea gulls and pelicans floated effortlessly above them, diving whenever the small fish came close to the surface. Everything looked just as it had the previous day, but the world seemed less interesting on this beautiful morning.

It was the same as when his father died, and when his mother passed, and just like that first morning after Veronica left and he knew he was alone again. But there is a difference between having your wife leave and losing your best friend. One of them you can live without, and the other you will miss forever. Then he wondered just how many good years he may have left on this earth, and resolved that he would not pass until justice had been served on the one who took Carl from him.

* * *

The parking situation around campus was as bad as Luther remembered. At 7:45 in the morning every space appeared taken. He turned off Tenth Street and began a fruitless search in front of the Brewster Building, pulling over for several minutes, hoping that someone might leave and provide him a place to park. As several other vehicles drove slowly by, hoping to win the parking lottery, he spied an enticing Handicapped space directly in front of the building.

'Was he not handicapped this morning?' he asked himself. 'Did he not lose his best friend, and was he not here to help?' He tried to find some rationale for taking the available space, but the fact that he might deprive a truly handicapped person from their needed space, plus the $200 ticket he would surely receive, deterred him.

Then he saw the red and clear lights of an old station wagon blink on, and like a gift from heaven, the vehicle began slowly backing out. "Thank you, Jesus," Luther whispered. "I wasn't going to park in that handicapped space. You knew that didn't you? You were just testing me, weren't you?" And he smiled as he gratefully accepted the gift of a front row parking space.

The History Department, known throughout the university as one of the most contentious and pompous academic sanctuaries on the entire campus, was also one of the liveliest. "Too many intelligent, competitive smart asses in one location," Carl would often say. A departmental meeting was as likely to disintegrate due to internal feuding as it was to end with uproarious laughter.

Luther rarely visited his friend in the 'Halls of Pomposity,' as he sometimes referred to the 3rd floor corner section of the building, because one or more of the aggressive professors would follow him in pursuit of special funding for pet projects or proposals for stories for even his small circulation paper. Not that their ideas were unwelcome, but they simply would not leave him alone to visit with Carl.

As he stepped out of the elevator, he noticed many of the professors were clustered at the door to the office of the department head. The loss of three staff members, even at a university with over 20,000 students and over a thousand faculty, was still a shock to the institution. But here in this one department, no one could conceive that any person might want to harm Carl Bowden, known as the 'gentle scholar' by his students and peers.

As Luther approached the door, one of the professors noticed, touched another on the shoulder, and like a tag team match they turned to face him. For the moment, all other departmental issues were tabled, and as Luther approached they separated for him to enter. Lucy Armstrong, long time History Department secretary and former romantic interest of Carl, came around the desk to hug the newspaper publisher.

"How could anyone do such a thing?" she asked. Her eyes were moist and mascara smeared from wiping her eyes. Luther could not answer and felt a sob well up within him, and he held on to the secretary until the emotional wave passed. At that moment, Dr. Cleveland Williams, department head and able administrator, entered to greet him, "Luther, we're so sorry for the loss of Carl. We're stunned and absolutely speechless. Is there anything we can do for you or the family?"

Luther cleared his throat and took another deep breath. "I spoke with Carl's cousin in Fayetteville, and she asked that I handle the administration of his estate."

"I know," the professor replied. "She called our office this morning informing us of the decision. And I called Major Bonner, to make sure that it was proper to give you a key to his office, so that you could examine everything in detail. He concurred," and Dr. Williams held the key toward Luther. "Please let me know if there is anything any of us can do to facilitate this investigation."

Luther accepted the key, thanked him, and smiled sadly at the secretary who held such fond memories of Carl, a man she still loved and admired. But she warned Carl from the beginning that she had a voracious appetite for men, and that he might only be the next in line. But who could resist the charms of Lucy's long blonde hair, beautiful smile and large breasts? Even now, she held her youthful figure, and because of her sophisticated presence hosted nearly all department functions. And if rumors were believed, also provided special favors for the portly department head.

She leaned forward and whispered in Luther's ear. "I'll talk to you later. Something I think you should know." Then she leaned back and smiled weakly. Luther nodded, turned away, and walked down the hallway.

Carl's office was at the end of the hall, next to the elevator, as far away from the antics of the department head's office as he could be. He had long ago given up any desire to become a campus administrator, especially after his short tenure as acting department head, seven years ago, after the untimely death of one of the more colorful leaders of the department. After six months of contentious meetings, feuding and rivalries, he was frustrated and ready to quit, just as a new head was announced. It had also given him a chance to renew a physical relationship with Lucy, an opportunity to scratch a primal itch that both of them had enjoyed. But when he moved back to his old office, her ardor cooled and her favors focused on the new department head.

Luther pushed the key into the lock, turned it gently, and it clicked. He turned the round brass handle and the door opened. It was like rolling the stone away and entering a tomb of relics. Everything was just as Carl left it the day before.

He felt lightheaded, wavering slightly as he moved around the desk and pulled out Carl's oak swivel rocker that he favored over the hard-backed side chairs provided by the university. Luther patted the golden oak arm rails then bent down and for no apparent reason gently rubbed the seat with his hand, feeling the emotions welling up within him. He stood quickly, taking several deep breaths. Then feeling better he sat down in the chair, knowing in his heart that it was the one item in Carl's office that he wanted for himself.

Carl used a desktop calendar to keep up with appointments and personal activities. He never mastered the art of personal digital assistants or electronic calendars on his cell phone. Besides, Carl would often say, 'At my age I don't have all that much to keep up with anyhow.' Then he would laugh good-naturedly and smile generously, an endearing quality that kept him on the guest list of so many friends and professional associates.

Luther was studying the calendar notation for yesterday, "Sunday, 11 AM, Brunch with Paskil." Then a note below that, "Special Collections, Joyner Library, see Ludie before she leaves."

'Paskil, who is that?' Luther asked himself, and then a flash of memory, 'The bibliography, it was copied from microfilm. Ludie may have made copies of something from microfilm for Carl, and that means she probably knew what Carl knew.'

Then he fell back in his chair with his eyes closed. 'So Carl and Ludie could have been killed because of what was on the microfilm,' and he sighed deeply to himself. 'And poor Sherry was killed just because she was with Ludie.' He was sitting there thinking to himself when he heard a voice.

"Luther, is this a good time? I know you're busy, but I have a few minutes," and then her voice trailed off. His eyes popped open and Lucy was in the doorway.

"The door wasn't closed, so I thought maybe it was okay to come in, but if you're busy now, I can come back."

Luther cleared his head, trying not to think that three people may have died simply because of some information on an old microfilm. 'But what was it about?' he asked himself as he said, "No, Lucy. I'm just reminiscing about the old days with Carl."

"So's everyone else around here, but you and me, I mean we've got special memories of Carl, don't we?" She smiled at first, and tears formed in her eyes. "And poor Dr. Worthington, and her friend, Sherry. Why, Luther, why would someone do something like that to such nice people?"

Luther had no answer and just sat for a moment until Lucy recovered her composure. "I talked with Jimmy, Major Bonner, you know him, and he said you were helping with the investigation. So I thought you may want to know, just between us for now, because it probably doesn't mean anything, at least I don't think so, but Carl," and she began to cry again.

Then she stopped and sighed heavily. "Well, Carl was seeing someone, Luther, someone here at the university."

Luther laughed to himself. Carl was always seeing someone at the university, and occasionally more than one faculty member at the same time. "Was it the lady in accounting or the music professor?"

Lucy laughed to herself. Carl was sometimes as busy with the ladies as she had with the men, but this time it was different. "Luther, he was seeing one of his students, very discreetly, but you know, you can't get anything like that past me, at least not in this department."

Luther's mouth fell open, "A student, Carl was dating a student?"

"Not just any student, a graduate student, his own graduate assistant. And they were doing it big time, Luther, know what I mean?"

Luther sat up, "But Carl knew what could happen if he got caught having a relationship with a student. He often said it was the ultimate taboo for a professor, and besides he stayed so busy with the women faculty he didn't have time for students."

Lucy smiled and even Luther had to laugh, and then she added. "But this got serious, Luther, and in a hurry. This is a really fine lady, and I think she and Carl are," and then she paused, "were in love. You see, he could hide this from the men, but women who know men, well, they can tell when there is a change, especially a man who is in love. And I'm telling you, our friend Carl was smitten. He was in love."

Luther fell back in the chair, happy for Carl that he had found someone, but saddened that he would never be able to marry. "Who is she, Lucy? Can you tell me?"

"I can tell you, but you have to promise me that unless it's absolutely necessary you won't tell anyone else. She's a graduate student here, and could lose her position and scholarship money if this gets out."

"Lucy, I promise, that unless it is absolutely necessary, I will not tell anyone."

"Okay, Luther, I'm gonna trust you on this." Then she paused and looked around the office. "I love this office. Spent a lot of time with Carl in here. He still keep that bottle of Jim Beam in the bottom right drawer?"

Luther pulled the drawer open. In the bottom was a half-full bottle of white label, and he held it up. "It's right here, Lucy. You want it for a remembrance?"

"No, but I like to remember the thought of just the two of us sitting in here, talking about life and people. We were a lot more than lovers, you know, we were friends. He helped me through a lot of personal issues, and I helped him get through those few months he was interim department head."

"Her name?"

"Oh, yeh, Roberta. Roberta Locklear. She's a Social Studies teacher from Cumberland County, forty-some years old, here to finish her master's degree. Her thesis work is on the Lost Colony. That's what brought them together, and almost from the beginning they had a thing for each other. Didn't surprise me at all when Ludie called one day and said she caught them doing it on her desk in the library. Those two really had it going on for each other, Luther, hot and fast. And then it sorta cooled down a bit so they wouldn't get caught. Know what I mean?"

"I should be so lucky," he replied.

"You're not the kind that gets lucky, Luther. You're just good. You plan it out and make it happen. Carl just kind of went with the flow. Women on the make, they can tell these things. Unless a woman is looking to marry, she probably wouldn't want to risk being rejected by a man like you. That's a pain we've had enough of and want to avoid."

Lucy was telling Luther something he probably needed to know, why he didn't have any luck with casual affairs the way Carl did. But right now he was focused on fulfilling a promise made over the body of his best friend the night before. "Where can I find Roberta? I need to talk with her."

"I'll get word that you want to talk. Probably a good idea if you aren't seen talking with her around the office, or even on campus for that matter. Tell you what, I have her address in my desk, I'll get it for you. But keep your promise, Luther. Don't drag the lady into this unless it's necessary, okay?"

Luther nodded in agreement, and as she walked out the door he studied her from the rear, with an appreciative smile upon his face.

THE ASSISTANT

As Luther left campus, he drove several blocks down Fifth Street. Following Lucy's directions, he turned left on Reade and continued over to Fourth, where he saw a two-story apartment building on the corner across the intersection. He pulled into a center space of the concrete parking lot and looked at the door numbers on both floors, until on the bottom right he found Roberta Locklear's apartment. He reached for Carl's old black briefcase, got out of the car and walked toward her door, realizing he was about to meet the graduate assistant, the person his best friend had fallen in love with. Then he knocked gently.

A moment later a woman with puffy reddened eyes opened the door. Her long brown hair was pulled back and held in place with a white bone clip, and her golden brown cheeks reflected the warm rays of sunlight drifting in over his shoulders. He immediately thought of a beautiful native-American woman chosen to play the role of Pocahontas in a film of the Jamestown Colony. And then he said, "I'm Luther Surles, Carl's old friend from Little Washington."

She smiled at the reference to the small town only a county away. It was a local term of endearment to distinguish the first town in America named for George Washington from its much larger metropolitan cousin to the north. Her hand rose up to wipe her eyes. "Yes, I know, from the pictures at Carl's house."

Luther stood for a moment, admiring the attractive woman holding the damp tissue in her right hand, then acknowledged her obvious grief. "I am so sorry for what has happened. I know it is a great personal loss for you."

Her head lifted and her eyes studied him carefully. "For you as well," and then she paused. "How much do you know about me and Carl? "

"Lucy Armstrong told me all she could this morning, and it's the first time I've heard your name. No one knows but us, and unless necessary, no one else needs to know. I promise."

Her chin fell and she began to sob quietly. He gently held the door open a bit wider, "May I come in?"

She turned, leading him inside, then walked to an old maple rocker that had seen better days. "This is my grandmother's chair. She used to rock me here, and I find it of such comfort. And now, I have lost my very best friend, the only man who truly knew me, and loved me in spite of it all." Then she looked at Luther as he sat down on the pull out sofa. "And I loved him, Mr. Surles. I truly did."

He nodded, certain that Lucy had it right. Carl and Roberta were in love. "Please call me Luther, and may I call you Roberta?"

She sat in the maple chair, rocking gently while staring at the black two-handled briefcase sitting at Luther's feet. "How could this happen? Who would want to hurt such a sweet and gentle man? And dear Ludie, who would want to harm her? She was so witty and helpful. She knew about me and Carl, and helped us keep our secret." She smiled weakly, and tears filled her eyes as she realized she would never meet Carl in the library again.

"I'm sorry," she said as she stood and went into the kitchen to retrieve another tissue. "Lucy called to say you would be coming over, but that is all she told me." She dabbed at her eyes then looked back at her guest. "How can I help, Mr. Surles, I mean, Luther? What can I do?"

Luther wasn't sure what to ask or where to begin. He wanted to meet her, but more importantly, he wanted to know exactly what Carl was working on, and if she knew anything about the microfilm documents. "Start by telling me a little about yourself, Roberta, your background."

She took a deep breath, walked back to the rocker and sat down. She leaned back, closed her eyes a moment and then began. "I'm from Red Springs, NC. I was born in a small farmhouse in January of 1958, the same day the Lumbee men ran the Klan out of Robeson County. It's an easy date to remember, and ironically, you and Carl were only ten miles away at the time I was born."

Luther laughed to himself. "That was the same day I first met Carl. He was just a young kid, fresh out of college, and it was his first story as a reporter." Then he shook his head. "Carl did a hell of a fine job. Won a critics award for his writing."

"I'll never forget how he kept after me that night to tell him everything I knew about the Lumbees and their connection to the Lost Colony. I didn't really know that much, and I've pretty much forgotten all I knew, but I remember something about a 'wild and lawless group of people' that were found in the swamps in the 1730s."

Roberta's eyes suddenly cleared. The social studies teacher and graduate student in her revived. "It was 1736, Luther, the first time the Lumbee ancestors were found living in the swamps of Robeson County. The settlement of Campbelton, along the Cape Fear River, where Fayetteville is today, wanted to expand. So they sent a surveying party out to the Northwest to look for land that could be easily cleared for farming. When they got into what is now Hoke County, they found a small, swift running river the local Indians called '*Drowning Creek.*'"

"Drowning Creek," Luther interrupted. "That sounds dangerous."

"Probably a lot of Indians drowned in the swift black water for it to acquire such a name. But today it's known as the Lumber River. It flows through Lumberton into South Carolina, into the Little Pee Dee River near Mullins, then on to Georgetown and the Atlantic Ocean."

Luther nodded as if he understood, and she continued. "The surveying party built rafts and floated downriver until they entered the swampy area of what is now the southern part of Robeson County. And that is where they encountered what you referred to as a 'wild and lawless people.'

"Actually they were neither wild, nor lawless. It was their reaction to the surveyors and their instruments, and the fact that they wanted to parcel up the land that the Indians had always held in common that got an angry reaction from the people living there. They didn't hurt the surveyors or anyone in their party. They just forced them to get back on their rafts and continue on their journey."

Luther nodded again then added, "But wasn't there something about some of them speaking English?"

"Not just English, Luther, but old English with the same Elizabethan dialect the Lost Colonists would have used. And not only that, the surveyors also noted that some of them lived in stone houses, and others had blue eyes and could grow beards, rare traits among the Indians."

"So in 1736, the people that were found in the swamps of Robeson County had already intermingled with English colonists?"

"At least some of them had, but probably not all of them. Runaway slaves and other small groups of Indians, trying to escape from war and diseases, had also come to live in the swamps. And surely they must have acculturated with the people who claimed their own ancestors had intermarried with early English colonists at a place called Croatoa near the ocean."

"So it probably was a mixed breed of people they found there in 1736?"

"It probably was," she replied, "but it was the first census in American history, in 1790, that established that some of these people were descended not only from English ancestors, but perhaps the very first colonists at Roanoke Island."

Luther sat enthralled not only at her story, but the way she told it. It was like having Carl sitting there, trying to help him understand something important. Had she learned Carl's teaching techniques, or was it just another trait the two of them shared that had helped bring them together?

"Of ninety-five surnames among the Lost Colonists, twenty-two were found in the first and last names of people living in the swamps along Drowning Creek. And if the census had been done correctly, there might have been more."

"What do you mean correctly?"

"In 1790, the census takers were more interested in an accurate count of the white population and black slaves than of the Indians. It wasn't that they weren't going to try and count everyone. It's just that they didn't go to as much trouble to be accurate with the non-white population. So when the census takers rode through the back-water areas of Robeson County, they didn't venture too far down along the riverbanks where the Lumbees lived, and they probably missed some of the names."

She paused a moment to see if Luther understood the implication. "Don't you see? Of ninety-five surnames listed among the Lost Colonists, twenty-two were found among a small group of people living in the swamps of Robeson County in 1790. Now what are the odds of that, Luther? And considering that many whites and most blacks avoided going into the swamps, because the Lumbees didn't take kindly to having strangers moving through their land, it's unlikely that many new English surnames were introduced to the Lumbees between 1736 and the census. Understand, Luther, those Lost Colony names were already there long before the census takers arrived in 1790."

"Okay," he said as if surrendering, "but one question that has always bothered me is why would the Croatans have relocated over 200 miles from Roanoke Island to live in the swamps of Robeson County?"

Roberta smiled. "Now you sound exactly like Carl. That was the basis of most of his research. He wanted an answer to that same question," and then she paused.

Her eyes clouded as she thought of Carl, and she blinked often to hold back tears. Her lips quivered as she tried to speak, then she stopped and dabbed at her eyes with the tissue. "Was it some kind of cruel destiny, Luther, that I should come here to meet Carl and fall in love, only to lose him? There should have been so much more to this story. It should not have ended like this."

Then Luther had a nervous thought, 'Who said it had ended?' He watched her for a moment, not sure how to proceed, and then decided to go back to her own story. "Tell me a little more about yourself, Roberta, if you don't mind."

She wiped her eyes and stared through the picture window that looked out over the concrete parking lot. "Until I was eleven, I thought I had an idyllic childhood. My father, though, suffered from an addiction to alcohol, and my mother and older brother tried to shield me from his drunken rages. But later, as I began to mature, he sometimes made lewd comments, and once he even molested me. So, I was sent to live with my aunt and her family, the Oxendines, in Pembroke. And my cousin, Ramona, and I became like sisters.

"After high school, both of us attended Pembroke Indian College. That's what some of the locals still call it," she added with a smile. "I majored in history, and after graduating in 1978, I got involved with 'AIM,' the local American Indian Movement. And because I was also a strong supporter of the Lumbees, I ran afoul of AIM's primary agenda, advocating for the native Cherokee and Tuscarora populations. Eventually they let me know I was no longer welcome, and made it clear that I should move somewhere else to become a teacher. That's why I relocated to Hope Mills, in Cumberland County, still close enough to visit my family.

After twenty years in the school system, I applied for a sabbatical to attend East Carolina and complete my master's degree. And here I am, Luther, so happy to have found Carl, and so miserable that he has been taken away from me. And for what, Luther," she added, her voice escalating, " for what? Why has this happened?"

There was a genuine sadness in her story, perhaps something more that she could not share with him. And there were also a few lingering thoughts in his mind. 'How could such a beautiful woman have escaped the attention of so many men who would surely have been attracted to her over the years? How could she have never married? And what did she mean that Carl loved her, in spite of it all?'

"I see you have Carl's briefcase."

Luther suddenly perked up, "Yes, and I have some information here that I would like to ask you about."

"Anything, Luther, ask me anything that you think will help."

He reached down inside the leather case he pulled up the three-ring notebook.

"Did you know that Carl was writing a fiction novel?"

She smiled, almost blushing. "Yes, last October, after we started seeing each other, Carl revealed that eventually he wanted to compile his lectures and write historical fiction, that conveyed essentially the same information. And I thought it a wonderful idea, a great way to teach history. But instead of waiting until he retired, I encouraged him to begin immediately."

She paused and looked softly at Luther. "You were his best friend, are you sure he didn't tell you about me?"

"Not a word, Roberta. Not even a slip of the tongue. And he never mentioned that he was writing a novel." Luther glanced down at the floor. "Guess he found a new best friend." Then looked up with a reassuring smile to let her know that he was okay with that.

He took a deep breath and added, "I just want to get to the bottom of this, find out what happened and make sure that whoever killed Carl, Ludie and Sherry is brought to justice."

"We're on the same side, Luther. I will do anything to help. What else do you want to know?"

"Anything else about the novel you want to share?"

"Well, as hard as I was working on my thesis research, I suggested that he begin with a story that included the Lost Colony, something both of us were interested in."

"And what has been the focus of your research?"

"Family names of the Lost Colonists." She smiled, "And not just those that were found in the swamps of Robeson County. Some Lost Colony descendants may have become part of other Indian tribes and relocated to other parts of North Carolina."

"Like where?"

"Belhaven, Washington, Chocowinity, Greenville, and even Roanoke Rapids. Carl emphasized that for my research to be credible, it needed to focus on more than a single group of Indians with an oral history that claims ancestry with the Lost Colonists."

"So it's not just the Lumbees that may be descended from the Roanoke colony?"

"No, Luther. The prevailing wisdom is that the colonists went to the island of *Croatoa* to wait for the return of John White and the re-supply ships. But the limited resources on the island could not support the Indians during the winter, much less the colonists. So, at least some of them had to move inland with their Croatan hosts. And eventually, they probably intermarried with the Croatans and were assimilated into their culture.

Even as late as the year 1701, John Lawson, Surveyor General of the North Carolina colony, found a small group of Croatans still living near Buxton, on the Outer Banks. And even then, they claimed to be descendants of early European colonists, but their numbers had been drastically reduced. Less than twenty warriors remained in the tribe. Even so, there is a prevailing theory that if you can trace the migration of the Croatan Indians in Eastern North Carolina, you may be able to locate some of the Lost Colony descendants."

Luther nodded, but then remembered that Carl had often discussed alternative theories. "What did Carl think had happened to the Lost Colonists?"

"So you knew Carl had his own theory?"

"Just some talk over dinner and a bottle of wine, but I honestly cannot remember what his theory was."

She was still smiling and Luther observed the simple beauty that Carl must have appreciated. She was not only lovely, but also sincere and engaging, and no doubt had filled the one void in Carl's life that not even a best friend could hope to make whole.

"Carl never doubted that the colonists went to Hattorask to live with the Croatan Indians for a time, or that some of them may have remained and eventually married into and became part of the Croatan culture. But the Outer Banks could not support such a large group during the lean winter months. Carl believed that a significant number of colonists had to leave Croatoa and seek support and safety from other Indians."

"What other Indians?"

"That's a very good question, Luther. It's part of what Carl has been researching all these years. What other group of Indians would take in the colonists? Where did they live? And how come the search party from Jamestown, only twenty years later, could find no trace of them?"

Luther interrupted, "There was a search party from Jamestown?"

"Yes. Captain Newport, Admiral of the small fleet that brought the Jamestown colonists to Virginia, also had orders from the London directors to send out a search party to locate or discover what had happened to the Roanoke colonists.

"In 1608, John Smith was told by the Pamunkey Indians of the Powhatan Confederacy that men and women, wearing clothes like the Jamestown colonists, were living in a village near the Chowan River. He sent a soldier named Sicklemore, with several Pamunkey guides, to the Chowan, but they only found the remains of a village that showed evidence of European settlement. And when they asked the local Indians what happened to them, they were told that the *Mangoaks*, or Tuscarora, had raided the village and taken the white men and women."

"Did Sicklemore pursue them any further?"

"He did, and went about thirty miles up the Roanoke River, but had to turn back because his guides told him the Mangoaks were going to attack, kill him, and steal his sword and gun."

"Did the Jamestown colonists ever make another attempt to locate the Roanoke colonists?"

"No. As far as we know, that was the only effort," and then she paused. "And when Carl called me last night he was so excited. He said he had found something he called the 'Tuscarora Connection,'" but before she could go on Luther interrupted her.

"Carl called you last night?"

"Yes, I was at my mother's house in Pembroke, visiting family. He called and said Miss Ludie had found a microfilm copy of a master's thesis that he had been searching for, and that it contained the final piece to the puzzle, the Tuscarora Connection."

Luther fell to one knee and he began searching through the leather briefcase until he pulled out a single sheet of paper. "Have you ever seen this before?"

He held it up for Roberta to examine, and she responded. "No, but it looks like it was copied from microfilm. Look at the sprocket holes on each side of the paper."

"It was, Roberta. Ludie found a microfilm, copied the document and gave it to Luther. This is the only page left of the copy. The killer probably took the rest with him, and whatever was on that microfilm may have gotten them both killed."

Roberta's face turned ashen, and Luther watched for a moment as the wheels turned in her head. She sat quietly, staring out the window as if something important had suddenly occurred to her, something she could not share.

Luther was certain that he knew why the three professors were killed, but he had no idea what information was on the microfilm. And though Roberta had been of help, he felt sure she was holding back information. Did she know who killed, Carl? Did she tell someone who told someone else? There was a lot more to Roberta Locklear than she had revealed, and he knew just the person to call and find out more about her. But first, he had to meet with Jimmy Bonner, Chief of the University Police Department, and give him an update on the investigation.

"Roberta, I have to go now to meet with an old friend. You have been a lot of help today, and I would like to come back and see you in a day or two. Would that be okay? Roberta, can you hear me?"

She continued staring out the window, "Yes, please call me anytime. I want to help, I really do, but I'm just so confused right now. It's too much to think about."

Luther rose from the sofa, let himself out, and was certain of two things. Roberta Locklear knew more than she had revealed, and may be connected to Carl's murder, whether she realized it or not.

* * *

Luther drove slowly past Umstead Dormitory on Tenth Street toward a stately old home that had been painted white and donated to the university years ago. It was now the headquarters of the ECU Police Department, and in a perfect position to keep an eye on the Kappa Sigma house across the street.

On some Friday afternoons the pledges would place couches from the party room on the front lawn. They would set a beer keg on the porch for 'Happy Hour,' and the brothers and pledges would holler and gesture toward the busy late afternoon traffic. Their hope was occasionally realized when one or more adventurous coeds would stand up in a convertible and bare it all to the boys of Kappa Sig, then speed down Tenth and up College Hill to disappear into the maze of dormitories.

'Don't know if they still do that or not,' Luther smiled to himself as he parked and walked around to the front of the house. He paused for a moment, not sure whether to ring the old doorbell, or if it even still worked.

"Luther," called a voice from inside. It was Wendell Harris, the detective from the Greenville PD. "Come on in. Jimmy and I were just talking about you."

They shook hands in the front reception area then Harris took him back to the Major's office. Jimmy Bonner was just hanging up the phone and stood to greet his guest, "You doing okay, Luther?"

"Okay just about sums it up, but I've got some information I need to share with you, both of you."

Wendell closed the door and pulled another side chair up to Jimmy's desk. "Good, Luther, 'cause right now we don't have anymore to go on than we had last night."

"What have you got?" Jimmy added.

Luther took a deep breath then looked straight at the two men. "Carl had two appointments on his calendar yesterday. One was to meet someone named Paskil for lunch, for what reason I don't know. But I'm assuming it may have had something to do with his research. If so, this person may live nearby and also may be connected to the university. So, Jimmy, could you do a search of current and former employee records and see if someone named Paskil is associated with the college? Sorry, I don't have a first name or initial."

"That's okay, Luther. I'll take care of this myself. Should have something for you later this afternoon."

Harris leaned forward. "What about the other appointment?"

"He was to meet Ludie Worthington in the Special Collections area of the library before six o'clock. It seems she had discovered a microfilm of an old master's thesis that had some information he needed for his Lost Colony research, and she had printed a hard copy for him." He glanced toward Jimmy. "The last page was the bibliography, the sheet you found under Carl's body."

"And the killer took the hard copy?" Harris asked.

Luther nodded. "I don't know what was on that microfilm, but it may be the connection between their murders. Ludie knew what Carl knew, and the killer wanted to make sure no one else got their hands on that information."

"What about the microfilm, Luther. Do you think the killer got that, too?"

"I have no idea, but for the moment I assume so."

"And Sherry," Jimmy added, "wrong place, wrong time?"

"That's the way I see it for now." Then Luther leaned back in his chair. "One more thing. I found out from Lucy, the department secretary," and he looked toward Jimmy who nodded and gave him an appreciative grin, "that Carl was working with his graduate assistant on some Lost Colony research. It was part of her master's thesis. So I went over to her apartment and talked with her."

"Suspect?" Harris asked immediately.

"Too soon to tell, detective, but she seemed willing to talk with me and share what information she had. The most important thing she told me was that Carl called her about seven o'clock last night at her mother's home in Pembroke."

The other two men leaned forward, certain that important information was about to be revealed. "She said he was very excited. He told her that Ludie had discovered the microfilm and printed a hard copy for him, and that it contained something he called the Tuscarora Connection."

"What does that mean?" Harris asked.

"According to Roberta, he said it was the final piece of the puzzle connecting the Lumbee Indians of Robeson County to the Lost Colonists of Roanoke Island."

"No shit," Jimmy responded. "She said that?" And he thought for a moment, "But how does that make her a suspect?"

"I'm not sure it does," Luther added, sincerely hoping that she was not part of this. "Look, she's pretty torn up, losing her thesis professor and a personal friend." He had decided not to reveal the true relationship between Carl and Roberta unless it was necessary. "She found it difficult to talk with me and eventually broke down, So I left her apartment, but " and he let the conjunction linger in the air for a moment. "I think I would like to find out a little more about her background."

"Good idea, Luther," Harris added. "I mean she may have told someone else about Ludie, the microfilm and that Tuscarora thing. And if she did, even if she isn't the prime suspect, she may be involved."

Luther nodded, "I agree, and that's why I want to go to Pembroke and find out more about Roberta Locklear."

"I know the Police Chief in Lumberton. I can give him a call."

"No, Jimmy. I want to do this quietly, just an average person making a few discreet inquiries. Sometimes it's better that way. People don't get as defensive and clam up as much as when law enforcement comes knocking on their doors."

"He's got a point, Jimmy. You got a contact down there, Luther?"

"Sure do, a good one, an old friend whose family owns *The Lumberton Herald*. He and I go way back to Duke University. I still see him occasionally at some of the newspaper conferences, and he knows everyone and everything that has happened in Robeson County for the past fifty years. If he doesn't know about Roberta Locklear, then he knows someone who does."

"Sounds like a good plan, Luther. I'll let the lieutenant know that you have this investigation well in hand, and that you're making great progress."

"Thanks, Harris, and also, for your kind words last night."

"I just told him the truth, Luther. You're damn good at this. If the newspaper business ever gets too tame for you, you can always join us in law enforcement."

"Had any time to check out the laptop?" Jimmy asked.

"So far, all I've found on the hard drive is his fiction novel about what the coastal Indians were like before the English first arrived in 1584. And I've got hard copies of all that in the notebook that was inside his briefcase."

"Good stuff?" Harris asked.

"Not sure. I haven't had time to read much of it. That's what I'm going to do this afternoon when I get home. So if you gentlemen will excuse me, I'm headed to the creek for some reading on the back porch." Then the three men shook hands and Luther headed out the way he had come in for the thirty-minute drive down east to Blount's Creek.

Indian Wood

Part Three

Arcadia of the New World

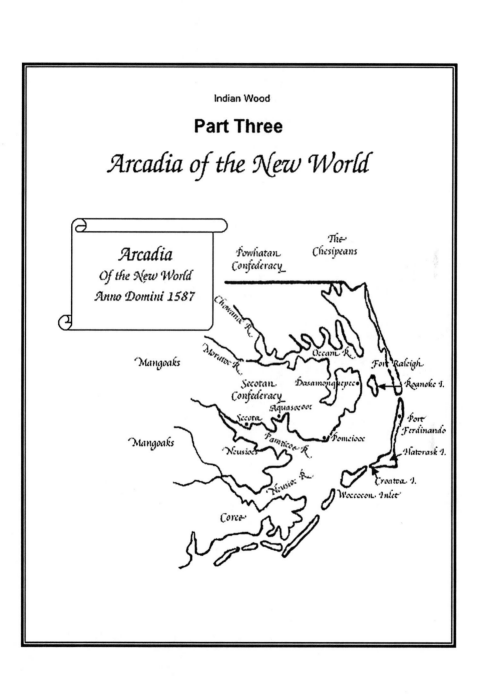

Arcadia
Of the New World
Anno Domini 1587

The
Chesipeans

Powhatan
Confederacy

Chowanix R.

Moratuc R.

Occam R.

Fort Raleigh

Mangoaks

Secotan
Confederacy

Dasamonquepec

Roanoke I.

Aquascecot

Secota

Pomeiooc

Fort
Ferdinando

Mangoaks

Pamticoe R.

Hatorask I.

Neusioc

Neusioc R.

Croatoa I.

Wococon Inlet

Coree

✤ ✤ ✤

LA NOVELLA

Heaven always seems nearer in a home by the water, and one of them sits on a point at the foot of Blount's Creek Bridge in Beaufort County, North Carolina. The silt laden creek took its name as the eastern terminus of colonial Governor Thomas Blount's private estate, spanning the distance between South Creek, near Aurora, and the brackish headwaters of Blount's Creek, some fifteen miles away. An old pull ferry had operated across the creek mouth since before the American Revolution, and the small beautiful bridge was now a quaint reminder of a long ago need for farmers, loggers and businessmen to have a reliable crossing of this once strategic body of water.

During the Civil War, Federal skirmishers had encountered Confederate pickets on the West side of the ferry, guarding the roadway to the gun emplacements of Fort Hill that secured the river approach to the town of Washington. Hurling insults across the creek, both sides postured and fired occasional shots until the Union force retreated to the safety of the highway back to New Bern.

The old store on the East side of the bridge had long ago rotted away. It was once the scene of countless conversations as men, young and old, fished, hunted, crabbed and scraped oysters from the riverbed. And all seemed to meet at one time or other on the wooden benches in front of the store; gas for trucks and boats, coffee on cold mornings, beer on warm afternoons, and candy, chips and sodas for the children.

While young boys and girls would test themselves by swimming to the center of the creek, climbing a rickety ladder of two by fours nailed to the center span, then making a leap of faith by jumping fifteen feet off the bridge into the black brackish water below, their fathers and uncles would sit around and tell humongous lies. And none was a bigger liar than Mr. Earl, owner of the country store. "I tell you, boys, I was wounded some kinda' bad back in the war. I was such a mess they had to put me on two stretchers just to get me to the aid station where they could sew me back together." And all the men would erupt in laughter at the outrageous story as another World War II veteran launched into an even bigger tale.

That was the way it had been for generations of young men and women on the South side of the Pamilco River, until Mr. Earl's wife died of leukemia, and he fell into a depression that not even his prized 'Coon' hunting dogs could bring him out of; and prostate cancer eventually took him away. Later owners tried to keep it running, but with the passing of time the old lapboard sided shotgun building fell into general disrepair and finally closed. And then developers took an interest in the small piece of property that jutted out into Blount's Bay. First, one with dreams of condos and a marina, then another with a dream of a ship's store and home lots, and finally the property ended up on the auction block of the courthouse steps. That's when Luther bought his seven acres of heaven on the water, four of marsh grass, and three of up ground, upon which he built the home of his dreams.

He always had admired the architecture of the old Life Saving Stations constructed along the Outer Banks of North Carolina in the late 19th century. During summers away from school, he also enjoyed the creature comforts of the Cape Cod style beach homes near Hyannis Port, Massachusetts, where he once lived and worked with two of his fraternity brothers, as assistant dock masters. It had been his intention to combine the best of the two styles into one plan, and that is the house he built on the point at the mouth of Blount's Creek. The river could take him ten miles up to Washington, or sixty miles East to Ocracoke, and out into the Atlantic to any place in the world where a boat could travel.

The house was elevated ten feet above the ground in case of flooding due to hurricane surges. Grey shingled siding covered the exterior, leading up to the porches and many gables on the roof, but it was the rounded 'Widow's Walk' on top that gave the home its unique character. Luther rarely walked up the circular stairs and ladder staircase that led to the door that would take him outside to enjoy the beautiful panoramic views of the Pamlico River. He was satisfied to sit in a wicker rocker on a twelve foot wide back porch that ran the length of the house, which offered just as satisfactory a view, and placed him closer to the sounds of the marsh grasses whistling in the breeze, singing an enchanting melody for anyone on the back porch.

While rocking gently in his chair, he stared at the wicker porch swing where Carl would sometimes lean a floral cushion against the right side so he could put his feet up and lay back facing out into the bay. The nearly constant breeze would move the swing back and forth and Carl would often fall asleep. It was as if his friend were with him now, swinging peacefully in the breeze, while Luther scrolled through the pages of Carl's novel on the laptop computer.

They were the same pages as in the notebook, and even though he was used to reading electronic copy on his computer at work, he preferred the feel and texture of hard copy whenever it was available. He turned the power off, gently closed the laptop, and reached for the white plastic covered notebook. It was not yet the novel Carl had intended, but a smaller version, a novella. He opened the cover, flipped past the title page, 'Arcadia of the New World,' and studied the chapter titles, including the ones not yet written. Then he turned the page to begin reading 'The Captain's Tale.'

✤ ✤ ✤

THE CAPTAIN'S TALE

London, Fall of 1583

The water taxi sculled easily up the Thames, trying to shoot London Bridge before the tidal surge rose and prevented even a small gondola from passing under the roadbed. The waterman pushed steadily on the long oars as he peered into a miserable fog, trying to avoid small barges and other tilt boats carrying patrons to all parts of the waterfront city.

Beneath the awning sat a graying sea captain; cheeks puffed and blistered red by salty winds, his hollow black eyes reflecting the disaster of his most recent voyage. He was deep in thought, hardly aware of the mist that crept under his cloak, chilling his aging bones. Occasionally his lips would tremble, and he would mutter softly as he rehearsed the report of his passage to the New World.

"Durham house on the left, Sir," the waterman whispered softly.

Edward Hayes leaned forward to view the old Norman towers that rose straight up from the river. In a small turret on the right he could see the light in Raleigh's study, and though he longed for relief of his report, he dreaded worse to face his patron.

As the tilt boat brushed the water gate, the captain rose from his seat and stepped out on the landing, turning to face the oarsman, "Two pence for this?" and he winced as he felt in his purse for the fare.

"Ay cap'em, a man 'as 'es livin' to make."

"Hay penny too much if you should ask me," he replied gruffly, and tossed the coins deftly toward the boatman.

"Shall I wait, Sir?" asked the boatman, hoping for a return fare.

Captain Hayes looked up at the light in the turret then glanced back at the young waterman. "Not this evening,' my boy. It's a woeful tale I have for Master Raleigh, so fetch yerself up to Whitehall for a royal fare."

Then Hayes turned quickly toward a large oak door that a servant had already begun to open.

Durham House belonged to the Queen, and she had consented to lease the upper apartments to Walter Raleigh, her new courtier from Devonshire. It had been a Bishop's home in London, just off the famous strand that ran along the Thames River. But after her father, Henry VIII, broke from the Papacy in 1532, all religious property in England was forfeited to the crown, and kept or doled out to friends according to the King's wishes. To his daughter, Elizabeth, he deeded Durham House for life, and to Raleigh she would lease the upper floors until her death.

Captain Hayes walked slowly behind Ephriam Turner, one of Raleigh's young house servants, and looked over the gardens on each side. 'How lovely the frail flowers, and so many yet to bloom' he thought as he recalled some of the Caribbean Islands he had once visited. A breeze whispered around the corner as they turned up a flight of stairs to the second floor. "Larger than it looks from the river," he said to no one as he gazed up and down the halls and over the courtyard. He took notice of the furniture and décor. 'More functional than ornate,' he thought as he considered the man who lived there. 'All the better to show off the peacock,' and for the first time that day a smile creased his lips.

Only two years before, the man from Devonshire, had been a penniless army captain, fresh from the brutal attempts to crush rebellion in Ireland. It was Raleigh's knowledge of colonial affairs that brought him to London and the attention of Francis Walsingham, special advisor to the Queen and head of her secret spy network. In a discussion on Irish strategy before the Privy Council, Raleigh had submitted a new plan to finance the struggle in Ireland, and this greatly impressed the frugal monarch. Always taking note of a bold new face and voice, Elizabeth took him aside and was charmed by the man and his West Country accent.

Other than his soldier half-brother, Sir Humphrey Gilbert, Raleigh had no other associations at court. At twenty-eight he was a tall fetching red-haired young man, a romantic poet, courageous soldier and a mystery to the Queen. He held her attention for hours while he spun tales of adventure and ambitious plans, so many of which took place on the high seas that she gave him the pet name, 'Warter.'

He stepped quickly from the shadows into the light of the Queen's favor. Country manors were granted to the new court favorite, and to give him a suitable income, the monopoly on the 'Farm of Wines.' His influence at court grew steadily, but the wealth and power one gained was the envy of all who sought it. Raleigh soon found himself one of the most hated men in London.

His only friend at Whitehall was the Queen herself. Others simply accommodated the arrogance and wit of the current favorite. For comfort and peace of mind he would travel to his home in Devonshire, two hundred miles west, but in London he would retire to his study in the turret at Durham House, and that is where Edward Hayes found him, late on a bleak afternoon in September, 1583.

"Come in, please," called a firm voice from behind the door.

Hayes dreaded to enter. It was the first sight of his face he feared, knowing he already knew and having to go over the whole miserable affair with him. Ephriam pushed the door open slowly and stood back for the sea captain to enter. The room was not so large as it seemed, but round and well suited for a study. The windows offered views up and down the Thames, an inspiring sight for a man who seldom came to London town.

"Come in, Captain Hayes, please don't stand in the doorway." Raleigh's eyes flashed and a sullen smile was on his face.

"My word, Sir," Hayes exclaimed as he entered the room. "It's that I am," and he paused as if seeking the right words, "somewhat speechless Master Raleigh."

Raleigh turned quickly to the servant at the door, "Ephriam, ale for the captain and a block of cheese and bread." The young man disappeared and Raleigh turned back to Hayes. "Speechless," he said, smiling curiously. "Not this day, my friend, for we have much to talk about. I want to know how it passed from the day you departed Plymouth Harbor till the day..." Raleigh suddenly turned away and stepped over to a window where he looked down the Thames toward Whitehall Palace, residence of the Queen.

Hayes stood still, considering the fortunes of this young man since they first met on an earlier aborted attempt to reach Newfoundland in 1578. Always a fancy in dress, he was now the word in fashion. He looked over the young courtier, dressed in a silver satin vest, brown velvet doublets, silk slippers and more jewels embroidered therein than ever a man saw in one place. Most interesting of all was the magnificent white pearl piercing his left ear, which was barely visible under the locks of course reddish hair.

The quiet made Hayes suddenly nervous, and he wanted to get on with his report, to be done with it, and he blurted out the facts that he knew to be close to Raleigh's heart. "Pooped from the rear she was. We tried to get him to come off the Squirrel, not ten tons draught, but Gilbert refused, you see."

Raleigh turned around quickly, his eyes ablaze. "But why, the general should have chosen the larger vessel for his flagship?"

"Ay, but there was them that feared to cross again in the pinnace, sir. And Gilbert sought to inspire them by leaving the Golden Hinde to sail home on the Squirrel."

"Go on," said Raleigh impatiently.

"Just off the Azores we come into high seas and a great storm blew over us. That evenin' just before dark, the Squirrel came astern and they was nailin' a chair to the stern castle for Sir Humphrey. Then he came over to the rail with his red hair flyin' and shouted for all to hear, "As near to heaven by sea as by land." Then he went and sat in that chair continuin' to read. So we trimmed sail to let the Squirrel gain ahead, intendin' to watch her light in the darkness, so not to lose sight of her."

Raleigh leaned against the small oak desk in front of the large turret windows, gripping the sides with his bare hands. "And then what happened?"

Captain Hayes let his hands fall to his sides and bowed his head slightly. "Near 'bout midnight of the ninth, still in heavy seas, the watch cried out, 'The General is cast away.' She just went down the front of a great sea and was pooped from the rear, she was. And we searched by God we did. Traversed the same till dusk next evenin' with every man on watch, but not a sign, Master Raleigh, not even a plank 'a wood in them heavy seas."

Raleigh was breathing heavily, as if he had just run up the stairs to his study. His head hung down and a watery glaze covered his eyes while he grieved for his lost half-brother by his mother's first marriage. Though fifteen years his senior, Humphrey had taken Raleigh under wing and filled his head with adventurous tales of gold-laden Spanish galleons and prospects for English colonies in the New World.

These were the same tales he told the Queen as if they were his own. And when she asked Gilbert not to sail on this attempt to plant a colony in Newfoundland, it was Raleigh who persuaded her to allow his half-brother to sail with the fleet; all the more reason for his guilt.

He stepped away from the desk toward a window to gaze down the Thames past Tower Bridge, and remembered youthful days at Hayes Barton, the old family home. He recalled trips to the mouth of the river Dart with his father and younger brother Carew, where they would sit around the docks for hours listening to stories of far away ports and glory at sea. Never did the sailors speak of hardship and death, only the riches and glory that awaited those who dared the adventure.

A fresh evening breeze rose up to the window and filled the room. Raleigh lifted his hand to his forehead, and without turning around said to the captain, "So tell me then, what may I say to the Queen of this voyage?"

Before Hayes could answer, Ephriam reappeared with bread, cheese and two pewter tankards. The captain cast a longing glance at the table where they were placed, but hesitated. Raleigh, quickly responded, "Please, Captain, my table is yours."

Hayes stepped forward and picked up a mug of ale. "And for you, Sir?"

"Nothing for me, now, except an answer for the Queen."

Hayes took a large gulp from the cool tankard, then set it down and began to cut a wedge of cheese. "Damnable weather from the start, Sir, just like in seventy-eight, you remember? We sailed into a gale the same day we lost sight 'a Lands End, and kept it till we got to Ireland. Then two days fair weather an' we struck a greater storm. We beat to windward forty to fifty degrees tryin' to make headway, and finally made St. John's on August three."

"We found fishing vessels there from several nations, but seeing our superior number and armament they readily agreed to England as sovereign of the lands there about. And to be sure of Master Cabot's claim to the land, Sir Humphrey held a special ceremony on a point high above the water in which all lands west to Oceana Pacifica were taken in the name of Elizabeth, for the glory of England."

With part of his story told, Hayes turned up the tankard and gulped heartily, and with a bead of ale in his beard continued. "Passed a fortnight in St. Johns, feasting in the company of fishermen, even the Spanish. But then Captain Browne of the Swallow and a number of his crew feigned sick and desired to return to England. Sir Humphrey, knowing they was set on pirating the fishing fleet soon as we departed, confiscated her cannon and sent her home.

"Then to aid in searching bays and rivers along the coast, he made the Squirrel his flagship, and had the Swallow's cannon set on board, overcharging the frigate with ordnance in my opinion. But you remember how Master Gilbert was, 'For show,' he said, 'in case we meet up with any of Frobisher's Eskimos.' And you recall what they did to the Captain and his crew?" Raleigh nodded glumly at the tragedy that befell Martin Frobisher

and his men after their ship was encased in ice on one of his many voyages in
search of a northern route to the land of Cathay, source of the valuable silk
trade.

Hayes glanced over toward the desk, hoping the story might bring
some hint of relief from Raleigh, but his patron continued gazing down the
Thames, offering only his back for an audience. "Seeing as how we discharged
so much pickled beef and dry provisions entertaining the fishermen on St.
Johns, we made for Sable Island to take what cattle and swine we could find,
remembering the French had left them years before to breed. Eight days
later we arrived off Cape Bretton and then a gale came over us. And the
Delight, of much greater draught than the Squirrel or Golden Hinde was run
aground.

Captain Hayes' voice became softer as he continued, "We beat about
miserably as the storm swept the shallops and rafts of the Delight away from
us; men drowning within sight, yet we were helpless to assist them. For two
days after we beat about more, seeking some sign of their salvation, but for
naught." Then he whispered, "Near a hundred good men were lost, along
with all the provisions for the colony."

Walking over toward a window he continued. "So the General held
a meeting on board the Hinde, and it was decided to turn back to England,
refurbish, and set out again next Spring. But then, the men on board the
Squirrel began to complain of her seaworthiness, claiming she wasn't fit to
face another storm, much less a return crossing. That's when Sir Humphrey,
against all better judgment, and to calm the fear of the crew, decided to return
to England on board the Squirrel."

Each man stood near a window, looking out over the Thames toward
Lambeth Marsh on the other side. Almost to himself, Captain Hayes whispered,
"He was a good leader, your brother, he was; if only he had lightened the
Squirrel of some ordnance."

Raleigh, still quietly grieving, heard the last words and commented,
"None of your guilt, Captain, for my brother Gilbert was of no hap by sea, and
met his fate by his own hand." Without turning again to face Edward Hayes,
he added, "My thanks to you for coming, Sir, and please put all this in writing
for the Privy Council."

Relieved of his burden, Hayes stepped quickly to the table and put
the tankard by the cheese. "Ay, Master Raleigh." Then he picked up his cloak
and walked quietly to the door. "My sorrow to you and the Gilbert family,
Sir," and with a soft clink of the latch the door closed behind him.

THE CHARTER

London, Spring of 1584

Early morning sunlight shimmered up the Thames toward London Bridge where farmers were carting fresh meats and produce to the great houses along the Strand. Raleigh had been up before the sun and taken a chair on top of the turret to watch the city rise and quicken to life. He shivered slightly in the cool morning mist. 'So different from the heat and stench of summer,' he thought to himself.

He inhaled a breath of fresh air and smiled softly as he considered the plan he had been cultivating for several months. With his right hand he pulled the fine reddish hair on his chin into a point, in the fashion of the day, and thought quietly to himself. 'To Durham House I will bring the finest minds of England, and together we shall plan the way.' His cool dark eyes lifted toward the blue morning sky and he spoke softly into the wind. "The path lay before us, and by the soul of my dear lost brother, England shall have her colony in the New World."

The clanging of a bell below caught his ear, and he peered over the wall to see a small barge coming up to the water gate, ringing to let the house servants know of its arrival. The great oak door swung open and out came Mary Clement, his cook and her scullery assistant. "Fetch me up a basket full 'a eggs lad, and a turn 'a butter." She stepped on board and began picking through the sparse early season fruits, then ale, and finally the vegetables that she always purchased by the basketful. As Raleigh watched the cook and her helper pick over the produce, he made up his mind to go before the Queen and seek Gilbert's letters of patent to explore and colonize in the New World.

He was very proud of his home in London, and the small fortune he had accumulated, but a dream to plant and cultivate a new England, in a new world, far away from the pomp and ceremony of court was stirring in his soul. It dined with him and slept with him at night, occupying his thoughts even in the presence of Elizabeth. He swelled with pride at the thought of succeeding in a new world where the power of England had not yet succeeded in Ireland.

His personal servant, Ephriam Turner, had joined those below carrying the day's rations into the house. Raleigh spied his curly brown hair and shouted down, "Ephriam, my horse upon the hour."

The young man looked up, "Ay, Master Raleigh, by the front gate upon the hour."

* * *

The man from Devonshire sat high in the saddle, cocking gently with the gait of the horse. To the criers in the street, selling their wares, he was a resplendent example of what it meant to be in favor at the Queen's court. Riding his magnificent grey stallion, he wore white silk doublets and shirt, a red velvet cloak laden with pearls, and hat to match, with a large feather plume trailing off to the side.

His aide from the campaigns in Ireland, Michael Butler, rode ahead to clear a path, "Out of the way for Walter Raleigh. He's to see the Queen, be off now."

Vendors and passersby stood aside to let him pass, women in swoon and men admiring, but casting curious untrusting glances at the court favorite. The horse labored over the cobblestones and pressed on toward the smooth brick way in front of Whitehall Palace, where Raleigh stopped beside a young girl selling flowers. He smiled as she stepped back, somewhat in fear of the man of whom she had heard so many tales. "White roses?" he asked softly. "Do you have any white roses for the Queen?"

Her face brightened and she completely forgot who the man on horseback might be. "The Queen," she squealed, "my flowers for the Queen?" And her hands flew up to cover her face. Then she quickly began searching in her cart, selecting only the finest white roses, and wrapped them in a bolt of green silk she saved for her very best customers. She held them up, knowing that it was possible the man on horseback might actually give them to the Queen. "A gift for the Queen," she whispered, "from one 'a her majesty's most loyal servants."

It never ceased to amaze Raleigh, the love and devotion Elizabeth commanded from her subjects. As surely as they despised her half-sister, Mary, they would give up their own lives in her service. "A good heart you have, dear lady, and I shall convey your kindness to Her majesty."

"Oh, my," she swooned back, and covered her mouth with her hands. Then she blurted out for all to hear, "God bless you, Master Raleigh, and God Save the Queen." And upon a chorus of "God Save the Queen," Raleigh was heralded toward the palace.

For several minutes after he passed the gates of Whitehall, the refrain could still be heard, and then it died away as business returned to normal in the streets of London. Captain Butler turned to Raleigh, "Be strong in your convictions, Sir, for she is stronger than a blade of steel in such matters."

"How so?" Raleigh queried.

"Took your brother twelve years to wrest Letters of Marque from the Queen, so do not feel poorly if you should not succeed in one day."

Raleigh smiled confidently and gave a mocking salute to his friend and confidant, "To the battle then," he whispered, and swung easily off his horse. "Meet me by the tennis court at noon, and we shall see how I have fared."

He walked quickly toward the palace staircase, the roses held gracefully before him and made a course for the Queen's private apartments. Other courtiers cast piercing eyes at the arrogant young man as he strode the halls, hardly acknowledging the admiring glances from the ladies at court.

Court life was an extravagant and elaborate affair in which every courtier went to great lengths to profess and demonstrate his hopeless love for Elizabeth. Raleigh was particularly well suited for such games. Young, handsome, intelligent and quick of wit, he appealed to her curiosity and intellect. He challenged and stimulated her mind as few at court could, with his passionate poetry and marvelous tales of adventure.

They would often play cards far into the night, with Raleigh reciting poems and calculating the means by which to lose his hand to Elizabeth. She was the radiant center of life at court, from which emanated all warmth, beauty, and wealth. And all who sought her patronage must learn to play her game, and play it well.

As the recently appointed Captain of the Queen's Guard, Raleigh stepped smartly toward her apartment door, waving off the four guards, placing the flowers behind his back and entering the small delicate antechamber. Seeing no one, he barely paused as he set off through the next door. He could hear the frivolity of the ladies in waiting on the Queen's person as he grasped the handle, then all became quiet. He paused and listened for a moment, then dared proceed into the inner sanctum where he found the Queen barely through her elaborate morning toiletry.

Raleigh had been in the Queen's bedchamber before, but never had he seen her without wig or make-up. 'Truly, she looked every one of her fifty years,' he thought to himself. Her frail hair, still mercifully streaked with red, was pulled back, awaiting her wig, and her pale sullen cheeks begged for a touch of color to give them life.

She rose from the stool and pulled her long elegant hands away from the attendants who were painting her nails. "Warter," she said, mocking his Devonshire accent, "must you engage a poor woman so early, before she is ready for court?"

He looked for more than a moment at Elizabeth, who was after all a mortal woman. Then he considered whether his daring entry should have been averted, or if indeed he was creating the effect he had planned. Surely the ladies in attendance would spread the story through court that only Walter Raleigh dared enter the sanctum before the Queen's toilet was complete.

'It mattered little,' he thought. His course was now set and he must proceed. "Glorianna, my fair, a blessed good morning," and he smiled brilliantly as he had planned.

The ladies attending the Queen normally retired when a courtier came into her presence, but under the circumstance they were unsure of her pleasure. All of them stepped quietly back awaiting the Queen's wishes, gazing admiringly at the handsome young Raleigh.

"I could, dear Highness, have waited I know, but the beauty of a white virgin rose must not." The Queen smiled to herself as Raleigh fell to one knee, bowed his head and pulled the roses from behind his back, and the attendants swooned together at his gesture.

She motioned for her lead attendant to accept the flowers, an obvious compliment to her regal virginity. As the young woman leaned forward to receive the roses, Raleigh's head lifted up, glancing at her brocaded bosom. Then their eyes met, and he was astonished at the beauty of Martha Throcmorton. Her auburn hair spilled round her pink youthful face, and her ruby lips were smiling back at him. This was indeed a woman whose chamber Raleigh would later visit, but for now both must play the courtly game.

Fortunately, Elizabeth held her head askew so as not to show too much of her aging face, and she missed the passionate glance between Raleigh and her lead attendant. But the other ladies of the court saw the blush in her cheeks as Martha found a vase in which to plant the roses. In mock frustration Elizabeth cried, "Be gone, Warter, be gone I say, till I am more suitable."

"As you wish, Majesty," he responded and began to rise.

Martha held the vase of roses up to the Queen and she took an admiring sniff of their delicate fragrance, then glanced at her courtier. "We shall break the fast of night together in the garden."

Raleigh stood and smiled, "Though it pains me to leave, Glorianna, I shall wait for you there."

She glanced quickly at him, a smile upon her face, "Till then, my Lord, now be off." Then she leaned slightly to catch a last glimpse of her handsome young suitor as he closed the door.

* * *

Sunlight was shimmering warmly on the table in the garden as Raleigh and Elizabeth made small talk over fresh fruit and the Queen's favorite bran cereal. "Your constitution requires it, Warter, now eat I say."

"I am sure it does," he responded with a smile, "but my palate refuses." He reached for a slice of freshly baked sweet bread and began to butter it generously. "Now this is fit for the Captain of the Queen's Guard."

"The day will come," she continued, "when bran will find a place in your diet, whether it suits your palate or not." Then she smiled knowingly to herself as she looked out over her well-manicured flowers, shrubs and trees, and the many brick paths that ran between them. She loved her garden where she could walk alone and admire each variety and fragrance of her natural subjects, while she contemplated the affairs of state. She leaned back in her padded chair with a silver goblet perched between her fingertips, filled with freshly squeezed juice, and stared casually at a vase containing white roses sitting in the middle of the table.

"A peasant girl asked that I give these to you."

"But only after you offered to purchase them for me."

Raleigh looked curiously at the Queen, "And how did you know that?"

"My dear, Warter, it is part of being the Queen of England to know what her subjects are thinking, and I know what you are thinking even now." He smiled sheepishly and looked deeply into the Queen's sparkling eyes as she continued. "Your brother's charter to explore and settle in the New World, you want it for yourself."

He sat amazed as she continued, "I am not so much a seer as I have Walsingham, and his 'friends' shall I say, who keep me well informed. He serves me faithfully, and is well rewarded for his service." She reached forward and plucked a single rose from the vase and twirled it thoughtfully under her nose, "And you also serve the crown well."

"Thank you, Majesty," he replied proudly.

"I so admire you, Warter, your courage, vitality, sense of duty and adventure. So tell me then, what would you do with Gilbert's charter?"

Raleigh's eyes cleared immediately, the moment was at hand and a fresh look of excitement covered his face. Now he must convince the Queen of England of his worthy plan, and he began to plead his case. "The reasons for a colony in the New World are few and simple, but very important to the future of England. Though we are not at war with Spain, the feelings are mutually hostile, and we attack each other's shipping openly on the high seas. Therefore, Majesty, a base in the New World from which to operate would be ideal. Drake and Cavendish would not have to make the perilous journey home to England after each successful sea forage; they could put into our new port to refit for another voyage."

"Yes, I have heard that suggestion from Drake himself, please go on."

"And with a colony, we can also explore our New World lands and may yet discover riches to rival those of Spain."

"That would indeed be of comfort to our treasury, but is that possible?"

Raleigh unleashed himself in reciting the tale of David Ingram who in 1569 had walked from the Spanish fort of St. Augustine in Florida to the fabled land of Norumbega near Newfoundland, "where the natives plate their houses in metal of such brilliance..."

"Oh come now, Raleigh," and for once she called him by his given name. "Enough of Ingram, now more of your plan."

"The Northwest Passage to Cathay, Majesty, which you did send Martin Frobisher in search of..." and he paused to observe the Queen's keen interest in a sea passage that could link England directly to the silk and spice trade of the Orient. "Consider how much further, and more fully, adventurous men like Frobisher might explore for the glory of England if they had a base in the New World from which to operate?"

"Indeed, his voyages were successful, but..." then her eyes suddenly lit up. "Did you see the Eskimo man and woman he brought back on one of his last voyages, and a child, too?"

"Yes, Majesty," and then he paused. "A pity they were filled with consumption and did not survive to return home."

"It is true, what you say, about a base for exploring in the New World," she continued, dismissing the deaths of the Eskimo natives from her thoughts.

"And Glorianna," Raleigh continued with increased enthusiasm, "consider how a colony could become an economic asset to England. Our debtors and the unemployed could be sent there, initially as servants to work off their ship's payment and debts, and then begin a new life in a new England. And as the colony grows and prospers, it could become a trading partner to help sustain the homeland.

He watched her eyes focus on some distant flower in the garden, and still holding her attention he continued. "And finally, your Majesty, the reformed religion of the Church of England..."

No sooner had these words escaped his lips than the Queen turned with glaring intensity. Raleigh was surprised by her grave expression and nearly stopped in mid sentence, but thought it better to continue, "... could be spread into the New World by each and every colonist from England."

A smile slowly appeared to lighten the Queen's face, and she sat quietly for a moment looking out into the garden before speaking. "Mendoza, do you know him?"

"Yes, the Spanish emissary."

"He sees and hears all. Walsingham tells me he has as many spies at court as I have courtiers. And for that reason, Warter, I ask that you be extremely careful with whom you discuss the details of these plans."

Raleigh's hopes grew expectantly high. "Then the charter will be granted?"

Elizabeth turned to look squarely at Raleigh. "Upon two conditions."

"Anything your Majesty wishes that is in my power to grant."

"One, that not a pence of royal fare shall be spent to support the venture. It must be financed entirely by your own means or that of investors."

"Agreed," he responded quickly.

"And that you, dear Warter, not sail on any voyage in support of this venture."

The smile vanished from Raleigh's face and a heavy sigh crept out before he could contain it. "But, Majesty, I..."

"Enough," she said sternly. "I have already lost one of Devon's sons in this cause and I shall not risk his brother. You must agree to these conditions or the charter will not be yours."

Raleigh stared sadly at the aging monarch, knowing her mind was set, but hoping it could later be changed. "Agreed, your Majesty."

* * *

The telephone phone rang inside the house. Luther frowned and shook his head as he looked up from Carl's novel. He forgot to bring the cordless extension with him out on the porch. 'It never fails,' he thought and decided to let voicemail take the call, until he heard Veronica's smoky voice.

"Luther, darling, are you there? Please pick up. The receptionist at the paper said you were at home, and I just wanted to ask you about," and then her voice trailed off. She could not find the words to speak of Carl's murder.

Luther jumped from his chair and ran inside, grabbing the phone and pressing the button for the recorder to stop in one motion. "Veronica," he said, his heart pounding slightly from the run inside, or was it the excitement of hearing her voice again. "So good of you to call."

"Luther, I don't know what to say," she said in exasperation. "I heard about it on the news this morning, and I have been crying ever since. Who would do such a thing to dear, sweet Carl? And Ludie, she was such a pleasant and feisty woman." Her voice trailed off into a moment of silence. "And you, dear Luther, how are you doing?"

Luther coughed slightly, clearing his throat. "I'm okay, Veronica. I just miss him. We've been best friends for over forty years and done so much together; fishing, hunting, archaeological digs."

"And all those parties at the river, Luther. You two were something special the way you carried on together. A woman could get jealous over such a friendship."

He smiled to himself at so many memories he and Veronica and Carl had shared together. "And you, how are you doing up there in Winston-Salem?"

She sighed into the phone, "Fine, Luther, just fine. You know the parties are a bit tamer here than at the creek. No one gets naked and runs up to jump off the bridge. They just get a little tipsy and call for their drivers to carry them home. But still," and her voice fell silent.

"Is it what you wanted, expected it to be?"

She did not answer for a long moment. "Well, I do miss some things about my life at the creek," and he could feel her smile into the phone. "Life was good there, it just wasn't everything I needed it to be."

"I understand," he whispered, wishing he could hold her again.

"Have arrangement been made?" she asked.

"We're in the process of finalizing things. There will be a memorial service and viewing. Then Carl wanted to be cremated and have his ashes spread in several places, including here at the creek."

"Could I please help, Luther?" she asked quickly, a quiet desperate tone in her voice. "Carl was a good friend, one of the finest people I've ever known; a bit of a ladies' man to be sure, but such a sweet gentlemen."

"Of course, Veronica. Carl would be pleased to have you here, and involved." And he thought to himself, 'So will I.'

"You will call me then," she said as her voice broke, "when arrangements have been made, so I can be there, for you and Carl."

"As soon as I know."

There was a slight pause in the conversation, as if neither wanted to be the first to say good-bye. But then it was done, and Luther went back out on the porch to continue reading. He sat down and opened the notebook to where he had stopped. And to his surprise, on the next page was a handwritten note from Carl.

Some of the Algonquian Indian names and locations in the following chapters may be difficult for readers to understand and recall. As an aide, I may include an alpha list and brief description of important characters and places, like the one below.

Carl L. Bowden

Algonquian	Indians inhabiting the coastal areas from Northern Virginia down to the Pamlico River in NC
Aquascogoc	one of the villages of the Secotan Indian Confederation, located near modern day Belhaven
Catuaga	the leader of a Neusioc Indian war party

Croatoa	island on which the Croatan Indians lived, primarily around modern day Buxton, NC
Dasamonquepec	...main village of the Secotan Indian Confederation, located near the modern day community of Mann's Harbor, NC
Hanowocta	the Chief, or Weroance, of Aquascogoc, and father of Kimtoc
Hattorask	area along the Outer Banks where the Croatan Indians lived
Kimtoc	son of Hanowocta; soon to wed Oshanoa of Croatoa
Mangoaks	Tuscarora (Iroquoi) Indians living West of the Secotans
Manteo	son of the village chief of Croatoa
Neusiocs	warring (Siouan) Indians, living across the Pamticoe along the tidal waters of the Neuse River
Oshanoa	a maiden from the isle of Croatoa who is to marry Kimtoc, son of the Chief of Aquascogoc
Pamticoe	Secotan Indian name for the Pamlico River
Secotan	Algonquian Indian tribes between the Albemarle and Pamlico Sounds, united together for trade and common defense
Verotacam	wife of the great chief, Wingina of Dasamonquepec
Wanchese	a Secotan Indian warrior from the village of Pomeioc
Wingina	the greatest chief of the Secotan Confederation
Wingo	another name the Secotans used for their great chief, Wingina
Weroance	Algonquian word for village chief

❖ ❖ ❖

THE VILLAGE OF AQUASCOGOC

Spring of 1584

A late afternoon sun burned through the plumes of smoke rising from the cooking fires of Aquascogoc. The women of the village labored over fire pits with steaming clay pots of meats and vegetables hanging from poles suspended above glowing coals, all in preparation for the evening's wedding feast. Kimtoc, son of the village chief, was to wed Oshanoa, the most favored maiden of Croatoa.

The chiefs of many important villages and an assembly of their warriors had been arriving during the day, but it was the greatest of them, Wingina of Dasamonquepec, Weroance of the Secotan Confederation, that gave the day such importance. It was his blessing that the chief of Aquascogoc sought for his son and his new wife. For the son of a chief who received such a blessing would surely have sons who would one day become chiefs themselves.

"He comes," cried a voice in a small canoe out in the river. "He comes," yelled the voice again excitedly. Manteo, son of the chief of Croatoa had positioned himself at the mouth of the creek for a strategic view of the river that led to the great waters of Pamticoe. With his long muscled arms he began to paddle furiously back to shore staying well ahead of the great canoe that carried Wingina. His brown skin glistened in the yellow light from a thin coating of bear fat that protected him from mosquitoes, and with each stroke of the paddle he gritted his teeth, further distorting the red and yellow bands of decorative paint that had been carefully applied to his face.

His canoe moved swiftly, the air drawing back a long mane of black hair in the middle of his head. The sides, long ago shaved clean by the sharpened edge of an oyster shell, and picked routinely to keep them smooth, glistened from growing beads of perspiration.

As his canoe came very close to shore he laid his paddle down in front and rose from his knees to a crouch. Just as the boat touched bottom he sprang forward to join his father and the other warriors of Croatoa. Word that Wingina was arriving spread quickly through the village, and everyone who could leave the cooking fires began to run toward the shore, seeking out the spot where the chief of their own village had chosen to greet their greatest weroance.

Manteo ran through the crowd till he found his mother limping through the chaos. As his hand touched her elbow she turned and smiled warmly. Only a few of her teeth had survived the chewing of animal hides to soften the edges so a bone needle could penetrate them. But still her smile was warm and beautiful to her only son, whom she loved more dearly than the withered old warrior she had for a husband. No words passed between them as they walked carefully among the others, seeking out the large gathering that had come from the island of Croatoa.

Though his was the smallest village of those gathered for the wedding feast, the bride was from Croatoa, and therefore, Manteo's village was second in line to Aquascogoc to welcome the great chief, Wingina. As he took his place behind his father, the large canoe came into view at the mouth of the creek. A greeting chant rose from among those gathered on the bank and continued until Wingina's boat was nearly ashore. "Wingo, Wingo," they shouted, as children peeked eagerly from behind their mother's deerskin waist wraps for a glimpse of a canoe that held thirty warriors stroking proudly in perfect rhythm.

Wingina sat kneeling in the center. His head was shaved on both sides, with a long mane down the middle, but unlike Manteo's, the long shock was braided and decorated with tiny wampum shells. Around his neck hung copper blades and turquoise stones that had come from trading with the Western tribes for Yaupon leaves, which were used to make a sacred, tongue numbing black tea.

The closer the large canoe came to shore, the easier it was for Manteo to see that the great chief was much younger than his own father. But then he remembered the leader of the Secotan Confederation was chosen from among the many weroances according to bravery and skill in battle. And Wingina, his father had often told him, had one other gift that made him a great leader, the wisdom to avoid war when it was not necessary.

Behind the main canoe were three smaller ones carrying the wife and family of the great chief, and many other warriors. Just as the great canoe touched bottom, Wingina stood and called to his people. Everyone fell to their knees to acknowledge their leader, except the other chiefs who bowed at the waist as a gesture of loyalty. Then all rose quickly, beginning the chant once again, but Manteo was slow to rise because he helped his mother stand on legs that now could only bend and walk with difficulty.

The chant continued vigorously as the other canoes arrived, and Verotacam, wife of Wingina, was carried by two warriors and placed beside her husband. Her long black hair was braided on both sides and decorated in a manner similar to her husband's. Her face was round and smooth with blue tattooed lips and cheeks. She had not suffered the harsh weathering effects of the other women who had to gather firewood and tend gardens, as well as care for their children and warrior husbands.

When Verotacam smiled, as she often did, Manteo could see that her teeth also suffered from disease, even though she did not have to chew skins the way his mother did. Covering the front of her gown were turquoise beads from the Cherokee to the west. Large pearls from the Pamunkeys to the north were sewn in delicate patterns down the sides. She also carried a precious gift over her left arm for the new bride. It was a wedding cape made from the precious skin of an albino deer, also laced with bits of copper and pearls and turquoise stones. Verotacam herself would attend the young bride from Croatoa.

Wingina walked slowly to the place where the chief of Aquascogoc stood waiting to greet him. The younger chief reached forward to grasp the arms of Hanowocta, sealing the bonds of friendship that held the many villages of the Secotan Confederation together. "Wingo, Wingo," rose the chant from the people of Aquascogoc, and the older chief smiled generously, pleased with the support of his people. Indians from each of the other villages were smiling also, knowing a spirit of friendship would prevail over the wedding feast.

Manteo stood behind his father, filled with pride at being a Secotan in the service of Wingina. Even the Neusiocs, across the Pamticoe to the South, acknowledged his greatness as a warrior chief. Manteo's gaze then drifted to the many warriors standing at the water's edge. They were lean and handsome with their painted bodies, covered only with loincloths. Their hickory bows and war clubs were always at their sides, ready for battle. Surely Wingina could use another young warrior, one from Croatoa, like himself. Soon, he promised himself, he would journey to Dasamonquepec and seek out the brother of Wingina, who was chief of his personal guard. There he would demonstrate his foot speed like that of a deer, his strength in wrestling, and above all his accuracy with the bow. 'He could not be denied,' he thought to himself.

The ceremonial greetings to Wingina by each of the village chiefs consumed most of the remaining daylight. The women and children returned to preparations for the wedding and left their men to sit around pit fires to tell stories of battles and hunting adventures. Manteo listened intently to one of the Dasamonquepec warriors as he described a trading mission to the Chesipeans, a large body of inland water to the North.

He listened intently as Wanchese described the great canoes with wings that could fly across water, and the men with glistening white skin who had sticks that made thunder, and fiery water that could make a man crazy. "I spoke to those who had seen them many seasons ago with their own eyes," Wanchese said. "They were like gods who wore colorful clothing where we have none, who smiled and roared with laughter and spoke in tongues which no one could understand. And they offered shiny metals and colorful stones to the Pamunkeys for pearls we find in abundance in oyster shells."

Everyone sat cross-legged around the fire pit passing a large clay bowl filled with a steaming black brew boiled from Yaupon leaves found on trees along the coastline. 'Enough of this potion and one might believe anything,' Manteo thought to himself. He slowly stood and walked toward another campfire, where stories were being told of the last encounter with the Neusiocs. "We tricked them into the open, just like they did to our brothers from Secota who went to make peace two planting seasons past."

Manteo had heard the story, and moved on to another fire, listening to stories of encounters with the dangerous Mangoaks to the west, and then of trade with the Cherokee. "They come from a land that reaches up to the sky, and travel all the way to the great waters. Here they offer us turquoise and yellow stones for our pearls and tiny seashells."

"And for Yaupon leaves to make the sacred black tea," another warrior added. And all of them laughed with their numb black tongues sticking out for others to see.

A sliver of moon was creeping in and out between clouds, and evening winds were whipping treetops as they often did before a sudden storm. "Not tonight," Manteo whispered to himself. "Nothing must disturb the wonder of this night."

He walked quietly among the thatched huts, thrown together outside the village for a few days entertaining for so many guests, until he reached the village entrance. It was an opening in the palisade of tall tree trunks that surrounded and protected Aquascogoc from intruders.

He entered the passageway that twisted first right and then left, and opened up to a compound of well-kept lodges and storehouses. On a large mound in the center was the temple house, where the wedding would take place. He walked slowly toward the entrance just in front of the village shaman's door when he heard a voice rise quickly. "Evil, it is evil. I have read the bones of our fathers and they say it is evil," shrieked the Shaman.

"But why have they spoken now? Why not before the wedding feast was prepared?" It was the voice of the village chief, Hanowocta.

"They speak when they are ready. I cannot make them say as I wish." The priest was speaking harshly to the chief, the only one who could do so and not be severely punished.

"But why is she not good enough to be the wife of a chief?"

"Because she is as much one of them as one of us."

"You mean of her father's kind?"

"Yes, the white skins. The bones say they will come to defeat us and take away our lands."

"Priest, you have heard too many stories of Wanchese and his trading adventures to the Chesipeans."

"Wanchese is from the village of Pomeioc, and he speaks the truth from his heart," answered the Shaman. "I fought with his father before I was priest and I knew him as a child. He has a gift for seeing what is truly in a man's heart, and he has seen those who have seen the white skins. He knows they will be our enemy, even more than the Neusiocs."

Hanowocta stared into a small fire in the center of the lodge, considering all that the spiritual advisor had said. "Again," he said to the priest. "Tell me the story again."

"Her mother was Ocona, who died in the child's third season. Her father was one of the five white skins found on the shore of the great water by our people at Hattorask. The white men lived there for half of one season, and always they worked on a way to leave and return to their own people. Finally, they tied two canoes together, lashed a small pole in the middle and a way to catch wind from their own clothing. They sailed away, leaving two of our women to bear their children."

"And what of the white skins?"

"Many days later their canoes were found on the beach, but no sign of them. I tell you it is part of a plan to bear their own kind among us and have their children become our leaders, to take our lands without ever having to fight us."

Hanowocta looked angrily at the Shaman, "Never will I allow the son of my son to become one of them." He rose quickly and cast a parting glance, "Never I tell you."

The priest pointed his finger at the chief, "I warn you, Hanowocta, the bones have spoken. If you allow Kimtoc to wed Oshanoa, evil will come upon our village."

"Too much has taken place to listen to bones that speak too late," and the chief stormed out of the hut.

Manteo stepped quickly to the side of the Shaman's hut to avoid being seen. His mind was spinning with what he had heard. 'Should he tell his father? Could Oshanoa be the evil thing the priest had said? What harm could she possibly bring to the village of Aguascogoc?' he asked himself, then looked up at the crescent moon and watched the dark clouds whispering above the blowing trees. 'Say nothing. It is Hanowocta's decision. And he is right, it is too late to stop whatever will happen.'

* * *

Sitting high in a great oak across the creek, the leader of a Neusioc raiding party had an owl's view of the cooking fires of Aquascogoc. Catuaga knew for days in advance of the wedding ceremony, and of the many important guests who would be gathering there. 'This is the time,' he thought, 'to avenge the slaying of my brother.'

Earlier that spring, Secotan warriors had crossed the Pamticoe and surprised a peaceful encampment at the mouth of a large creek that ran south into Neusioc territory. The men, women and children would go there early in the season, before planting, to dig hard clay from a large mound to form the clay pots and bowls to replace those that had been broken and lost. The women would use small sticks and the hulls of acorn shells to make distinctive markings around the outside of each piece, first with village symbols and then with their own personal markings.

The men would build and tend a large rectangular fire pit to create a great bed of coals to fire and harden the clay vessels. After many hours, each piece would be removed and inspected for cracks or broken areas. Those that passed inspection were packed away for the village, and those that did not were simply tossed away, leaving beds of pottery shards for later generations to ponder over.

It was at such an encampment earlier that year that a Secotan raiding party found the Neusiocs. The raid was swift, with swinging clubs and flying arrows, warriors screaming and women wailing as some of the children were captured and carried away by the Secotans. Catuaga's brother, unable to bear the loss of his child, pursued the raiders back to their canoe. Just as he reached them, an unseen Secotan swung a stone axe, knocking a deep hole in the back of his head, and he fell face down in the water.

Catuaga's blood ran hot within him for revenge. Raiding forays across the great river had been a sporting event between the Secotans and Neusiocs for generations, giving warriors of both tribes opportunity to practice skills that had not yet been tested in larger battles. It was possible that he may even be attacking his own relatives from earlier raids; captured and grown up as Secotans, but it did not matter. On this raid he would try to avenge himself by killing the bravest of Secotans, their great chief, Wingina.

He would be patient and wait until after the feast, when the bellies of the Secotans would be too full to fight and many of them would be possessed by the black tea and unable to resist. 'When they lay down to rest,' he thought, 'that is when the Neusiocs would attack.'

✣ ✣ ✣

WEDDING OF OSHANOA

The time for the ceremony was at hand. Men and women of importance were seated before the temple, while all others were squeezed inside the palisade walls to view the events. Kimtoc sat beside the Shaman's lodge, the sides of his head freshly shaved, picked clean and painted black; while the mane of hair down the center was braided and decorated with tiny shells and turquoise beads.

A double row necklace of larger wampum shells, indicating wealth among his people, lay across the ceremonial woven vest. It was a gift from the Croatoans to the new husband. His loincloth and foot coverings were made of deerskin with the fur of black bear sewn around the edges. Though not as handsome as some of the other warriors, Kimtoc was lean and strong, and had proven himself in many forest battles. And one day, it was rumored, he would take the place of his father as Chief of Aquascogoc. This alliance was vitally important to the Croatoans, who often ran short of corn during the winters and stayed in neighboring villages to survive 'til the next season's harvest.

The priest suddenly ran out of his lodge, scowling as he screamed, "Begin the ceremony!" Hands clapped together and sticks beat a wooden rhythm while the women hummed a melody passed down from generations of mothers. Directly across from the Shaman's lodge was the temple. It was here that Oshanoa and her attendants had passed the day; the older women instructing her in the ways of pleasing her husband while the younger ones giggled in delight at the prospects.

When the humming melody started it was a sign for the bride to leave the temple and join her husband before the priest who would present them to Wingina. Except for those from Croatoa, few had seen the bride of Kimtoc, and rumors had spread among the lodges and around the cooking fires for days. "Blue eyes," they said. Secotans with such eyes could be counted on one hand, and it was considered a good omen for the husband.

"Teeth as white as the clouds and as strong as the beaver," they whispered among themselves. "Light brown hair that turned red in a bright sun, and skin as soft as that of deer hide chewed many times. And when she smiled it was like sunlight shimmering on the water. Surely there was no maiden more beautiful in all the villages of the confederation." Tall and graceful, she was considered capable of bearing many children, caring for a large garden, preparing food and making clothes for her family. "Such a maiden would be a great blessing to Kimtoc and the village of Aquascogoc."

First to come out of the temple was Verotacam. The wife of Wingina was glowing as she smiled at the many women humming the song that at one time had carried her to the side of her own husband. Then the humming faltered and whispers seemed to replace the melody. Verotacam turned around, but it was the appearance of Oshanoa that had replaced the song. 'Never,' thought Verotacam, 'had a Secotan maiden ever been more beautifully adorned for her wedding.'

Flowers and colorful beads lay around her head and cascaded through her long brown hair to the albino deerskin-wedding cape. Blue eyes peered out and greeted everyone with a beautiful smile, and all agreed that it was just as they had heard; Kimtoc was indeed a fortunate husband. Smiles and whispers continued to follow Oshanoa across the small yard as the wedding song started again. She walked slowly toward the young man she had met only once before when his father had led a trading mission to Croatoa. She could forgive his scarred face and broken teeth, injuries from Neusioc war clubs, because she knew he was very kind and generous to his mother. 'If only he would be as kind to me and my children,' and she smiled for her husband as she turned to the unusually stern face of the Shaman.

Wingina stepped away from the side of the priest toward Kimtoc and Oshanoa. He took each of them by the right hand then placed theirs on top of his. He raised his left hand and the humming stopped, and he gazed intently into their eyes to see if there was any reason why he should not bless their union. Finally he smiled at them and cried loudly, "Shaman, this couple is blessed." In spite of his personal feelings, the priest could protest no more, at least not in front of Wingina. He immediately began the fertility chant and even Hanowocta noticed that for the first time he was performing as he would for any other marriage ceremony.

Soon after, the ceremony was over and the celebration began. While the young couple stood in front of the temple accepting gifts from those who had come in from other villages, the women of Aquascogoc carried in clay pots filled with meats and vegetables and bread cooked in shallow clay pans from the meal of crushed corn. Summer fruits, roots, and sassafras flavored water covered the small yard as the guests turned to feasting. Gourds filled with Yaupon tea were passed among the warriors, the taste of which numbed their tongues to the sweet taste of melons and hot meats the women had prepared.

While the darkness of the forests enveloped the compound, cooking fires cast shadowy figures up into trees, where night birds were perched on small limbs, waiting their chance to steal to the ground for a morsel of food. Other creatures of the night had also begun their hunt for prey, and across the river there was movement at the bottom of a great oak tree.

ATTACK OF THE NEUSIOCS

"Catuaga," whispered a voice from the forest floor, "we are ready. By the time we get to the village, all will be asleep."

"Except for the guards," answered a voice from up in the tree as he eased himself down, limb by limb.

The leader of the raiding party jumped to the ground and stood before twenty-one Neusioc warriors, painted for war and hungry for revenge. Slowly he went over the details of the plan he had carefully devised. Just upstream, at a narrow point in the creek, they would float across with logs. Then they would form into small groups of three warriors. Two would carry war clubs with large stones held between the split ends on top, securely fastened with strips of deer hide. The third would be the archer, protecting the club warriors who would strike as often as possible.

A sliver of moonlight cast barely visible shadows over the water as the Neusioc warriors waded silently into the creek and floated across. Catuaga was the first to crawl up the bank and scramble into the trees without disturbing the vines or leaves. His warriors followed as quietly, stepping through the forests without a sound. They followed the water down to a place where all the canoes had been lashed together, and were guarded by two warriors from the village. It was part of Catuaga's plan to capture the small boats, not only to assure that his men would have a means of escape, but also to prevent his enemy from following. Any canoes not used by the Neusiocs were to be cut free and pushed into the river where the current would carry them away.

Catuaga motioned for two teams to go forward. They moved to within accurate bow range and set their arrows. The two guards were standing a few feet apart, passing the long night away in conversation. With a sudden whack, an arrow struck one of them high in the back and his mouth fell open as he reached out to his friend. The other guard's eyes grew wide with terror when he saw the feathered stick protruding from the back of his friend. He cocked his head to sound an alarm, but before he could a small pointed rock on the end of a shaft tore into his throat.

The sound of footsteps came rapidly up behind them and two stone war clubs delivered smashing blows to the heads of the Secotans. The skulls cracked and the clubmen were splattered with blood as the bodies of the guards twitched violently. The Neusiocs smiled perversely at the success of the first part of the mission.

Immediately, other warriors ran out of the forests and began cutting vines that held the canoes in place. All but the largest, Wingina's great canoe, were cast off into the river to be carried away downstream. Catuaga grinned wickedly as he considered how great his name would be among his people. It would be enough to capture Wingina's personal canoe, but to kill the great chief and avenge the death of his brother would make his name part of Neusioc legend, a story that would be told around campfires for generations.

Catuaga and another warrior would go inside the walls of the compound to find the resting place of Wingina. With his clubman at his side, he stepped quietly through the temporary lodges, hearing the bloated snoring of warriors full of black tea. The other Neusiocs positioned themselves around their sleeping enemy, and when the sounds of fighting erupted inside the compound, they would strike their victims swiftly before they could recover from their sleep.

As Catuaga neared the gate he called to the guard inside, "We have come to find our relief."

A head peeped over the wall at the two dark figures below. "You should not have left the canoes unguarded. Our chief will have you punished for this."

"Come down and let us in. We are too tired to worry about that."

As they stood in front of the gate, the guard climbed down and pulled the heavy log door aside. Catuaga had already strung an arrow, and as the guard became visible he pulled back as far as the bow would bend and released it. The arrow sliced into the man's chest, burying itself up to the thistle bows used to guide it, and before he could fall to the ground, the clubman smashed his skull against the door, sending an eyeball sprawling from its socket.

Immediately, the two warriors crept into the compound, quietly searching for Wingina's resting place. The clubman pointed at the temple, suggesting he might be sleeping there. Catuaga agreed, but between the gate and the temple was a small lodge with a fire burning inside. The Neusiocs crept up behind the hut and peeped through the woven branches and packed mud.

Inside, Kimtoc lay on his back, and kneeling beside him was Oshanoa, washing her new husband with ginger water to prepare him for their first night together. Catuaga had never seen such beauty. Her long brown hair fell loosely over her breasts as she rubbed her husband's chest and thighs, and a primal heat stirred in Catuaga's chest.

A sudden chill from a cold hand on his shoulder reminded him of his duty. He could barely pull his eyes away from the sight before him, but he knew that time was short and he must complete his mission. Looking into the clubman's eyes he could see the man was unaffected by what he saw in the lodge. 'How could it be that a man not be moved by such a sight?' he thought to himself as he peered across the yard to the temple entrance.

They made their way across the open area, and just outside the temple another arrow was strung. Again he looked toward his clubman, making sure he would be ready when they sprang inside. Dim light from glowing embers in the center of the temple revealed a man and woman lying against the back wall. Still not sure it was the great chief, Catuaga cried out, "Wingina!"

The chief of the Secotans woke from his sleep to look up and see a bowman about to let an arrow fly. Confused he thought, 'Why would one of my men want to do me harm?'

Catuaga savored the confusion on the great chief's face, but for a moment too long. The instant before his arrow was loosed a string of wampum shells, thrown by Verotacam, struck him in the face. The arrow landed with a smack in the left thigh of Wingina, causing him to scream in pain. Already the clubman was racing toward the chief with his club raised to deliver a deathblow, but just as he reared back to drive the club forward, Verotacam leaped from her knees and drove a long oyster shell strapped to a wooden handle deep into his chest.

The clubman fell backward, mortally wounded, and Catuaga could hear the screams and war cries outside the walls as his warriors attacked the sleeping Secotans. He quickly picked up the war club, determined to kill Wingina and his woman, but just as he raised the club he heard a warrior entering the temple. He stepped back to the side of the entrance, prepared to strike as he came in.

In spite of Verotacam's warning scream, the young warrior ran into the temple. "Wingina, are you safe?" were the last words he would utter, as Catuaga swung the war club into Kimtoc's forehead. The new husband fell back against the wall and slumped down as if he were sitting on his hind legs. Catuaga recognized him as the same man who had been with the beautiful young woman only moments before. And now he sat in a dying heap while blood spurted over his face and ran down onto his chest.

Verotacam sprang to her feet, charging the Neusioc warrior while he looked at what had been a promising young husband. Catauga raised his leg and kicked her violently in the chest, throwing her backwards over her wounded husband. Then he looked at Wingina and screamed, "I am revenged, great one! Now you live to tell of my greatness!" Then he grinned wickedly at Wingina and Verotacam and turned away to run out of the temple.

There was confusion everywhere inside the compound. It was easy for Catuaga to make his way to the gate, but outside the wall, there was bitter fighting. Two of the Neusioc warriors had been killed, but the rest had made it back to the great canoe, leaving only a few archers at the edge of the camp to defend their escape.

As Catuaga ran from the gate he was spotted by Wingina's men. "Another one," they screamed. "Kill him."

Catuaga told his men that if he could not escape they were to leave him behind, that he would fight to his death rather than be captured. He immediately sprinted toward the point where the great canoe was waiting, but three Secotan warriors stood in his path. He looked to the right and saw that he would have to run back through the camp. Then he glanced to his left and the safety of the forest. He ran blindly into the darkness, and never saw the war club that caught him squarely in the chest.

Air gushed from his lungs as his feet left the ground, and he was enveloped in a spasm of pain, choking and gasping for breath. As the Secotans approached with war clubs raised to deliver deathblows, another club was held out over the Neusioc.

"I am Wanchese, and this man is my prisoner. He will be taken before Wingina who will decide his fate." To invoke the great chief's name brought immediate obedience from the other warriors. Then Wanchese said to them, "Tie him before his strength returns."

❖ ❖ ❖

REVENGE OF THE SECOTANS

Daylight was still hours away as the damage was being assessed. Mourning cries were heard throughout the encampment as news that six Secotan warriors had been killed, three more severely wounded, and another five suffered minor injuries. But none wailed so loudly as the women of Aquascogoc who mourned the death of Kimtoc, son of their village chief.

"Had he not come into the temple," moaned Verotacam, "surely my husband would be dead,' and she continued to speak of his bravery while never mentioning that she was the one who had killed the clubman. She looked sadly at the widowed face of Oshanoa who could not comprehend the cruel fate that had befallen her. A warrior husband with whom she had not yet slept, would never come to her bed. To whom did she belong? Could she escape this nightmare and return to Croatoa to be among her own people? Her head was spinning with fear over her own fate when she turned and saw the Neusioc leader strapped upright to stakes in the center of the compound.

Catuaga sneered at those who held him prisoner, like a snake trapped against a log. 'If only I could free my hands,' he thought, 'I would strike as swiftly as the black moccasin.' "To the death," he whispered viciously to himself, knowing that before sunrise it would be so.

Oshanoa looked at him, firelight reflecting off his lean body, the way Kimtoc looked as he ran from their bed. She watched in disgust as the Neusioc worked up saliva and spat upon the women who stood in front and taunted him. One of them raised her hand with a sharp flattened rock that had once been the tip of a spear. "For my son," she screamed as she leaped forward to drive her blade into the enemy heart.

The hand of a Secotan warrior swiftly reached to grab her arm and restrain her. "No," he said softly. "Wingina saves him for the wife of Kimtoc."

The words struck Oshanoa's ears like fire. Her hands flew to her mouth as she suddenly understood that Catuaga's death was to be a rite of revenge for the women who lost their husbands. The gory prospect caused her head to spin as she stared at the man staked to the poles in the center of the compound. Not only would she be expected to participate, but as the wife of the chief's dead son she would have to initiate the ritual.

The Shaman began to dance before the captive, and the flickering firelight cast his eerie shadow against the heavy foliage of the trees above. His wailing song was picked up by the women and a deeper incantation was started by the men, while the priest pretended to chip and saw the edges of oyster shells in preparation for the delicate cutting of flesh that would follow.

Oshanoa's head throbbed and vibrated with the rhythm of the Shaman's song, and her stomach was churned with fear. Her lips fell apart and her eyes grew wider as she moaned softly to herself. She felt the cool presence of someone behind her and turned to find Hanowocta and his wife. "It is your duty," whispered the mother of Kimtoc as she choked back angry tears.

The temple gate swung back and a litter bearing Wingina was carried out to witness the death of Catuaga. The Shaman's song rose to a feverish pitch while the women who would participate in the ceremony were brought before him. He looked them over and realized the mixed breed from Croatoa was not there. His wailing grew long and weary as his eyes roamed over the compound searching for the wife of Kimtoc. When his eyes found hers he leaped into the air and brought the sharpened oyster shells down swiftly and deeply into the dirt at her feet.

She stood before him, frozen, unable to move at the thought of what was to follow. Surely they could not expect her to do this. Only a few hours before she had been a bride, and then the cool hand of Kimtoc's mother touched her shoulder. "You must begin the ceremony," she croaked angrily, sensing that Oshanoa's hesitation would reflect badly on the honor of her son.

The Shaman, wearing the hat of a bear's skull with a face painted gruesomely red, began to dance around her. He shook a small gourd filled with the teeth of his ancestors in her face. "The spirits call upon you, Oshanoa. They will not allow Kimtoc in to the great afterlife unless you avenge his wounded spirit."

Verotacam looked pleadingly across the compound at the young girl who was being asked to perform the duty of a mourning wife, something she did not feel. The great chief's wife saw her heart and walked slowly across the yard to offer support. She reached out to Oshanoa with her eyes, "You must do this my child, for the honor of your husband and his family, you must."

Oshanoa was still looking into her eyes, accepting her fate, when the Shaman grasped her right hand and pressed a long sharp piece of oyster shell between her fingers. Then he pulled her toward the stakes in the center of the compound that held the defiant Catuaga. She walked numbly beside the Shaman, barely hearing the rising chant around her.

They stopped in front of the Neusioc leader, but Oshanoa, seeing the face of the man who killed her husband, turned away. Behind her she saw the angry faces of the women who would truly avenge their husbands by stripping the flesh away from Catuaga's body until he bled to death. It was better for him, she understood, than living as a slave, and in death he could demonstrate the courage of the Neusiocs. But still she wanted to run away from this nightmare.

The Shaman spun her around, "Evil one," he whispered. "You have brought death to the village of Aquascogoc. Now save your husband's honor as well as your own."

'What did he mean?' she thought to herself. 'What evil had she brought to the village?' The Shaman let her go and backed away, picking up the wailing chant and inciting others to follow his lead. He shook the gourd high over his head as a signal to the women who stood behind Oshanoa, and when his arm fell, they would join the ritual.

Oshanoa stood several feet in front of the Neuisoc warrior. "Woman," he sneered, "let me die with honor, the same way your husband died."

She could not believe that he wanted to die. "Death I can accept, but the waiting," and he grinned at her. "It was I who killed your husband," he said tauntingly. "I crushed his skull with my war club, and his blood ran at my feet."

Her eyes narrowed as she recalled the image of Kimtoc's body slumped against the wall, his face covered with blood. Her face contorted and she stepped forward raising her right hand to strike him. The frenzied chant grew even louder in anticipation of the spilling of Neusioc blood, but she stopped inches from his head, with the sharpened edge of the oyster-shell knife glistening in his eyes.

The chant slowed to a moan and she could feel the great disappointment behind her. "Strike, Oshanoa," they screamed, "for Kimtoc's revenge," but still she held the blade in front of his face.

Even Catuaga began to scream at her. "He was no warrior. He could not have given you sons, only weak daughters like yourself. He was a coward. Even in death he tries to run away." The chant was ringing in her ears, and the insults from Catuaga were too much to bear. "And now he has left you a widow without knowing him as a man."

The fire flushed through Oshanoa's face and ran down her arm. She drew her hand back and struck, but her grip was poor and the blade spun, cutting her own fingers. She screamed and stepped back as the oyster knife fell from her hand, then looked at the scowling face of Catuaga. She had opened a small cut on his cheek and blood began to trickle down his neck.

The Secotans were in a frenzy. "More, Oshanoa," they screamed, but her anger had vanished at the sight of his blood. She began to feel dizzy and rocked unsteadily on her feet. Sensing her weakness, the enemy warrior screamed, "She is like all Secotans, afraid of a great Neusioc warrior," and he laughed cruelly in her face.

The chant died away and the tide of sympathy for Oshanoa turned to anger. The Shaman, sick of her disgraceful performance, dropped his arm and the other widows sprang into action. With slow deliberate movements, from years of dressing rabbits and squirrels, they scraped the skin away from his face then peeled back his hair, leaving the bloody skeletal head screaming in hysterical agony. The women continued to shave layers of flesh away from the neck and shoulders until Catuaga's gaping mouth fell silent and his bloody head rolled to the side. As his body hung limply from the ropes that constrained him, the women continued stripping away flesh to feed the hungry dogs that were always around for any scraps of food.

The sight of the Neusioc warrior's mutilated body sickened the young woman from Croatoa. She bolted from the side of the priest and ran into the temple, where only hours before her husband had been slain. She fell in the doorway and crawled against the wall where Kimtoc fell, her eyes filled with salty tears while her mind raced in confusion. Only the day before she had been the beautiful maiden of which all Croatoa was proud to have marry the son of the chief of Aquascogoc. And now she was a virgin widow who had disgraced her people before their enemy.

Flames licked the darkness outside the temple as the other widows continued to sack the carcass of Catuaga. The frenzied chant echoed against the trees and rang menacingly throughout the forest as small groups of warriors from each of the villages listened to new ideas for raiding the Neusioc villages on the South side of Pamticoe.

Manteo stood quietly outside the gathering from the village of Dasamonquepec and listened to the rants of Wanchese, the young warrior who had captured Catuaga. His eyes flashed and he beat his chest fiercely describing how he would capture and kill more of the Neusiocs. There was something admirable about the courageous young man. He had come from Pomeiok, another small Secotan village, and had already achieved a position of importance with their great chief. 'Soon,' Manteo promised himself, 'he would go to the main village and seek his future with the warriors of Dasamonquepec.'

RETURN TO CROATOA

Early morning rays of sunlight filtered through the overhead trees and several women below prodded hot coals back to life to restart their cooking fires. Many of those who had gathered for the wedding feast now stood before the temple mourning the warriors who had died in the raid. Inside, the bodies were laid out so that each of the Secotans could enter and see what the Neusiocs had done. The village chief sat behind the body of his son murmuring a prayer for the dead. The great chief, Wingina, lay behind them, partially upright, but painfully aware of the arrow that had been broken off and pushed through the side of his leg.

Outside the compound, Manteo sat with his father discussing what must be done. After the disgrace of Oshanoa, during the ceremony to revenge Kimtoc and the other warriors who had died, it was no longer an honor to be one of the Croatoans. "We must take her back to our village," his father said. "It is where she belongs."

"But Father, is not our custom that the wife of a dead warrior go to his brother?"

"Yes, my son, but Kimtoc has no brother, and the father is unwilling to take her. And worse, there is no warrior here that will have her now. Word will soon spread through all the villages, and her name will be shunned among our people. There is little to do except take her home."

"But her mother is also dead, and that means..." Manteo watched his father carefully, unsure of what to say. But he realized that Oshanoa would now become the burden of the village chief and a member of his father's lodge.

"She will serve my brother's wife and help with the children and garden."

Manteo thought for a moment and realized there was little choice. "Yes, Father, a wise decision."

They sat together watching the door of a small hut that had been quickly thatched together to serve during the wedding celebration. As they spoke, they observed two blue eyes peeping out to see who might be near. Assured that only her people were close by, she stepped out into the early morning mist carrying a garment in her hands. Though her eyes were red and swollen, she was still more beautiful than any flower in Aquascogoc.

As Oshanoa stepped toward them, Manteo was deeply saddened to know that she would never have a Secotan warrior for a husband. 'Perhaps one of the Pamunkey or Cherokee with whom they traded would take her for a wife,' he thought, 'but a great loss for his village. She could have brought much honor to her poor relatives on the outer islands who had to scavenge for shellfish and beg for corn just to survive the winters.'

Oshanoa walked over to Manteo's father, and with her head bowed she slipped to her knees. In her arms she held the wedding cape given to her by the wife of Wingina. "Please," she barely whispered, "return this to Verotacam. I am no longer worthy."

She held the cape forward and the chief motioned for Manteo to take it. "We will see that it is returned. Now gather your things and help the others prepare to leave. As soon as our men return with the canoes, we will depart for Pomeiok."

Without lifting her head she started to rise, but as her hands touched the ground to lift herself, she paused. "Thank you for taking me back to Croatoa. I know that I have brought dishonor to our village." She pulled one knee up then lifted her head, revealing the tears brimming in her eyes. "I have no husband, no friends, and only through your kindness, a home. I live only to serve my people." Her lips trembled slightly at every word, but through it all she did not surrender dignity. Manteo felt strongly that one day, a worthy warrior would come to save Oshanoa from the great misfortune that had befallen her.

Though blood had been spilled and warriors killed, life went on as it had for hundreds of years in Aquascogoc. The cooing of morning birds and the barking of squirrels filled the misty air in the forests as white plumes of smoke began to rise from cooking fires throughout the village. Women carried pots of thick sodden venison, raw melons and roots to the warriors who seldom ate with their women and children. They returned to their fires to feed the younger ones and then themselves. Afterwards, they washed and packed their belongings in skin pouches and carried them to the boats where their men balanced the load to make rowing easier.

As the sun began to rise above the trees the men grumbled at the lateness of the hour. They knew the sun's rays would heat the water and air above it, creating surface turbulence that would make rowing all the more difficult. As the women of Croatoa cleaned their campsites and prepared to leave, they looked back and realized they had been fortunate. None of the death and injuries had been visited upon their warriors. But even so, they were saddened to return with the one they had so proudly brought to Aquascogoc.

Manteo lifted Oshanoa and placed her in the middle of his canoe. He would have none of the Shaman's story that she brought bad luck to anyone who touched her. She sat on her hind legs between pouches filled with cooking pots, while Manteo stood in the water, waiting for his father to return from the temple. It was the custom for a village chief to escort a visiting weroance to his boat and wish him well on the journey home, but no one came from Aquascogoc. With the death of Kimtoc and Oshanoa's disgrace, it was too much to expect.

Voices could be heard coming from the path, and Manteo leaned back to catch a glimpse of an old man and woman walking slowly toward the water. He could tell by the limp of the woman that it was his mother trying to keep pace with the cheerless gait of his father. They walked alone, with the old chief suffering the indignity of sharing Oshanoa's humiliation.

When they reached the boats, he had one of his men carry him to his canoe and then return for his wife. After everyone was made ready he looked over the canoes that had been rescued from the river and were now bound for Pomeiok, then he waved his arm toward the great Pamticoe. Each of the men standing in the shallow water pushed off, then jumped in back and took up their paddles, drawing long even strokes in rhythm with the warrior rowing in front.

In minutes they were at the mouth of the creek, rounding the point that would carry them out to the waters of Pamticoe, but no one looked back, preferring to forget the tragedy at Aquascogoc. Instead, they began a low churning song to occupy their minds while they rowed toward Pomeiok. They would rest there until the next morning and continue their journey home to Croatoa the next day.

* * *

Luther lifted his head and turned to the left. It was the phone ringing again. "Dammit, why didn't I bring it out with me the last time?" Then he remembered it was Veronica who had called. 'Could it be her again?' he thought hopefully as he got up from his chair and ran inside.

"Luther, how are you doing?" It was Harry Hughes from the newspaper.

"Fine, Harry. I mean…" and his voice trailed off.

"I know what you mean, Luther. I was just calling to check in, let you know that everything is okay here at the paper, and…" then he paused. "Well, everyone keeps asking if I've heard from you, and well, I just wanted to let them know that we had talked and everything is okay."

"Thanks, Harry. Tell everyone I'm fine, just missing my best friend, a lot."

"Jimmy Bonner called, from the ECU Police Department. He gave me an update on the investigation, what he could tell me for now. Said to tell you hello and that you should stay in touch with him."

Luther smiled, "I will, Harry. I'm reading Carl's novel right now, and if I find out anything I'll call him."

"Carl wrote a novel?"

"Well, he started one, on what the Indian culture was like here on the Pamlico before the English arrived in 1584. He was making good progress, too, but I guess it will never be finished."

"Sounds interesting. Carl was one hell of a story teller."

"That he was, Harry," and Luther sighed heavily into the phone. "Tell everyone I'm doing okay, under the circumstances, and I will call you soon."

"Take care of yourself, Luther, and I'll take care of the paper."

"Thanks, Harry, you're a good man." Then Luther said goodbye and went back out on the porch to finish reading the few remaining chapters of Carl's novella.

DURHAM HOUSE

London, Spring of 1584

"Gentlemen, please, quiet, " Raleigh pleaded above the din in the small banquet hall at Durham House. He tapped a silver knife lightly against his Venetian crystal. "Finally, to have all of us together at one time," and he smiled brilliantly for his guests while his eyes sparkled from the effects of the claret he imported by the barrel from the Bordeaux region of France.

For months each of the men had been coming to Durham House, for days at a time, developing plans for England's first colonial venture in the New World. But never had all the principals been gathered in Raleigh's home along the Strand. Following the Queen's advice, the plans were being made in secrecy, and yet all of London was buzzing about what might be taking place in the turret overlooking the Thames.

Raleigh stood before them, looking over the men who had given so much of their time for planning the details and logistical requirements of the venture, not to mention their financial support. To his right sat the venerable William Sanderson, one of the most respected men of the London financial community, who had invested and agreed to act as treasurer for the company. Beside him sat Francis Walsingham, the rotund eyes and ears of Elizabeth, who had invested over a thousand pounds of his own money and personally represented the Queen.

Next to Sir Francis sat Ralph Lane, a young army captain who had recently returned from the fighting in Ireland. Lane had been personally chosen by the Queen on advice from Walsingham to be the military governor of the first colony.

Next to Lane sat Thomas Harriot, the brilliant young scholar who had given up his career as a math professor at Oxford to participate in the planning. He, along with Hakluyt, would pore over the known maps of the new world to select a site for the colony. And beside him sat one of the most suspect intellects in Elizabethan England. John Dee, a philosopher and astrologer, would select a date for the venture to set sail. It would be a time in accordance with the accumulated wisdom of experienced sea pilots, and nature's seasons in the New World.

At the opposite end of the table was Richard Hakluyt, a clergyman who was well regarded by the sailors of every nation. It was not his eloquent sermons that held him apart from his peers, but rather his hobby of collecting and translating the nautical adventures of explorers from all European nations, with particular emphasis on those from England. His support had given Raleigh's effort enormous credibility, and his promotional literature would soon flood London, telling investors of the wonders and fortune to be gained in the colonial venture.

Raleigh looked to his left, and at the far end of the table sat his own cousin, Sir Richard Grenville, who not only made an investment but had agreed to put his military experience to use for the benefit of the venture. Pompous and arrogant though he was, his courage and seamanship were well regarded by all.

Sitting beside Grenville was Michael Butler, Raleigh's personal aide who was in charge of the stores accumulating in the warehouses of Plymouth. It was there that all the supplies for the voyage were being gathered. Next to him sat a short paunchy man, an experienced sea pilot named Simon Ferdinando. Not only had he been the pilot for Raleigh's first naval command in 1578, but also his brother Gilbert's ill-fated voyage to Newfoundland. Ferdinando had also been on several expeditions to pirate the Spanish plate fleet, from the Azores to the coast of Florida. Experienced pilots with New World rutters, personal books and knowledge of the coastline of the Americas, were difficult to find and Raleigh felt fortunate to retain the services of the man from Portugal.

Between Raleigh and the Portuguese pilot sat two young men from Devon on the Southwest coast. Phillip Amadas was a raven-haired sailor of great ambition. His father had invested heavily to earn his son a position as captain of one of Raleigh's ships. Arthur Barlowe, the other ship's captain, was a striking contrast to the more flamboyant Amadas. Quiet and observant, he had also served with Raleigh in Ireland. His family, somewhat disappointed by his efforts in the military, had invested to secure Arthur a position in the colonial venture. Adept at scholarship, he was chosen to lead the smaller ship and fully record the details of the voyage to the New World.

Looking over his distinguished guests, Raleigh raised his glass to eye level, "Gentlemen, may I propose a toast to the memory of my dear bother, Gilbert, whose dream did lead us here this night." Each of the men stood and held their wine glasses toward Raleigh. "To Sir Humphrey," they whispered together, then sipped lightly in his honor. Slowly they sat down and looked up at the excited face of their host.

"For these past months, we have labored to plan every detail of our effort to plant an English colony in the New World. And even so, the Queen has wavered in her commitment to sign the 'Letters of Marque.'" Then Raleigh flashed another smile as he unfurled a paper scroll and held it before them. "But now in my hand, sealed in the presence of our Lord Walsingham on the Twenty-fifth of March, 1584, is our charter."

"To the charter, gentlemen!" shouted Grenville as he raised his glass, and the others followed suit. "To the charter!" they shouted together, eager to empty their glasses of the red claret and hold them out toward Ephriam Turner and the other servants, who replenished the goblets while Raleigh continued speaking.

"Gentlemen, we sail for the new world in less than a fortnight." He could see the excitement spreading in their faces as they looked at each other and then back at their host, hardly believing their plans could be put into effect so early.

"But how," queried Sanderson, "can ships and colonists be made ready in less than two weeks?"

"There has been some reorganization in our plans, Master Sanderson," Raleigh answered. "There will be no colonists on the first voyage."

Most of the men at the table were not aware of the change in plans, and their confused looks suggested to Raleigh that he must put their concerns at rest. "Our plan, gentlemen, is simple and sound. There will be three voyages. The first will be to reconnoiter the coastal areas granted in the charter and to select a site for the colony that will be safe from the elements, as well as the Spanish, and provide a base for prosperous growth."

"But Raleigh," cried Sanderson, "we've only enough resources for the two voyages that had been planned."

"Yes," responded Raleigh confidently. "But if we do not succeed in our first voyage, a second will not be necessary, nor a third. Would you have us fail because of a poor location such as the Spaniard Ayllon at Chicora? Would you have us send men, women and children and lose half the company in the first year to disease? No," he continued with a grave expression. "We must plan more carefully for the future of our colony."

There was a general nodding of heads as his guests agreed with his thinking, and the ever money-conscious Sanderson asked another question. "What, then, of the second voyage?"

"A military effort," Raleigh responded quickly. "Master Lane will be governor of a company of soldiers and investors whose mission will be to secure the site of the colony. They will construct a fort and build houses, and explore the territory there about for the future benefit of England."

Sanderson began to nod his head in approval as Raleigh continued. "And the third voyage will carry our well provisioned planters for the colony. Men, women and children, masons, smithy's, coopers and all manner of trades and crafts to support the farmers and merchants. Our colony, gentlemen, will not merely be an English outpost in the New World, but a New England that will one day become a great trading partner in support of the crown."

Raleigh reached for his glass and lifted it high. "A toast to a New England in the New World," and everyone stood quickly as a surge of energy swept over the room.

"To a New England in the New World!" they shouted together and drank deeply from their glasses.

Raleigh allowed his guests to savor the excitement a moment longer before he asked them to take their seats. "Now, my friends, on the first voyage will be two small barks captained by our able sons, Phillip Amadas and Arthur Barlowe. And their pilot will be Simon Ferdinando. They are charged with discovering a suitable site for our colony."

"And where might they seek such a site, Master Raleigh?" ask Walsingham. "Surely, not in the frozen North where your brother sought to plant his colony," he said with some concern.

Raleigh laughed. "The North is much too cold, Sir Francis, and the South is full of Spaniards and man eating Caribs." He paused a moment to observe the expression on the faces of Sanderson and Barlowe.

"You mean there are savages among the islands that eat human flesh?"

"Tis, true, Master Sanderson. More than one sailor has survived shipwreck only to be hacked to pieces as he crawled upon the beach, and have his flesh devoured even as his body twitched in death."

"Enough of the Caribs," said Walsingham. "Now tell us where it is that we are to plant our colony."

Raleigh smiled seeking out the venerable clergyman whose name had become synonymous with New World exploration. "Reverend Hakluyt, would you please speak to us on where we will explore for a colony site."

Hakluyt gingerly wiped his beard with a white silk napkin, set it across his plate and began to speak in the measured tones of an accomplished pulpit orator. "In 1524, the Italian explorer, Verazzano, in the service of Henry of Navarre of France, sailed along a thin strip of land which he named Arcadia, in honor of the ideal land of natural beauty found in Jacopo Sannazzaro's novella, *Arcadia*. At thirty-six degrees north latitude, this land is precisely in the mild and hospitable Mediterranean climate. So it is to this goodly land of plenty that we will send Captains Amadas and Barlowe, where they will seek an inlet through Verrazano's isthmus, and beyond that a deep water port hidden behind the barrier islands, well protected from Spanish eyes." Then Hakluyt picked up his glass to sip his claret, signaling to his host that he was through speaking.

"But, Raleigh," Walsingham inquired. "Did not the Spanish attempt to plant a mission in El Jacan some ten years ago, barely one degree north of where you seek to plant our colony now? And were not those missionaries murdered by savages?"

"True, Lord Walsingham, the Spanish mission did fail in the Chesipeans. And that is why we seek to locate just South of that area, in hopes of finding more wholesome neighbors." And with a smile he glanced around the room, sensing acceptance and satisfaction of the group with Hakluyt's reasoning. Then all eyes turned toward the young captains and their Portuguese pilot who would explore the land of Arcadia and discover the exact site upon which to plant the first English colony in the New World.

"A toast," Raleigh said excitedly, to which all of the men gathered around the table rose to their feet. "To the success of the voyage of Amadas and Barlowe!"

"To Amadas and Barlowe!" they echoed with confidence in the future of their New World venture.

* * *

The Port of Plymouth, April 27, 1584

A crescent moon barely lit the morning sky above the harbor, where blue water ships were tied to docks awaiting cargo or ballast stones. Creaking wood and lapping water had long since lulled sailors to sleep, but at the far end of the wharf where two small barks of barely fifty tons berth were tied, deck hands began quietly going about their work. From the coals of a cook's fire a small flame erupted, and using a stick of lightwood he signaled to a sister ship that the time for casting off was at hand.

Immediately a small bellows on the second ship produced a flame, and the cook began preparations to feed the hungry crew. A dozen men from each ship crawled over the side to their long boats to labor at the oars, pulling the barks quietly away from the docks and clear of the harbor. Only then would the sails be unfurled to capture the wind and carry them out to sea.

Arthur Barlowe sat in the stern castle of the second ship, determined to record in his log everything that transpired on the voyage. Knowing that Amadas was better suited to physical pursuits, he wrote with special diligence, feeling the surge of the oarsmen as they pulled with the tide. The rowing suddenly stopped, and he could hear men scrambling back on board. He saw the longboat swing behind the bark, securely fastened for the month's voyage across the Atlantic. Then he lifted a small tankard to his lips. "To the pinnace," he whispered to himself. "We shall need your shallow draft to explore behind the barrier islands."

He gently opened the map that John Dees and Thomas Harriot had prepared, and with his right forefinger traced southwest toward the Azores off the coast of Spain, then down to the Canary Islands off the coast of Africa. There they would pick up the Easterly Trade Winds and be blown across the ocean to the West Indies, where they would stop for fresh water, meats and valuable fruits that enriched the health and well being of sailors.

Though under orders to explore Arcadia and furnish Hakluyt with information for his *Discourse on Western Planting*, Barlow knew that neither he nor Amadas would be able to resist the temptation of taking any Spanish merchant ship that happened to cross their path. He smiled at the thought of dividing up the share of spoils, as he lifted the tankard and watched the longboat drift lazily in their wake.

VOYAGE TO DASAMONQUEPEC

Croatoa, Summer of 1584

Manteo moved quietly in the warm dark waters behind the barrier islands that barely came to his knees. As a small boy he had come here with friends to spear the elusive seakanuk in the darkness of the early morning hours. One would carry a long fat pine stick that burned brightly enough to see the puff of sand as their prey tried to escape. Another would carry a long hickory spear, sharpened to a fine point, and when the fish would move the point was driven through the pulpy flesh.

Oshanoa eased quietly alongside, holding the fat pine branch just in front of them. Over her shoulder hung a reed basket with several of the tender fish, wrapped in sea grass to keep them moist. She held the fiery end so close to the water that the flame was nearly extinguished, but it allowed Manteo to see the bottom clearly. "When can you see him?" she asked excitedly.

"Sometimes he looks like a mound of sand, but usually only when he tries to escape," he answered above the flaming light. A cloud of sand erupted at his feet and, gauging the direction, Manteo drove his spear downward until he pushed the tip through the flesh and into the sand.

Oshanoa squealed as she held the spear while Manteo bent down in the water to grab the fish. He stepped on the center of the back to hold it still, then reached for the tail with one hand and the head with the other and wrestled the fish out of the water and into the basket on her shoulder.

"A big one," she squealed with delight as she threw on another layer of grass to keep the fish moist and fresh until they returned to the village.

They fished in the sound until the sun began to climb out of the ocean and over the great sand dunes that sheltered Croatoa from the salty winds of the sea. By then the basket had become too heavy for Oshanoa, and as they made their way back to the cooking fires, Manteo took her load and carried it himself.

"You are very kind, Manteo. Most of our warriors would not consider helping a woman carry anything, much less a basket of fish."

He smiled as her thick brown hair swirled in the morning breeze. "But you have carried it long enough," and instead of walking in front, let her walk beside him.

She dragged the spear in the sand for several minutes before speaking again, "Must you leave us?" she asked sadly.

Manteo stared ahead, not wanting to answer, but felt he should. "I go to serve Wingina in Dasamonquepec. It will bring honor to our village if I serve well."

"But he has not fully recovered from his leg wound. Must you leave now?"

He walked on silently, not wanting to speak more of leaving the village. Oshanoa reached out and softly touched his arm, and as he turned he saw tears in her blue eyes. "But you are my only friend. What will I do after you are gone? No one speaks to me unless to tell me of some work to do. Even your father hates me," and the spear fell away as she reached up to wipe the tears that gathered on her cheeks.

"Oshanoa, my friend," whispered Manteo. He gently touched her cheek and lifted her face to look at him. "The people of our village understand. How can a lovely young doe be asked to strike at a growling bear? Instead she flees and seeks the shelter of her home. Too soon they know you were called upon to serve your people. But dishonor is a sickness that does not heal. One day you must leave our people and seek a new life, and I know in my heart that you will find a great warrior worthy of you."

She pressed his hand against her cheek while tears silently crept down her face. She knew in her heart that he spoke the truth, that one day she would leave Croatoa to live among a new people that did not know or care of her dishonor at Aquascogoc. "But when?" she whispered. "When will such a warrior come for me?"

They walked on together in the cool morning air, silhouetted against a brilliant sunrise that shimmered across the water. Somehow they sensed a new beginning, but knew little of the greatness that would come to embrace them.

* * *

The smell of baking fish filled the morning air as women throughout the village worked to prepare seakanuk in their own special manner. It was roasted whole over some fires, while at others the large chunks of tender white meat were stripped from the backbone and stewed into a mush along with the colorful pagatour kernels, potatoes and openauk roots found in the low marshy areas.

Manteo and two other young warriors, who would escort him to Dasamonquepec, would be leaving after the morning meal. They were busy packing their canoe with war clubs, bows and arrows, spears and necessary foods such as dried meats, fresh fruits and deerskin sacs of water flavored with the root bark of sassafras trees.

"Manteo," cried a voice from the path leading to the village. "All is prepared at your father's lodge. Go and eat."

Manteo looked over his canoe once more, and satisfied that all was prepared for his departure from Croatoa he turned and ran up the path toward his father's lodge. As he stooped down to enter the door he saw his mother ladling bowls of her fish stew that he loved so well. She smiled at her son in a way to let him know that she had made the effort more to please him than her husband. Lumps of freshly baked bread from the colorful corn meal and ground roots lay among the grapes and melons that had been picked the same morning by Oshanoa.

"It is good to see my son again, before he leaves on the great journey."

"It is an honor to share my father's lodge before I depart." Manteo looked over at his mother as she rose to leave. "Father, I will not be here to see my mother for a long time. Could she share this meal with us?"

The grumpy looking chief looked up at the old woman whose leathery skin reminded him that he too was growing old, then motioned toward a reed mat. Manteo's mother fell to her knees beside her son, honored to share a meal with the two greatest warriors in her life.

"Wingina is still at Aquascogoc," the chief said.

"I know, Father."

"His elder brother, Granganimeo, is chief in his place until Wingina returns. You will see him when you arrive and give him my greeting."

"Yes, Father, I remember Granganimeo from the winter hunt of great white birds. He is a man of honor, and much good humor."

"True, my son," and his father reached behind and pulled out the albino deerskin cape that Verotacam had given Oshanoa for a wedding gift. "Ask the great chief's brother to accept this."

"I am pleased that you allow me to return the cape, Father."

"Eat!" cried a voice beside them. "Enough talk, fish go bad." His mother flipped her hand limply toward the bowls on the woven grass mat.

Manteo smiled at her and picked up a small bowl. He held it to his mouth and with two fingers began to slurp the mushy meat and potatoes. After devouring several bowls, more to please his mother than to satisfy his hunger, he wrapped the wedding cape carefully in another deerskin. Then he said farewell to his parents and walked quickly to the canoe that would carry him from Croatoa to great adventure at Dasamonquepec.

Manteo had asked two of his friends to accompany him and bring his canoe back to Croatoa. He would have little need of a personal canoe, and it would take his people at least one great moon to replace it by finding a downed tree in the forest, suitable for burning out and carving the interior with flattened stone axes. "Kineton," he shouted as he neared the water. "Is everything ready?"

"Yes, Manteo, we are ready."

"Then let's go," he shouted back with a large grin on his face. He stepped into the water beside the canoe and placed the wrapped wedding cape under several layers of animal skins, then hopped in the center and picked up a paddle. Hoctoba was in the front, his paddle ready to begin the long strokes. Kineton sat in back, holding the larger paddle that was used to steer as well as propel the canoe. And as they pushed gently off the bottom to send their boat out in the sound, the people of Croatoa gathered along the shore.

"Good-bye, our son," the women sang to him.

"Good hunting," shouted the warriors, and all were smiling and waving except the lone young maiden who stood apart from the others. Her arms hung at her sides and tears filled her eyes as she watched her only friend in the village row away to the north.

Manteo glimpsed her but looked away. He knew her life in Croatoa was one of hard work and shame, but he felt in his heart that one day she would be rescued by a great warrior from another village or tribe. 'Soon,' he thought to himself as he and his friends became a small peak on the northern horizon.

❖ ❖ ❖

PORT FERDINANDO

Late July, 1584

For more than a month, the English barks sailed the Southern route across the Atlantic, arriving in Puerto Rico by way of the Dominican Passage. There they refreshed food and water supplies then weighed anchor and set sail for the Florida Channel.

The pilot, Simon Ferdinando, miscalculated the strength of the great current and for several days they were carried eastward out to sea. Discovering his error, he brought the ships about and headed west for the coastline, where upon sighting land he could take a reading and adjust his course.

"Land ho," cried the watch at sunrise on July 4, 1584. For two days the sailors smelled the sweet greenery of landfall, a sharp contrast to the salt spray they knew so well. All hands ran forward to catch a glimpse of the land Verrazzano had named Arcadia. As the sun crept up their backs, they could easily make out a low rise of sand and trees on the western horizon.

Barlowe sent below for his mariner's ring and declination tables. After several attempts to shoot the low eastern sun he estimated they were still several minutes south of the latitude they wished to reach. He was hardly surprised to see Amadas' ship bear off to the north and parallel the coast.

He watched carefully as the lead was cast off the port side, and again as it was brought up at the stern. He wondered cautiously at the depth of the water and contents of the lead as it was retrieved. 'Would it be pebbles, shells, sand or mud?' he asked himself as he prepared to note in his log for the benefit of future sailors who would pass this way and sound the same waters. The lookout on each ship peered relentlessly toward the shoreline seeking a break in the land indicating a possible cut or river flowing out to sea. They sailed a northern course with southerly winds at their backs, and for several days eased along the coast until finally an entrance was sighted.

The ships turned slowly toward land and tacked within a quarter mile of the inlet where finally they dropped anchor. The longboats were pulled alongside where a crew from each bark scurried over and took up the oars. For several hours they sounded the entrance, with men in front casting lead every few yards. They found the inlet to be shallow and full of dangerous shoals, but on an incoming tide of sufficient depth to allow the barks to enter.

With the assistance of oarsmen in the longboats, the ships passed carefully between the sandy banks, and with slackened sail, they moved half a league south and settled in a bay with trees sufficient to hide their masts and rigging behind the barrier islands. Barlowe noted carefully in his log the events that had taken place that morning, but had not yet agreed with Amadas to name the shallow inlet after the Portuguese pilot.

He put the quill pen aside and closed the logbook, putting off the decision until the land about had been reconnoitered and taken possession of in the name of Elizabeth, Queen of England. He rose quickly and ran up to the stern castle where he called his men to gather round the mainmast. There he would lead them in prayers of thanksgiving to the Almighty for a safe arrival in the New World.

As the men gathered on deck and fell to their knees, an ocean breeze whistled through the rigging, and Barlowe began to pray aloud. Between amens the sailors cast their eyes about from the barrier islands at their backs to the mysterious land toward the west. At the final amen, the crew rose and began clamoring to go ashore for fresh victual and adventure. Amadas, as well as Barlowe, began delegating tasks and before their instructions were complete the first two groups of men began to fill the longboats.

First ashore were the hunters. They spread along the waterline and into thick forests as the boats returned to their ships for water casks and the men who would dig the shallow wells. On board, other men furled sails and tied off rigging in preparation for an extended respite from the sea. A shot rang out in the forests near the shore as cheers rose through the trees, and the cooks on board fired their ovens in anticipation of preparing a meal of fresh game.

A spirit of adventure had swept over the crewmen as they explored the lands near about them. For two days they gathered the fruits of summer, conies and squirrels, but saw not a sign of life. It was on the third day, late in the morning, when a native canoe was seen rounding the point of land that sheltered the bay from southerly winds. It was on that day of innocent discovery when the New World opened itself to incursion by the English.

* * *

A sun-warmed breeze buffeted the shallow water near the leeward shore, but not enough to slow the progress of Manteo and his friends. Though peaceful, the long hours of continuous rowing had begun to drain their strength. As the sun fell out of the Western sky their canoe began to ease into shore, seeking a safe shelter for the night. A small sandy shoal rose out of the water and Manteo pointed in that direction. Kineton eased the large flat paddle to one side to guide them easily toward the small island, where an evening breeze would help blow away pesky mosquitoes.

Manteo rolled a long reed mat out on the sand, while his two friends began laughing together. "With you out of the canoe, Manteo, there is room enough for both of us to sleep here, among the deerskins."

"Warriors do not sleep in canoes," he teased them. "Not when there is good hard sand to lie on."

"Yes, but if the water should rise before morning, you may find the ground not only hard, but also wet." And they laughed at their friend who was leaving their village.

'It is good,' thought Manteo, 'that old friends who had grown up in the same village should spend their last night together, in pursuit of great adventure.'

There was something in Manteo's thoughtful eyes that held Kineton's attention. "Don't worry, old friend. We will look after your parents. And if any warrior visits our village, we will make sure that Oshanoa is presented as available for marriage, just as you have told us."

"Here, eat," said Hoctoba. "Your mother prepared dried venison and bread."

Manteo took the meat and bread and laid back on his mat, looking up at quivering stars that slowly began to fill the darkening sky. "I am ready," he said confidently to his friends. "I am prepared for this adventure, whatever it will be."

"Tomorrow," said Kineton, "you will begin a new life as a Secotan warrior, in the service of Wingina of Dasamonquepec."

"And your name will be great in our village," added Hoctoba.

"In all the confederation," teased Kineton.

Manteo smiled with his friends at the prospect. He had considered that his name might well be remembered by his parents, the people of Croatoa and his friend, Oshanoa, As the sky grew darker, talk between friends died away and the three young warriors gave in to slumber their bodies required. The sound of water lapping against their canoe was the last thing they heard before a twilight sky greeted them the next morning.

Manteo pulled the deerskin cover up to his face as he often did in his lodge back in the village. His arms stretched out above his head and his toes pointed out below the cover. With a loud grunt he shook his body awake and stood in the cool morning air. "Get up," he shouted to his friends who were still asleep. "We don't have far to go."

As the sun rose, warm air created mists in the treetops along the shore, but they evaporated quickly in the ocean breeze that curled over sand dunes and into the forests of cypress and oak. Crabs scurried underfoot as the canoe was dragged into the water and small schools of fish darted away as paddles dug into the sand, pushing the canoe out to deeper water.

As Manteo and his friends eased away from shore they began rowing steadily northward. For hours, seagulls swarmed over their heads searching for some morsel of food to appear. And then one of the gulls folded its wings and began to dive headlong into the water, to attack a wounded fish that had strayed too long near the surface. Just as the gull was about strike, its head cocked back to drive its beak with greater velocity, the sound of thunder ripped through the treetops of the island and out over the water.

The Croatoan warriors jerked upright in alarm, looking around for the source of the great sound. Cranes rose noisily from the shoreline, flapping wildly to escape from an unseen threat. Manteo looked overhead in the deep blue sky, but could find no cloud dark enough to carry such noise. Then he looked at his friends in confusion.

The sound of thunder exploded again from the small point of land jutting out in the sound ahead of them. Excited voices followed the explosion, but in a tongue that none of them had ever heard before. Kineton looked quickly at Manteo and Hoctoba, waiting for word that would send them on to Dasamonquepec to report the strange noise and voices, but Manteo whispered cautiously to them. "I do not know what they say, but it is the sound of hunters, rather than a raiding party."

"But such a great noise," said Kineton. "We must go to the village and tell them."

"Tell them what?" asked Manteo. "That we heard the sound of thunder in the forest and strange voices, but were too afraid to discover who it was that made the sound. No, my friends, we must find out who is on the island and what is the source of the thunder. Then we will have something to tell in Dasamonquepec."

Slowly the canoe began moving toward the point of land. The strange voices had gone away and all that could be heard were the sounds of the forests, the wind blowing through cypress and oaks and squirrels barking along their branches.

An instinctive fear kept them alert to potential danger as they began to round the point of land to a small bay, and they were suddenly frozen in the panoramic splendor of two of the greatest canoes that could be imagined. They rose up from the water to taper in long thin limbs covered with all manner of decorations. The young men sat in wild-eyed amazement as Manteo suddenly realized these were the great trading canoes from another world. These were the vessels of the god-like men, who possessed the great thundering sticks they heard in the forests. And with a foreboding curiosity Manteo accepted that the white men had finally come to Hattorask.

Part Four

Revelations

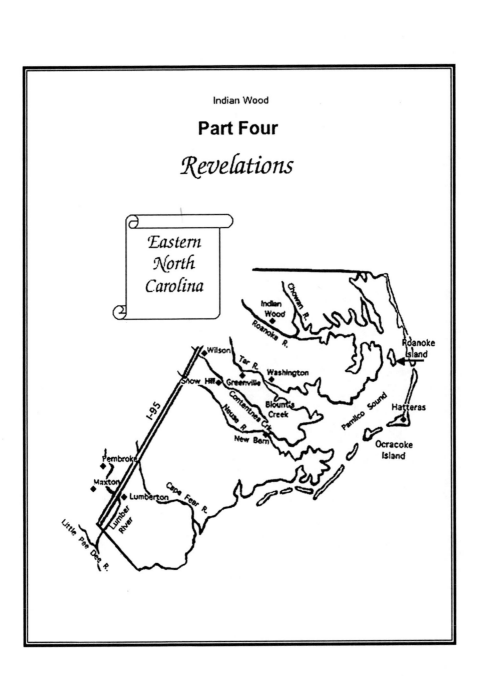

THE LUMBEE INQUIRY

As Luther sped silently along the four-lane highway toward Wilson, he was accompanied by endless thoughts of Carl and the mystery that surrounded his death. At the Hwy 301 over pass, he glanced north to where only a mile away stood a small concrete block restaurant that served the best rib-eye steaks in Eastern North Carolina. He was still smiling as he reached the I-95 intersection, recalling memories of Carl, driving with his date beside him, while he and Veronica sat in the back, sipping 'Seven & Sevens' on the way to a plentiful salad bar and great steak dinner.

As he turned south on the interstate toward Lumberton, the milepost markers passed like silent sentinels, and he was surprised that he could drive ten miles in thought without even being aware of the time that had passed between them. He was thinking of another friend, Langdon Bryant, who hailed from an old Southern family that had lived in Robeson County since the early 1800's.

At five feet ten, Langdon was neither short nor tall, with curly brown hair, streaked with gray, which framed a portly face. And like Luther, he had been in two luckless marriages that left him reeling through a series of casual relationships. But he was such a charming fellow, with good humor and wit, and that special vocal twang of a southern gentleman, that he was always welcomed in social circles, all the way up to the Governor's Mansion in Raleigh.

Luther and Veronica had also been included on the list to the annual Media Gala held at the Governor's house, but after a few years he tired of such events and much preferred the company of close friends for intimate dinners on the back porch of his home. But not Veronica; it was the highlight of her social calendar, and with flowing black hair, pale skin, and red gown, she commanded the attention of admirers from all over the state.

Men such as Langdon Bryant fawned over and pampered her with compliments. They danced elegant waltzes with her over the parquet floor of the ballroom, while Luther was content to network with peers in the newspaper business, smoking an occasional luxury cigar and drinking the governor's expensive whiskey on the grand patio overlooking the back lawn. And while she would seek out and plan for such events, he would sit comfortably at a table in the den, with men such as Carl and Harry Hughes, and one or two neighbors, playing poker into the wee hours, content with life at the creek.

Though she was intelligent and beautiful, it was her need for public affirmation on a grand scale that had eventually tarnished their relationship and led her into the arms of a cigarette baron in Winston-Salem. 'And by God, he could afford her much better than I,' were his last thoughts as he pulled off the interstate.

The downtown area of Lumberton was larger than he remembered, and he passed through several intersections searching for Fifth Street. Looking up, he saw an impressive building he assumed was the legal center of the county. He recalled that Fifth led right up to the courthouse steps, and *The Lumberton Herald* was only half a block away.

"Luther," Langdon shouted with a grin as he greeted his old friend from *Little Washington*. "How's life on the Pamlico?" Though Langdon had never been to his home on the river, Luther was certain Veronica had embellished its beauty to him. It was her way of rationalizing being tucked into such a lonely corner of the world, so far away from the city lights and ardor of her friends.

"Life is good at the creek," he responded with a generous smile, because when necessary he could play the game almost as well as Langdon.

"Come into the house," his host said as he pointed toward his corner office with a fine view of the street leading west toward the Lumber River. As they entered, Langdon began removing stacks of papers and booklets from two side chairs next to his desk, the stock and trade of men in the publishing business. "Sorry about the mess, but you know how it is."

Luther smiled and nodded knowingly, recalling the organized chaos that seemed to bedevil his own office. "Well at least you have room for two side chairs, Langdon. I barely have room for one."

The conversation drifted into small talk of the newspaper business, especially circulation numbers, advertising rates and the day-to-day operational issues that vexed small town newspapers. Finally Langdon leaned back in his large chair, folded his hands behind his head and said, "Your friend, Carl, was also a friend of mine, Luther. Hell, everyone liked him. He was just that kind of person, always pleasant and ready with a good joke to liven things up." And then his voice trailed off.

"So you think there may be a connection to his death, down here in Robeson County? And this woman, Roberta Locklear, you think she may know something?"

Luther suddenly felt uncomfortable, as if he were in a foreign place, an outsider about to interrogate an old friend. "Do you know her, Langdon?"

"I know of her," he responded. "Don't know her personally, but I know someone who does, a lady by the name of Ramona Oxendine. She's Roberta's cousin; heads up the foundation over at the university, fund-raising, special events, that sort of thing."

Luther fell back in his chair, a serious look on his face. "Do you think she would mind talking to me?"

"Already called her, and she said if we could get over there by lunch time, she would meet us under the bell tower. That's where she likes to take her lunch break, right there in the middle of campus."

"So you'll come with me?"

"Sure, Luther, anything to help. And like I said, Carl was my friend, too."

Luther felt a sudden welling of emotion in his chest, and rose from his chair. As it lifted up inside his throat he swallowed hard and tried to smile. "Think I'll go to the bathroom and get rid of some coffee."

"Sure, Luther, right down the hall on your left. And when you get back, we'll head over to Pembroke."

Luther nodded and walked slowly down the hall, searching for the small icon of a man's silhouette painted on the smoked glass panel of a wooden door. Then he disappeared for several minutes.

* * *

Langdon drove his white Cadillac Escalade down Fifth until they arrived at the busy I-95 intersection, then he looked over at Luther. "Before we go over to Pembroke I'd like to show you something." And instead of driving west, directly toward the university, he turned left on the ramp leading down to the interstate.

"Big plans going on here in Robeson County, Luther. Looks like both houses of congress may approve legislation to designate the Lumbees as a federally recognized Indian tribe."

Luther had a curious look on his face. "What will that mean to the Lumbees?"

"It means they can designate some of the land around Pembroke, maybe from I-95 to as far West as Maxton as their official reservation."

"And how will that affect the non-Indian population living there?"

"It won't, Luther. Everything stays pretty much the same, except that as a federally recognized reservation, the land can be developed for the benefit of the Indian population. Just like it has for other Indian tribes across the nation." Langdon paused a moment while he grinned at Luther. "You know what that means don't you?"

"Casinos, just like the Cherokee Indians have in the mountains."

"Damn right," Langdon shouted. "Real estate in this county is gonna take off. Casinos, hotels, motels, service industries, housing, schools, and every other kind of development that goes along with it. And by the time the Cherokee get the gaming commission to approve table games like Black Jack, Craps and Roulette, this place could become the Las Vegas of the East Coast." Luther noticed the vehicle had veered off the interstate into the right turn lane of the Highway 74 intersection.

"This the place?" Luther asked.

"That's right, Luther. Right here on the West side of I-95, and on both sides of Hwy 74.' This is the land the Lumbees will need to build their casinos and hotels. Its adjacent to one of the most heavily traveled interstate highways in the nation." Then he looked at his friend with a great big smile. "It's a marriage made in heaven."

"But who owns the land around the interstate?" Luther asked as he looked at the gas stations on either side of the road and the farmland behind it.

"Doesn't matter. The Lumbees can pay top dollar to anyone for however much of this land they want, and the banks will line up to loan them whatever they need." Then he continued on enthusiastically. "Can you imagine what this will do for the tax base of Robeson County, one of the poorest counties in North Carolina? And what about the money the Lumbees can earn for themselves and their university in Pembroke? I'm telling you, Luther, unless something unusual happens, the Lumbees should be designated as a federal Indian tribe within the next few years and that will be the catalyst for the rest of the development in Robeson County to take off."

Luther was surprised at the enthusiastic presentation offered by Langdon. But he could understand the potential this opportunity might afford the people of Robeson County, especially the Lumbee Indians. He was also the publisher of a small town newspaper in Eastern North Carolina, and if something like that were on the horizon for his likewise poor county, he would be just as enthusiastic.

"That's great, Langdon. It will be just great for the people of this county."

"Yeh," Langdon murmured under his breath. "If we can just keep from screwing this thing up, it can be good for everyone." They drove west on Highway 74 for several miles until they turned north and headed into Pembroke.

* * *

They drove into town on Third Street, passing by the old Indian Normal School on the corner of University Drive. Langdon kept going until he came to Faculty Row, the main drive leading into the heart of the campus. "We'll park beside the library," Langdon said, "and walk the rest of the way."

The two men left the vehicle, walking on the sidewalk beside the road and turned into the heart of the campus. Luther was impressed. Like every fine college there was a large green area where students, faculty and staff could gather on sunny days to sit and enjoy the landscaped beauty of their facilities. At Pembroke State University there was a large square bordered by the Sampson-Livermore Library on the south, and Lowry and Locklear buildings to the North. A small pond, with a crossing bridge, was in front of the library, while concrete risers anchored the center of the green, seating for special programs that were often presented by students and faculty. In the far corner was the Lowry Bell Tower, a four columned structure with great clocks on each of its sides, and Ramona Oxendine was sitting on one of the benches below the tower.

As they approached she turned and recognized Langdon, then stood and held out her hands. Langdon took them and kissed her lightly on the cheek, and Luther thought he noticed something more than friendly recognition in Ramona's eyes. Though not as pretty as her cousin, she had a round attractive face and engaging smile. Her skin was a shade between pale white and light brown, and freckled splotches ran across her nose, from one cheek to the other. She turned toward Luther and extended her hand. "Hi, I'm Ramona. Langdon tells me you would like to know something about my cousin, Roberta, her background, is that correct?"

She was pleasant and disarmingly direct. "Yes, I guess you know what happened in Greenville on Sunday night?"

"Everyone does, Mr. Surles. It is rare for a professor to be murdered on campus, but when three are lost in one night…" Then she paused and glanced away for a moment. "It's a very sad tragedy, but I don't see what this has to do with my cousin."

"Why don't we sit down, and I'll explain." Langdon and Ramona sat on one bench and Luther on another. "Roberta was Carl's graduate assistant," he said cautiously. He paused and looked straight into Ramona's eyes to gauge her reaction to his next statement. "And she was also his lover."

The look on Ramona's face revealed genuine shock. "Roberta was what," she said, almost as a question, and looked at Langdon as if for confirmation.

The look on Langdon's face was almost as remarkable. "I didn't know, Ramona. He didn't tell me anything before coming over. This is the first I've heard of it."

The distress in her eyes was real, but then she suddenly sat up. "Still, I don't see how she could be involved in this."

"I'm not saying she is, but she did mention something yesterday that I wanted to follow up on. She said Carl was the only man who knew her for who she really was, and loved her in spite of it all." Then he paused a moment for dramatic effect. "And that was such an intriguing statement, Ms. Oxendine, one that I felt I should inquire about. So I was hoping you could help me understand what she meant, and determine if it has any relevance to the case."

Ramona sat for a moment, staring out over the pond in the center of the square, not sure what to say or where to begin. He saw the hesitation in her eyes and decided to prompt her with a delicate fact that he already knew. "She said that she came to live with your family about the age of eleven, after her father tried to molest her."

"Molest her," she nearly shrieked. "Is that how she put it, Mr. Surles? Well, that old man didn't molest her, he raped her. He had sex with his own daughter. That's why she came to live with us." Then she leaned forward as if to whisper, " To get away from that drunken bastard that was her father."

She leaned back, composing herself before continuing. "But that's how things were handled back then. Families kept their skeletons in their own closets. Secret things were just handled quietly, so that no one would know, and no one would go to jail. And that's why my family took Roberta in, because we knew what she had been through. We never discussed it. It was just known between us that something terrible had happened, but that she was safe, and my family would take care of her." She took a deep breath and let out a sigh.

"So she grew up and turned out to be the most beautiful and smartest girl in school. She was 'Little Miss Everything;' homecoming queen, honor society and even Miss Pembroke her freshmen year in college. And any of us other girls would have been jealous, except that she was so nice, so caring and giving, the very best sister I could have hoped for. I tell you, Mr. Surles, Roberta Locklear is a rare and gifted woman, but then another tragedy befell her that I could not protect her from; none of us could."

Luther sat up and stiffened his back, in preparation for the controversial new information. "Did it have something to do with the American Indian Movement in the late 1970s?"

"My God," Ramona exclaimed. "Did she tell you about that, too?"

Based on Ramona's reaction, Luther realized there was much more to Roberta's relationship with 'AIM' than had been revealed in Greenville. "Only that her advocacy for the Lumbees was not well received by the local 'AIM' chapter. She also said that there was some intimidation, and even a suggestion that she move to another county to become a teacher."

Ramona glanced at Langdon hoping he would tell her that she didn't need to continue, but he simply nodded as if to say, 'Tell the whole story.' Ramona's head fell slightly as she took another breath, shrugged her shoulders and began. "My sister, my beautiful sister was raped again, by those ruffians in the *American Indian Movement*. They weren't the leaders, just the young hooligan element that hangs around the fringes of good causes, to bring a little credibility and respect to themselves."

Ramona stared out over the pond as she continued. "Roberta was not only beautiful, but was also an effective speaker, not afraid to advocate for what she believed in. And she felt the Lumbees needed to seek state and federal recognition as a separate Indian tribe in Robeson County, and that is where she ran into conflict with 'AIM.' At first the Tuscarora and Cherokee tried to reign her in, but when they found she could not be controlled, they ostracized her from the movement, and even threatened her. But she would not back down.

Then one night in June of 1979, she was driving home by herself after a rally held in the old auditorium of Vardell Hall, an old girls school over in Red Springs. A car passed and swerved, intentionally running her off the road and into a ditch. Four young Tuscarora men pulled Roberta from her car, bound her and took her to an isolated part of the county. They taunted her for what she believed in, sexually assaulted her, and left her there the rest of the night.

The next morning, just after dawn, my father got a call and was told where she could be found. I went with him, and we drove down an old logging road until we found her tied upright and naked to a tree, crying and screaming in delirium."

Ramona paused for a moment, staring up into a blue sky filled with white cumulus clouds, hanging over the campus like giant cotton flowers. "A month later, humiliated and disgraced by what had happened, she packed her things and moved away. We didn't hear from her for almost two years.

Then one night she just appeared at her mother's house with a beautiful little boy beside her. And all of us new the father had to be one of those evil men who had raped her in the darkness of that summer night. But she was different, cool and distant, and often spoke quietly to me of one day taking revenge on the Tuscarora men who had defiled her. But as her little boy grew up, the memories faded and her heart softened, She became more like the old Roberta I used to know. She took a position teaching in Hope Mills, a small town just below Fayetteville, only a few miles from here."

"Luther, you all right?" Langdon asked.

The look on his face was one of utter surprise. "Roberta has a son?" And in the back of Luther's mind another suspect had been added to the list.

"Yes, I had not seen him in years until last Sunday," she added. "Camron was at his grandmother's house for the family reunion, and he is such a fine looking young man. You don't even notice the effects of the cerebral palsy that afflicted him as a child, unless of course you speak to him for awhile, and then you observe some of it in his critical thinking skills."

"He's what we call a slow learner, " Langdon added.

"Special Education, all the way through school," Ramona said.

Luther fell back against the bench, his head spinning with the new information about Roberta. "And where does he live?"

Ramona thought to herself for a moment. "I think Camron said something about living in Manteo, on the Outer Banks, but I cannot recall what it is that he does."

Luther stared out into the center of the green for a moment, trying to collect his own thoughts. 'Roberta was Carl's graduate assistant. Both of them were working on Lost Colony projects. Carl discovered something he called the 'Tuscarora Connection' on Sunday afternoon and called Roberta at her mother's house in Pembroke. Her son was at the house. Roberta was raped by several Tuscarora men in 1979, and at one time wanted to take revenge against them. Could this be her revenge,' he asked himself, 'depriving the Tuscarora of whatever connection Carl had found? And could she have used her mentally challenged son as an instrument of her revenge?'

"Luther, what are you thinking?" Langdon asked. "Your eyes are just fluttering around in your head. And you've got a mighty curious look on your face."

"I don't know, Langdon. I think I need to go back and talk with Roberta." Then he looked at Ramona. "Thank you both for all your help. Ms. Oxendine, you have shared so much with me, and I sincerely appreciate it, but now I feel I must get back to Greenville."

"Mr. Surles, surely you don't believe that my cousin is involved? She is such a dear, sweet person. I simply cannot fathom how Roberta could be part of this."

'Hell hath no fury like a woman scorned,' he nearly blurted out, but held the thought at bay. "I sincerely hope not," he said as he stood to leave.

❖ ❖ ❖

THE LONG RIDE HOME

Thoughts and memories churned through Luther's mind as the miles slipped by and the sun dipped lower in the western sky. Even in his classic old Jaguar, the ride home seemed much longer than the drive down to Robeson County. Normally he would tune into an oldies station beamed out of Rocky Mount, but thoughts of Carl and Roberta swirled through his head, and he focused on the fact that she had an adult son that could be involved in Carl's murder.

The sound of his cell phone suddenly interrupted him, but instead of a traditional ring, Harry and the boys at the paper had downloaded a custom tone, the first nine notes of the Drifter's version of 'White Christmas.' The melodic base tones of 'Da-doo, da–doo, doop-doop, doop-da-doop,' would sound four times, until he either answered the phone or it switched to his voice mail. As he glanced at the digital readout on the front of his phone he saw that it was Jimmy Bonner calling from ECU.

"Hello, Jimmy."

"Luther, where the hell are you?"

"Just passing south of Wilson, headed back to Greenville to see you."

There was a short pause on the line. "Find out anything useful?"

"Maybe," he responded cautiously. "I'm mulling things over while driving home, but yeah, I think I have some interesting information that I need to share with you and Detective Harris." Luther decided he needed to tell them of Carl's involvement with Roberta, and that she had an adult son that could be involved. Then he asked, "Did you find out anything on Paskil?"

"Sure did," Jimmy responded enthusiastically. "Wesley Paskil took his masters in history at East Carolina College in 1956, and went on for a doctorate at UNC in Chapel Hill. Then in 1962, he came back to 'EC' as a professor in the history department and retired in '92. According to a friend in Alumni Relations, he's living over in Snow Hill, in Greene County. He's working as an adjunct professor with the archaeology groups excavating at *Fort Nooherooka*, an old Tuscarora Indian site."

"Another Tuscarora connection," Luther whispered.

"Yeah, this Tuscarora thing keeps popping up. Do you think Paskil is the one who wrote the thesis?"

"Sounds like it to me, and I want to talk to him if he's still alive."

"What do you mean 'still alive'? I just told you, he lives in Snow Hill."

"Yes, but whoever killed Ludie may go after Paskil to keep him quiet."

"I hadn't thought of that," Jimmy said thoughtfully. Then as he gave Luther an address for Wesley Paskil, he typed it into his GPS locater. "Take Highway 58 into Snow Hill. When you get to Fourth Street turn right. Then go on to Harper and turn left, and it should be about two blocks."

"Thanks, Jimmy. I'm going to stop at The Beef House in Wilson and have dinner, then drive over to Snow Hill and try to find Paskil. I'll call you on my way back."

"Luther, you still got that pistol?"

"Sure do, a Colt .380 automatic in the glove box. But you know I couldn't hit the side of a barn with it, not with that two inch barrel," and he laughed.

"But it makes a hell of a noise, and that may be all you need to scare someone off." Jimmy's voice sounded low and concerned. "You take care out there, Luther, and let me hear from you as soon as you get back to Greenville."

"Will do, Jimmy," Luther answered as he hung up and took the 301 Exit into Wilson. He hardly noticed the headlights of a faded blue Chevy pick-up that pulled off and followed him for nearly a mile. As Luther turned into the restaurant, the pick-up drove casually by, but the head of the man driving was turned hard watching Luther pull into a parking space next to the small brick building.

For decades Wilson had been a dry town, so patrons had made a practice of pulling into the parking lot with brown bags of bourbon and scotch. They put their names on a waiting list for a table and had set-ups delivered to their vehicles by the wait staff. And on more than one occasion, when their names were yelled from the steps of the restaurant, people in the cars would scream back, "Not ready yet, put us back two tables," because that was the kind of partying that often took place in the car bars.

Luther walked inside and directly in front of him stood a large middle aged man wrapped in a white apron, grilling custom cut rib eyes. "Luther Surles, you old son of a gun, where in the heck have you been?"

"Working, John, hanging out at the creek, you know how it is."

A large paw swept toward him and grasped his right hand. "Well grab yourself a plate and fix a salad. I just put out some more of those little smoked oysters you like. How about a big ole rib-eye?"

"How about a small rib-eye? I can't eat those 16 ounce steaks like I used to."

John held onto Luther's hand, looking him in the eye. "Sorry to hear about your friend and those two ladies at the college. I remember how you and Carl used to come over here once or twice a month and make a real big party out of the trip. Can't imagine how a thing like that could happen to such nice people."

Luther took another deep breath as he felt an emotional dam surge within him. Then he let it slowly out and the waters receded. "Thanks, John. I see my old table is available," and he pointed toward the far corner where he and Veronica, and Carl and anyone of his many dates, had often sat.

John let go of his hand, walked him over to the salad bar and handed him a plate. "This one's on the house, Luther, in memory of our good friend, Carl Bowden."

Luther nodded graciously, accepted the plate and began grazing over the items on the salad bar. He made a small bed of lettuce, added a few slices of tomato, green olives, cheddar cheese, a few of those little ears of corn and a mound of smoked oysters, all smothered in blue cheese dressing.

'Veronica would die if she saw me eating this,' he thought to himself, recalling the lettuce and tomato salad she would eat with just a dab of vinegar and oil to flavor it. 'But that's how she kept her ballerina figure,' and he smiled in remembrance of her light and graceful form dancing around their gourmet kitchen.

He thought of her more in the two days since Carl's death than he had in the past six months. As difficult as she could be when pursuing her own agenda, she more than made up for it in the personal attention she paid to his own needs; that is, after she had gotten her way, or whatever it was that she wanted. Still, he missed her, and even more so now, after losing Carl. He wanted someone to fill the glaring void in his own life.

Luther sat down in her old chair, the one she often sat in on the left side of the table, and looked around the room. Everything was the same except that she wasn't there, nor Carl, or any of the lovely ladies that he brought along for the party.

He was feeling his age, munching on salad when a pretty young girl walked up to him with an opened bottle of red wine. "John said you might like to try this," and she held the label forward for him to see. "He said to tell you it's a Cabernet Franc, from Fox Meadow, one of the new wineries he found on his last visit up the Shenandoah. It's pretty good," she added with a smile as she poured a generous portion into a boli glass, a round, slightly oversized wine goblet.

Luther held the glass up as if it contained a fine brandy, swirled it around and looked for the legs clinging to the sides, just the way Veronica would have done. Then he held his nose over the edge and inhaled deeply. It offerred a rich aroma, and finally he took a small taste. He let it run over his tongue and down the back of his throat where the flavor of pepper and black berries wafted through his nostrils.

"Very nice," he responded with a generous smile. "And thank John for me. I really appreciate it." She gave him a sparkling grin and country girl shrug of the shoulders, then walked away to take care of other customers.

Luther attacked the salad with gusto. And just as the lettuce was giving way to a white porcelain platter, she reappeared with a sizzling rib-eye, steaming baked potato, and a piping hot grilled onion on the side, topped with a slice of garlic buttered Texas toast. For only a moment Luther thought he might be too full to eat such a large meal, but within fifteen minutes the steak, onion and baked potato were gone. The only thing left was a small piece of bread that he simply could not finish. He struggled to his feet, laid a ten-dollar bill on the table, and walked slowly to the door.

"Did you get enough to eat, Luther? Can I fix you one for the road?" John asked as he beamed a smile toward his old friend.

Luther extended his arm, expecting a handshake, but instead John stepped forward and engulfed him in a great bear hug, nearly lifting him off the floor. "Don't be a stranger, Luther. We'll look forward to having you back for another visit."

Luther patted his full belly. "I'll be back, John. You know I can't resist a great steak dinner, and the wine, that was very good."

"Thought you would enjoy it, Luther; now be on your way and God speed."

Luther was grinning as he walked out the door and into the cool dark evening air. The old green Jaguar was waiting, purred to life and rumbled slightly as he backed away from the building. Still, he didn't notice the headlights of an old blue pick-up truck parked across the street, waiting for him to head back to Greenville.

Luther turned east on Highway 264, a four-lane that was sparsely traveled at this time of night. He noticed another set of headlights pulling out behind him. Thinking little of it, he continued to search for the Hwy 58 exit to Snow Hill. Just as he spotted his turn, the lights behind him began closing rapidly. He glanced down and saw that he was running 70 miles per hour. 'Someone must be in a big hurry,' he thought as the vehicle began to pass on his left side. And as he often did, Luther glanced over just as the blue pick-up truck began swerving into the side of his vehicle.

"Holy shit!" Luther screamed as the rear fender of the truck made contact with the front edge of his precious Jaguar. He felt the initial push to the right as the truck glided past and he could hear his tires squealing as he overcompensated and turned hard to the left. His car was sliding sideways along the shoulder, the front tires leaving streaks of smoking rubber on the pavement while the back wheels chewed up grass in the rear. He instantly realized that if he continued sliding sideways his car would flip over and be torn apart as it rolled and bounced along the shoulder. And with a slight turn to the left he did the only thing possible, he put the vehicle in a dizzying spin.

There was no way to count the number of revolutions, but with every turn Luther could feel the car slowing down, until it eventually glided to a stop, the headlights pointing awkwardly into the woods. Luther could feel the engine purring, almost as if nothing had happened, and he gently released his death grip on the steering wheel. He turned his head to the left and saw that the pick-up truck had pulled onto the shoulder about 100 yards in front of him.

Before he could think of what to do next, the door of the truck opened and he saw the dark figure of a man exit, reach into the bed and pull something out. 'What is that?' he asked himself, thinking it was a rake, or maybe a pitchfork, and he was suddenly filled with the dread of imminent danger.

The man walked slowly toward the Jaguar with tool in hand, silhouetted in the taillights of his own truck. Luther began to panic then remembered he had a gun. He leaned over and pressed the button on the glove compartment box. As it fell open he reached for the stainless steel pistol and yanked it out with his right hand.

As he pulled back on the carriage with his left hand to load the first round, he recalled from many practice sessions at the river that if you pull too quickly the bullet could jam before entering the chamber. He took a quick breath and willed himself to pull slowly and steadily until he saw a small copper nosed round slip into the chamber, then he released the carriage and felt it snap into place. The Colt .380 automatic was loaded, with another four rounds in the clip. All Luther had to do was slide the safety off, point the weapon and fire. But he had never pointed a gun at a human being before.

"Stop," he yelled at the man. "I have a gun, and I will shoot."

The dark figure paused for a moment, about halfway to the car, and Luther heard a small grunt and then a laugh. Then he started moving forward again. Luther could not bring himself to aim directly at his target, so he pointed down and to the left so the bullet would strike the roadbed and skip harmlessly away.

"Stop," he yelled one more time, but the man kept moving forward. Luther turned the safety off and squeezed the trigger. He only meant to fire one round, but with his grip tighter than he calculated, three rounds fired in quick succession.

Fire leapt from the barrel and thunder roared as the rounds skipped harmlessly to the man's side. He jumped back in such shock and confusion that he fell over, but quickly got up and ran to his truck. Luther's hands were still shaking as he thought it a harrowing, yet satisfying, moment to see the man drive away in a panic. 'Jimmy was right,' he thought to himself. 'The sound of the gun was enough to frighten him, but what to do now?'

He nervously opened the car door and got out to inspect the damage to his vehicle. In the darkness he could see very little, but noticed the bump from the truck had left a scrape of several inches just above the tire well. "Damn," he whispered, as he bent down and rubbed the scratches in the metal, recalling how difficult it was to match the British Green paint.

He stood and looked down the highway, wondering if the pick up truck may be waiting for him further down the road. Then he got back into his Jag, put it in reverse, backed up to the Highway 58 exit and raced off to the South. He still wanted to talk with Paskil.

As he drove into Snow Hill he looked for Fourth Avenue, turned right and headed for Harper Street. Jimmy's GPS was right on target; the small brick house was exactly two blocks from where he had turned, but the professor was not at home.

"I'm sorry," said the older gentleman who greeted him at the door, "but Dr. Paskil is away conducting field research." Luther carefully explained whom he was and what he was trying to accomplish. After several minutes of bewildering discussion, George Mackey finally allowed Luther inside the house.

While the man went into another room, to communicate with Paskil by phone, Luther walked around the living area studying walls covered with framed historical maps of North Carolina. He was staring at one of them when his host returned.

"That's a very nice copy of Edward Mooney's 1711 map of North Carolina," Mackey said with the trained voice of a museum tour guide "Mooney was a member of Colonel Barnwell's expedition, up from Charleston, to fight the Tuscarora. A little further up you can see Fort Barnwell, where the Colonel and his men gathered supplies and arms for the final attack on Hancock's Town, where the first war ended in 1712." Then he lifted his finger and pointed further up Contentnea Creek. "Here you can see Fort Nooherooka. That's where the second war ended in 1713."

Luther studied the drawing for another moment. "Some of the place names on this map look familiar. A few years ago Carl gave me a copy of John Lawson's book, *A New Voyage to Carolina*. I think it was published just before the Indian Wars started."

"Ah, yes, the poor unfortunate Mr. Lawson." Then George pointed back at the map. "See here, at Contechna, where Hancock lived, near the confluence of Contentnea Creek and the Neuse River. This is where Chief Hancock and his followers stripped the Surveyor General of the North Carolina colony naked, stuck his body full of pitch pine splinters, then lit them slowly from the head down, turning him into a human torch.

"But that punishment wasn't contrived just for Lawson. It was common practice for Indian tribes to test the mettle of their captives by sending them to their deaths through gruesome means." Then he paused and smiled pleasantly.

"Right after Lawson's death, in early September of 1711, the Tuscarora Wars began. The first war ended at Contechna, when Chief Hancock agreed to stop fighting, and to free his captives and return the plunder. And even though Barnwell and his men destroyed most of the Southern Tuscarora's crops and supplies, it had done little to diminish their fighting strength.

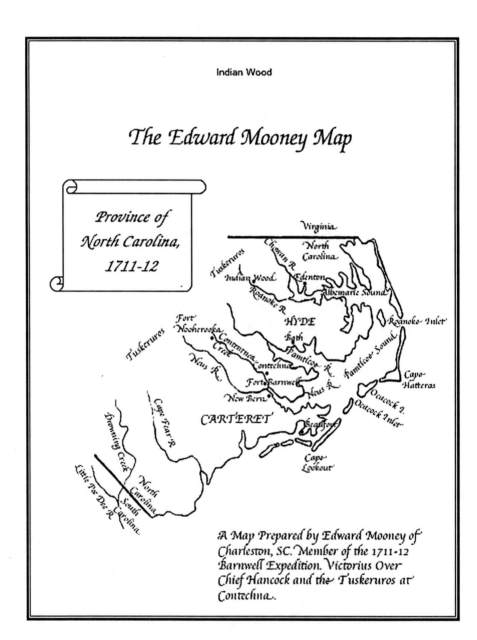

Indian Wood

The Edward Mooney Map

Province of
North Carolina,
1711-12

A Map Prepared by Edward Mooney of
Charleston, SC. Member of the 1711-12
Barnwell Expedition. Victorius Over
Chief Hancock and the Tuskeruros at
Contechna.

Then his finger trailed further up Contentnea Creek. "The second war ended here at Nooherooka in 1713. This is where the Southern Tuscarora were effectively destroyed as a fighting force. Hancock escaped, but over 500 of his warriors were killed in the battle." Then George added, "By the way, I got in touch with Wesley, and he has agreed to meet with you, tonight if you like. He's at the dig site, at Fort Nooherooka.""

"Then he's not far away?"

"Not at all, it's only five miles North of here. You passed it on your way in. He often stays at Miss Peninah's old home when he's in the middle of a dig. It's a small clapboard building next to the site where 'Aunt Nine,' a wonderful old black woman, lived until her death in 1960. Her children stayed there for some years, helping tend the farmland for the owner, but they have all moved away. Now-a-day's it's not much good for anything except a shelter to get out of the rain during digging season. But Wesley likes it there, so close to the dig site and all."

Luther looked seriously at George. "How's he doing, with all that's happened?"

"Frankly, he's a bit concerned. Since Dr. Bowden came over for brunch on Sunday, Wes thinks he may become a target for whoever killed Carl. So he is sort of hiding out, you might say. And had he not agreed, I surely would not reveal where he is staying. I trust you will keep the location in confidence."

"I will, George. I won't tell anyone unless I clear it with you and Dr. Paskil."

"Well, good. Come along, then, and follow me out to the site."

Luther took one last look around the room as they headed for the door. "Love the maps," he said with admiration.

THE PASKIL THESIS

They got out of their cars and stood in the darkness along a dirt and gravel road. George waved his arm toward a field of soybeans growing beside a line of trees that followed Fort Run Branch in a wide curve half a mile down to Contentnea Creek. "It was here, near the end of March in 1713, that 558 Tuscarora, 52 Yamassee, and 21 colonial militiamen died in the battle of Fort Nooherooka."

Luther peered into the darkness and could see little except a light in the window of a small frame building that stood thirty yards out in the field. "Just in front of Miss Peninah's old house, running northeast to southwest is part of the first road from Snow Hill to Wilson. Most of it followed the old Indian foot path that ran between the five Tuscarora villages along Contentnea Creek."

Luther was amazed at the amount of knowledge George seemed to carry in his head. "I forgot to ask earlier, but what is it that you do for a living, George?"

He turned with a smile. "I'm a retired school teacher. Geography and history were my subjects, and they are still my passion, especially anything to do with Greene County and Eastern North Carolina." Then he waved his hand in the air and said, "Follow me up this path to the house and I'll introduce you to Wesley."

Just as they approached the steps leading up to a wooden porch that ran the length of the small frame house, the front door opened and a man with balding head and wire rim glasses stepped out to greet them. He was wearing worn blue jeans with a long sleeve blue cotton shirt and red suspenders. "Mr. Surles, I presume?"

Luther accepted the rough hand that was extended toward him. "Yes, sir, I am."

"Well, come on in the house before the bugs take over," Wesley said with a grin. The three men settled around a small oak table in the kitchen. Wesley Paskil was short and stout but not a fat man. He was rugged and thick in the way old fullbacks aged as they tried to keep in shape in spite of the ravages of time. "I've got beer, wine, soft drinks and bottled water, Mr. Surles. What will you have?"

"I'd better have water for now," he replied with a grin.

"I'll have a Bud," George added."

"Okay, two Buds and one water." He opened the small refrigerator, grabbed three beverages and settled down at the table with the other men. "Sorry about your friend, Mr. Surles. Carl was an old colleague of mine from the History Department at the university." He took a big slug from his bottle of beer.

"Please, call me Luther."

"Sure, if you call me Wesley," he said with a smile. "Out here on the dig, we drop all the usual campus formalities and just work together to make a little history. Don't we, George?" he said with another big grin.

"That's right, Wes," then he looked at Luther. "We go back a long way, like you and Carl. So we understand how you feel, to lose one of your best old friends. One day all of us will pass, but hopefully, not like that."

Luther took a long drink from his bottle of water then set it down and looked intently at the two men. "Someone murdered Carl, and I want to know why. Then I want to make sure they pay the price; that justice is done. And that's why I'm here. I'm working informally with the investigation team, gathering information that can help Major Bonner at the ECU Police Department.

There was a quiet moment in the kitchen while George and Wesley took long swigs from their bottles. Then Paskil rose from the table and walked over to a small box on the counter. He thumbed through several items then turned around with a stack of neatly bound papers that had browned around the edges, and curled up at the corners from years of being stored away.

"Luther," he said with a profound sadness. "I'm afraid that I shared something with Carl that may have gotten him killed. But for all our discussions on Sunday, I'm still not sure what it was we discussed that would have been so egregious as to kill someone for the information."

Luther pushed back from the table. "I don't understand. You shared something with Carl and you don't know what it was that may have gotten him killed?"

"This, Luther, this is what I shared with him. It's the original copy of my master's paper that I presented to my thesis committee in 1956. And I never imagined that what I learned about the Indian slave trade in the early 1700s could ever shed any light on the mystery of the Lost Colony.

"But Carl looked over the paper, and then he called Ludie Worthington at the ECU library. He wanted her to locate the microfilm copy in the vaults and make a copy of my thesis so he could study it later that day."

Paskil walked over to the table, laid the old withered pages down and sat in his chair. "This is about the Indian slave trade that was taking place in the colonies in the late 17th and early 18th centuries. It was not only a lucrative business for the traders, but also facilitated the colonial government's desire to get rid of the Indians who raided the farms and communities of the colonists.

Indians would capture other Indians and sell them to traders for rum, guns, powder and ball, and other essentials they were becoming dependent on, like knives and copper pots and pans. The traders then carried their captives to Charleston where they were re-sold to the slavers who had just brought over their human cargoes from Africa."

"And what happened to the Indians sold to the slave ships?" Luther asked.

"They were taken to the Caribbean and re-sold in the slave markets of Cuba, Jamaica and the Dominican Republic. Eventually, they disappeared into the local labor force. And while everyone knows the story of the ante-bellum slave trade in America, very few know anything about the Indian slave trade. That's what my thesis was about, the selling of the Tuscarora captured at Indian Wood."

"Wait a minute, I'm confused. The battle took place here at Nooherooka, and over five hundred Tuscarora were killed. So who was left to be taken into slavery at Indian Wood?"

Wesley leaned back with beer in hand. "Luther, this is Nooheroka, where the second war ended in 1713. The story you want to hear is what happened at the end of the first war in 1712." Then he looked over at his old friend. "It's your turn, George."

George Mackey was ready and tried to curb his enthusiasm for the story he was about to tell by speaking in a slow, deliberate manner. "There were two Tuscarora Indian cultures in Eastern North Carolina in 1711, Luther. The Southern Tuscarora lived in five villages along Contentnea Creek, running from Wilson to where the creek enters the Neuse River, just below

Grifton. They were led by Chief Hancock, and only the Southern Tuscarora fought in the two wars.

The Northern Tuscarora lived along the Roanoke River in Bertie County. They were led by Chief Tom Blunt, and they did not fight against the colonists in either war." He paused a moment, nodded his head to make sure Luther understood then continued.

"The first war began in September of 1711, right after John Lawson was murdered by Chief Hancock at the village of Contechna. But Governor Hyde and the government at Bath were so weakened by internal bickering and dissension, they were in no position to fight a war. In just three days, Hancock's warriors, and a few allies, nearly cleared the Pamlico and Neuse Rivers of colonists. Over 200 settlers died, men, women and children. Dozens more were taken as captives to Contechna. Only those who made it to the barricaded homes of neighbors were able to survive.

"The North Carolina colony was hanging on by its fingernails. And they had no money or supplies to furnish provisions for the militia that Virginia offered to send. So they got little help from their northern neighbors, who had gone through a similar war with the Pamunkey and Mattaponi Indians of the Powhatan Confederacy in the 1640s.

"Governor Hyde then pleaded his case to the South Carolina colony. They sent a small militia, led by Col. John Barnwell, along with hundreds of Yamassee Indians from below Charleston. They arrived in late 1711 to defend the desperate colonists of North Carolina. After a short but intense war, culminating with the last battle fought at Contechna, Chief Hancock and Barnwell agreed to a cessation of hostilities. All the captives and most of the plunder were returned, and the Southern Tuscarora pledged to stop raiding the colonists. But Governor Hyde wasn't satisfied.

"He wanted Hancock and the Southern Tuscarora soundly defeated. And he was bitterly disappointed with Barnwell's effort. Hyde even went so far as to tell the Colonel that neither he nor his Indians would be paid anything for their service. So, Barnwell and his Yamassee warriors came up with a devious plan to win payment.

"Since the war was over, Barnwell graciously invited the Tuscarora to a peace celebration, where he told them the North Carolina government would furnish blankets and corn to see them through until their next harvest. And having lost so much of their supplies during the fighting at Contechna, many of the Southern Tuscarora agreed. The place chosen for the event was on neutral ground at a place called Indian Wood. It was a village located just north of the Roanoke River, where a large group of Chief Tom Blunt's people were living."

Hearing the words Indian Wood, Luther leaned forward, listening intently to whatever the retired high school teacher had to say. "Nearly a thousand Tuscarora were gathered there in late May of 1712. And on the day of great deception, Barnwell himself signaled the start of the attack. Unprepared for battle, the Tuscarora warriors were easily cut down by the guns and war clubs of Barnwell's army. In less than an hour, more than a hundred Tuscarora lay dead in the field, massacred by the Yamassee."

Paskil interrupted. "And that's where my master's thesis picks up the story, Luther. After the massacre, the Yamassee rounded up everyone that had not escaped, nearly five hundred men, women and children. They were mostly Northern Tuscarora, Chief Blunt's people living peacefully at Indian Wood. And that's what Carl referred to as the 'Tuscaora Connection.'"

"That's it! The 'Tuscarora Connection.' That's why Carl was killed," he said emphatically. "But what does it mean?"

Paskil turned up his bottle and drained the last few drops of beer. "I never would have guessed it myself, Luther. I only knew half the story, Carl figured out the rest. But let me tell you what happened to those people taken captive at Indian Wood." And he began an unknown tale of a thriving Indian slave trade in early colonial North Carolina, that Carl believed embraced the descendants of the Lost Colonists of Roanoke Island.

❖ ❖ ❖

DROWNING CREEK

"How 'bout another beer, George?"

"No, one's enough for me, Wes.

"Luther, you need another bottle of water?"

Luther was sitting at the table, deep in thought. "No, I'm good. I just want to hear the rest of this story and see if I can figure out how it relates to Carl's murder."

Paskil twisted the top off another Budweiser, sat back down at the table and continued. "Consider the situation in the North Carolina colony after Barnwell's treachery. Neither Hancock nor his warriors from Contechna were at Indian Wood, and so the raids on settlers started up again, setting the stage for the next Tuscarora War. And when Barnwell left in early June of 1712, it was not with the good will of Governor Hyde in Bath, nor the colonists of North Carolina.

They knew what they would be facing from Hancock and his followers. Because of Barnwell, they also faced the possibility that Chief Blunt and the Northern Tuscarora might join the fighting. And if that happened, it would mean the end of the North Carolina colony. Fortunately, the rest of Blunt's followers did not join with Hancock, and Carl said he had an explanation for that, too, but he didn't share it with me."

He took another long drink from his bottle and continued. "They say the shortest distance between two points is a straight line, and if you draw a line between Indian Wood and the slave markets of Charleston, you have, more or less the quickest route home for the Yamassee and their Tuscarora captives.

"And consider the logistical problem of moving 500 people, roped and tied together, through the forests, and having to ford streams and float on crudely made log rafts across several large rivers. And at every crossing they would lose a raft or two, and the captives, who probably drowned. But it was at the Little Pee Dee River, near Mullins, South Carolina, that the Tuscarora revolted.

They knew what was going to happen to them, because in the past they, too, had sold captives to white traders, who told them of the slave markets in Charleston. They knew that if they did not escape, they faced life as slaves. So they decided instead to chance death by drowning, in hopes of getting away.

The oral tradition among the Yamassee tells the story. In a coordinated effort, the Tuscarora rocked their rafts until they flipped in the swift brown waters of the Little Pee Dee. Many of them drowned, along with their captors, but the ones who made it to shore disappeared into the forests and sought help from local natives.

In groups of threes and fours they made their way up the river to a large creek. They call it the Lumber River today, but at that time it was known as Drowning Creek, because the waters were swift and black and took many Indians to their deaths."

Luther's head began to nod. "I've heard of Drowning Creek, about a survey party that floated down in 1736 and found," and he paused for a moment. "What did she call them, 'a wild and lawless group of people' living in the swamps?"

Wesley laughed. "So you've heard that story? Then listen to this," and he continued his tale. "It was well known among the Indians of that area that a series of large hummocks existed in the swamps, and that if they could get in there, they would be safe from pursuit. And that's where the escaped Tuscarora headed, for sanctuary in the swamps of Robeson County.

What they found when they got there was that other Indians, from various tribes in the Carolinas, were already living on some of the hummocks. They were trying to survive warring against larger Indian tribes, and the colonists, and also the new diseases that the white men brought with them. There were also a number of slaves, who had escaped from the plantations around Charleston. They had followed the same route into the swamps. And in 1712, to this previously mixed group people was added the bloodline and traditions of the Tuscarora. Then little more than a generation after they had arrived, a surveying party floated down Drowning Creek, where they found the mixed race of people you just mentioned."

"Some of them speaking the Elizabethan English," George Mackey added.

Luther sat back, considering for a moment everything that had been said, but still he was confused. "I think I can understand how the Tuscarora got into the swamps of Robeson County. But I still don't know how the descendants of the Lost Colonists got to Indian Wood."

Paskil smiled and relaxed in his chair. "The challenge for Carl, or anyone trying to prove what may have happened to the Lost Colonists, is to find a chain of evidence to document their movements from Roanoke Island to where any descendants might be living today. But no one to date has been able to do it.

"However, there is a group that is doing some DNA studies. They're going back to England, finding the graves of relatives of the colonists and getting permission to take DNA samples from bones and other tissues. Then hopefully, they can identify good prospects in Eastern North Carolina and match samples, genetic markers, to prove these people are descended from one or more of the Lost Colonists. That may not tell us how they got to where they are living today, but it will be a clear indication that at least some of the colonists survived.

And then there is the Bowden theory," he said with a huge smile on his face. "Carl told me that he believed he could place a large number of Lost Colony descendants at Indian Wood in 1712."

Luther's eyes lit up and he grinned. "The Tuscarora Connection," he shouted out, but this time with understanding. "I get it now. Carl believed that some of the descendants had assimilated with the Tuscarora and were living at Indian Wood."

"That's right," George chimed in. "And when the Yamassee took the Tuscarora as captives, they also swept up the descendants of the Lost Colonists."

"So," Luther summarized. "When the Tuscarora escaped on the Little Pee Dee and went up Drowning Creek into the swamps, the descendants of the Lost Colonists were already living among them. And that could be the basis for the Lumbee Indian claim of a connection to the Lost Colony."

"It could be," Wesley responded with a wink, "if you can prove that there were Lost Colony descendants living at Indian Wood in 1712."

"I thought you said Carl could prove it."

"He told me he could, but he didn't tell me how. He only said that after the colonists left Roanoke Island and went to Croatoa, they had to split up into several groups, because the Indians on the Outer Banks couldn't take care of all of them."

"Then where did they go?"

"Skico," he replied with a curious grin.

"Where's that?" Luther asked with a very confused look on his face.

"Somewhere on the Chowan River," Wesley answered. "Carl said that Skico was the key to where the colonists went after Croatoa, and what may have happened to them after that. That's all he would tell me. He said that Indian Wood was the pivotal point in the story of the Lost Colonists. He knew what had happened to them up to that point, and that I had inadvertently discovered what had happened to them after 1711. But again, I had no idea. My focus was entirely on the story of Indians selling other Indians to white traders, who would re-sell them in the slave markets of Charleston."

George then asked the glaring question, "Well, with Carl gone, does anyone know what happened to the Lost Colonists between Croatoa and Indian Wood?"

Luther's eyes squinted and his face darkened. "I think I know someone who may have the answer to that question," and then he stood up. "But I'll have to go back to Greenville to get it."

He spent the next few minutes recounting what had happened to him on the way to Snow Hill and cautioned Wesley and George that their suspicions were right. There was someone who may still be trying to silence anyone who could solve the mystery of the Lost Colony. He didn't know why, but he knew the two men should keep a low profile for the next few days. And then he left, bound for a small apartment in Greenville.

THE APARTMENT

It was approaching nine o'clock when Luther passed the Greenville city limit sign. He had already called Jimmy Bonner at the ECU Police Department to tell him of the day's events, that Roberta had a son who could be involved, and especially of the dark blue truck that tried to run him off the road. Luther was certain the man meant him harm, but could offer little in the way of a description. Rather than confuse Jimmy with the details of the Tuscarora Connection, he just let him know that he understood it now, and that he needed to go back to Roberta's apartment. He gave Jimmy the address and suggested that someone might want to observe the outside of the building while he talked to Carl's graduate assistant. He wasn't sure, but he suspected the man in the blue truck might be nearby.

Ten minutes later Luther was driving East on Fourth Street, and just as he drove up to the intersection where the apartment building was located, the parking lights of a black Ford that had backed into a driveway flashed at his green Jaguar. He turned his head and saw a hand lift up off the steering wheel to wave at him. It was Detective Harris of the Greenville Police Department. Luther felt a sudden wave of relief, knowing Harris had his back in case any trouble should arise, inside or outside the apartment.

As he drove into the concrete lot and got out of his car he saw that Roberta's living room light was on. He walked slowly to the door. Only the day before he had stood in the same spot, meeting for the first time the woman his best friend had come to love. 'How could she be involved in Carl's murder?' he asked himself as he knocked gently. 'But revenge is a such powerful motivator,' he thought as he heard someone come to the door.

"Who is it?" a soft voice queried.

"Roberta, it's Luther Surles. I need to speak with you, please." He was almost whispering so neighbors could not hear.

The deadbolt turned, a chain unlatched, and then she opened the door. Roberta stood in the doorway, her dark brown hair flowing over a white terry-cloth robe covering red silk pajamas. Luther paused a moment, reconsidering every negative thought he held that day of the woman Carl had fallen in love with. 'Surely she could not be involved,' he thought to himself as she pulled the door open for him to enter.

"How can I help, Mr. Surles?" she asked as he sat down on the couch, and she retreated to the comfort of her old maple rocker.

He didn't know where to begin. He needed to tell her that he had been to Robeson County, but before he could say a word she started. "I've been expecting you, but the later it got the more I thought it might be tomorrow before you came by."

The curious look on his face suggested an explanation. "My cousin, Ramona, called this afternoon. She said that you and Mr. Bryant had been to see her. She said she answered all your questions as honestly as she could, including the personal matter of my son, Camron."

For a moment she looked like an innocent doe in the headlights about to get run over with the discussion to follow. But like her cousin at Pembroke, she took the initiative. "The incident with the young Tuscaorora men was terrible and painful. When I discovered I was pregnant, I went to Baltimore to live with relatives and to have an abortion. But they were fundamentalist in their beliefs and persuaded me to have the child and place it for adoption.

The birth was complicated. The umbilical cord wrapped around my son's neck, and he was deprived of oxygen for part of the delivery. The couple who were waiting for him decided not to accept a child that may have already been damaged." Then she paused, tears creeping into her eyes. "Those were the words the woman used. She called my son 'damaged goods' and refused him."

Roberta reached for a tissue on the small table next to her chair and wiped her eyes. "As much as I hated the circumstances of his birth, I could not abandon an innocent child. So, with the help of my cousin and her husband, I kept my baby and named him Camron. Two years later, I moved back near my home, to Cumberland County. I accepted a position teaching at a high school in Hope Mills, and when I was self-sufficient, I took my son to meet his grandmother.

Roberta took a deep breath, sighed and smiled to herself. "My mother was weak in so many ways, especially when it came to the drinking and philandering of my father. But when it came to her children and grandchildren, she had the strength and resolve of a mother bear. That's why she was able to send me away to live with the Oxendine family after my father molested me." She paused and looked at her guest, "I suppose Ramona also told you about that?"

"Yes, she did, and how much she came to admire you for your strength and courage as you grew up."

"You're being kind, Mr. Surles, and I appreciate it."

Luther interrupted. "Please call me, Luther. I feel so much older when you address me as Mr. Surles."

She smiled pleasantly, "Okay, Luther. Is that better?"

"Much," he replied, and he sat quietly as she continued.

"When it became serious between me and Carl, I mean, more than just a sleep-over," and then she blushed at the description. "I'm sorry, I don't mean to diminish the depth of our..." and her voice trailed off as she stared into a dark television screen.

She wiped her eyes and then continued. "When it really got serious I decided to tell Carl everything. And if he still loved me after that then I knew I had found the right man to spend the rest of my life with."

She paused and stared at the curtains covering the front window, waiting for Luther to respond. "So Carl knew about your son, Camron?"

'Yes, but he never met him. Our plan was to keep things just as they were until I completed my graduate work. Then I would relocate to Greenville and move in with Carl."

"Did your son know about Carl?"

"No, I never mentioned that I was seeing anyone special at ECU. I have always dated a lot, so Camron was used to seeing me go out with other men. It would not have been a problem for him to learn about Carl, except that we decided no one should know," and then she paused. "Because of his position at the university,' she added. "And also, because Carl was my thesis advisor."

Luther decided to press on and ask about any lingering desire for revenge against the men who had long ago assaulted her. "Ramona mentioned that when you first moved back you talked of one day taking revenge against the Tuscarora who... " Then he paused, not wanting to use the 'R' word.

"Yes, Ramona and I have always been very close, and I felt I could tell her just about anything."

"But not about Carl?"

She smiled. "No, not Carl. That is the one and only secret I never shared with her. But as for revenge, time has a way of healing old wounds.

And besides, I had a wonderful child to love. Camron had special needs, did she mention that?"

"Yes, I think she referred to him as a slow learner."

"It was a result of his difficult entry into the world. But he is such a wonderful young man, tall and strong, kind and loving, and he keeps his long red hair tied back in a neat ponytail. Only when you are around him for a while do you realize that he processes thoughts and ideas more slowly than others. And that, of course, has rendered him a bit shy, but is, in itself, an endearing quality.

"He was such a wonderful little boy, Luther, that he became the center of my life. So, I decided I could not let my hatred of those men become part of his, and one day I let go of it. In my heart, I forgave them for what they had done, and the burden was lifted from me, just like it says in the Bible."

'Roberta was wonderful, beautiful and sincere. No wonder Carl had fallen in love with her.' He considered for a moment how much fun it would have been for her to have been with them in the car-bar at the Beef House in Wilson, instead of the 'short term ladies' Carl so often brought along. 'Veronica would have enjoyed you, too,' were his last thoughts before she interrupted with a suggestion.

"Would you like to meet my son, Luther? Would it help for you to meet him and discover what a fine young man he really is?"

"Yes," he replied with a smile. "I would love to." And that is exactly what he had in mind, find her son and ask him a few questions, like does he drive a blue truck? "Ramona said he might be working in Manteo?"

"Yes, he's a stage hand on the set of the Lost Colony. He's working very hard, helping prepare the sets and seating areas for the summer season."

"Nice job, but so far away from home."

"Not for Camron. He has always been fascinated with stories of the Outer Banks of North Carolina. He truly believes that our ancestors lived on Croatoa and helped the first colonists at Roanoke survive while waiting to be rescued by the English. And when they were not rescued, that they married into and became part of the Croatan Indian culture."

"And I guess you were the one that told him his ancestors may have included the Lost Colonists of Roanoke Island?"

"I did," she confessed with a smile. "And so did my mother, who first told me. You see the story is deeply imbedded in the oral tradition of the Lumbee people, and it is part of my mission as a student of history to discover the truth. It was a shared passion for the study of the Lost Colony that brought Carl and me together.

"He had been studying the subject ever since the night of the Klan rally in 1958. Then I came along, and we have been working together since last October. While I was conducting research for my thesis, he was writing his book."

Luther leaned back finally comfortable in the conversation he was having with Roberta. And now that the subject of the Lost Colony had been broached, he wanted to pursue what she knew about the Tuscarora Connection, and discover what Carl knew of the movement of the Lost Colonists prior to Indian Wood in 1712.

* * *

Luther apologized for the lateness of the hour. "The reason I'm so late getting back is that I stopped in Snow Hill to visit Wesley Paskil… "

Before he could finish the sentence she exclaimed, "Wonderful, because he's the only one who understands the Tuscarora Connection."

"You don't know?" he asked her in surprise.

She leaned forward in the rocking chair with her hands folded together. "I know what Carl knew, 'The Bowden Theory,' his personal thoughts on what may have happened to the Lost Colonists between Croatoa and Indian Wood. But this new thing he discovered, the Tuscarora Connection, I only got a brief description over the phone." She sat back and her eyes clouded.

"You should have heard him, like a little boy who found something extraordinary in a sandbox. And he wanted to share it with me, Luther." Her voice choked with emotion as tears welled up in her eyes. "But I only heard a brief description before he suggested I hurry back to Greenville."

Luther was anxious to learn what she knew, but was trying to be considerate of her feelings. "Please, if you can, tell me what he said."

She sniffed then cleared her throat. "He said that he found it, that he had finally discovered the Tuscarora Connection. He could not appreciate at that moment how personal it was for me to hear him use the word Tuscarora in connection with a solution to the mystery of the Lost Colony. I never doubted his theory about them moving up the Albemarle and Chowan, and later, migrating

South through Tuscarora territory, but I had hoped it would only have been that they passed through and had not assimilated with the Mangoaks."

"Mangoaks?" Luther asked in surprise.

She smiled at him and slipped back into teaching mode. "The Secotans lived on the coast and along the rivers and estuaries of the sounds. They were Algonquian in culture and language. The Tuscarora, living in the Coastal Plains, were of the Iroquoian culture and language. The Secotans called them Mangoaks, which roughly meant fierce warriors. Any trade in gold, copper or turquoise that passed from the mountains to the coast had to pass through Tuscarora territory, and they always received tribute for safe passage through their lands."

"So you didn't want the Tuscarora to be part of the solution to the Lost Colony mystery?"

She took a deep breath and sighed heavily. "Even though I had forgiven those men for what they had done, I had hoped the solution would not involve the Tuscarora. It was just a small personal matter for me, but Carl always suspected otherwise. And Paskil's thesis was the answer he had been searching for all these years. He believed he knew the path of migration from Croatoa to Indian Wood, and he said that Paskil had discovered the path from Indian Wood to the swamps of Robeson County."

"Would you like to know Paskil's thesis?"

Her hands slipped to her face and she nodded her head. "Is that why someone killed Carl and Ludie, because they may have found documentation to solve the mystery of the Lost Colony?"

"Hardly seems possible, but it may be so. And who ever killed them must have a good reason why they don't want the mystery to be solved."

"Tell me, then," she asked. "What happened to the Lost Colony descendents who were living at Indian wood in 1712?"

Luther proceeded to tell her all that Wesley Paskil and George Mackey had conveyed to him earlier in the evening. And when he mentioned the word *Skico*, Roberta's eyes lit up in recognition.

"Do you know where Skico is?" he asked her.

"I know who he is," she responded with a smile.

When Luther finished telling his story the history teacher was enthralled. "So there is a foundation for the oral history of the Lumbee Indians? There may be a factual basis for our claim of being related to the Croatans and the Lost Colonists of Roanoke Island," she repeated. "And Carl discovered it."

"Only," Luther repeated cautiously, "if Carl's theory can show there were Lost Colony descendants living at Indian Wood in 1712," and then he paused. "So now it's your turn, Roberta. Tell me the Bowden theory."

⚜ ⚜ ⚜

THE BOWDEN THEORY

Roberta leaned forward in her rocking chair and began speaking with the authority of a scholar, and the pacing of a practiced teacher. "This may be a lot of information for you to absorb in one sitting, Luther. But I'm sure if I move slowly and speak of events in a chronological order you'll be able to follow."

"Go ahead. I need to understand everything that Carl knew, that may have led someone to want to kill him."

He stared coolly at Roberta, as if she were going to reveal some amazing clue that might unravel the mystery of Carl's death. She understood the intensity of his desire to solve the crime, but his gaze unnerved her. "Carl's theory begins with the Roanoke Voyages that took place between 1584 and 1590, and ends at Indian Wood in 1712."

The First Voyage to Roanoke: Exploration, 1584

"The first voyage was one of discovery, to the 'Land of Arcadia' as it was first called by Raleigh and his investors. It was led by Captains Amadas and Barlowe, and their mission was to find a suitable location for planting the colony."

"I read about that in Carl's novel, and the planning that took place at Raleigh's home in London."

"Durham House," she added with a smile, and then continued. "While at Roanoke they had good relations with the local Secotan Indians, and even took two of them back to England as guests. One of them, Manteo, had a generally positive impression of the English, especially their guns and technology of the day. The other, Wanchese, was less impressed with English culture, and probably conveyed as much to his chief, Wingina, when they returned the next year. There is an old engraving of that period by *Theodore de Bry* of an Indian village called '*Roanouc,*' on the north end of the island. It was based on a drawing by Captain Barlowe, and is no doubt the first view Raleigh had of the location for his new colony. And it also provided the island its English name, Roanoke."

The Second Voyage to Roanoke: Fort Raleigh, 1585

"The second voyage took place in the spring of 1585. Sir Richard Grenville, Raleigh's cousin, was admiral of a small fleet that carried Captain Ralph Lane, his following of military men, and a host of young English nobles and entrepreneurs. Lane referred to them as 'ne'r- do-wells' who hoped to seek their fortunes in the New World.

Probably the greatest contributions of Lane's colony were the natural and scientific observations recorded by Thomas Hariot, the illustrations of John White that adorn nearly every book on early English colonization, and the explorations of Ralph Lane. He was the one who determined Roanoke Island was not a good location for the colony, because it lacked a reliable deep-water access for larger ships. But, according to Carl, one of his lesser-known accomplishments may have been the saving grace for the Lost Colonists."

"What was that?" Luther queried intently.

"I'll explain, Luther, but please let me continue in chronological order."

Luther nodded, and she continued.

"The first of many conflicts between the English and Secotans took place at the village of Pomeoic when one of the Indians took a silver cup from Grenville's tent. When it was not returned, Grenville had their entire crop of corn burned in retribution. Lane, on the other hand, while also an experienced military man, took a more measured response to minor indiscretions by the Indians. And while he could direct the men under his command, he could not always control the 'ne'r- do-wells.' Rather than help build the fort on the north end of the island, or plant crops to see them through the winter, they harassed the local Indians about the source of their small supply of gold jewelry, then pursued their own dreams of exploring for fortune.

"While Lane was away in the late winter months, exploring the Albemarle Sound and Chowan and Roanoke Rivers, the men left at the fort behaved poorly toward the local Indians. Having planted little to sustain themselves, and with the Secotans furnishing less because their own supplies were running low, the men at the fort resorted to strong arm tactics to force Wingina's followers to provide them food. And when some of the warriors resisted, violence followed and relations deteriorated.

"By the time Lane returned from exploring the Roanoke River in March of 1586, there was open hostility between the English at the fort and the Secotans. Many of the Indians wanted to take revenge against Lane and his men, but there was one young warrior Lane had befriended on his trip up the Chowan River that not only ensured the survival of Lane's men, but according to Carl, may have also saved many of the Lost Colonists at Roanoke." She paused to observe the curious look in Luther's eyes.

"Skico?" he asked curiously.

"Yes, Skico of the Chowanocs. He was the son of Menantonan, Chief of all the Chowan Indians, and he was the key figure in Carl's theory. When Lane had explored the Chowan, and visited the great village of Chowanoc, he had Manteo with him on the pinnace."

"Pinnace, what's that?"

"A small boat, with sail and oars, that could carry twenty to thirty men and their supplies," she answered, then she went back to her story. "Manteo presented Lane and his men to the Chowanocs as traders, so they were well received. Lane even held Chief Menantonan as a captive guest for two days, but instead of generating ill feelings, the two got along very well.

"As was custom among the Indians, to ensure good will between trading partners, the sons of chiefs were often taken captive, but treated very well in the villages in which they were held. They were more like ambassadors than captives. Menantonan's son, Skico, had just returned from an extended stay as guest of the Mangoaks in one of their villages on the Roanoke River."

"Mangoaks?"

"Yes, the Algonquian word for the Tuscarora who lived West of the Secotans." Then she continued her story. "Lane, seeking to establish good will with Menantonan and the Chowanocs, took Skico as a captive guest back to the fort at Roanoke. The chief's son remained with Lane for several months. He was treated well, learning much of the English ways, especially of their guns and pikes and swords made of hardened metals, which the Indians had little of. And according to Carl, none of the English advantages in warfare and metallurgy were lost on the young warrior.

"By late May, hostilities between the Secotans and the English had risen to a level where Wingina was now being called by his war name, Pemisapan."

Luther interrupted. "Wingina... wasn't he the great chief who went to Aquascogoc for the wedding of the young woman from Croatoa, and got wounded there in a surprise attack?"

"Yes, it was the wedding feast for Oshanoa, the maiden from Croatoa." She smiled warmly. "Very good, Luther. You did read Carl's story." Then she continued. "It was now a year after the incident at Aquascogoc. Wingina was making plans with several other tribes to attack the fort on Roanoke Island. Skico learned of the plot and told Ralph Lane, perhaps saving the colony. Lane then made his own plan to attack the Secotans at their village of Dasamonquepec, on the West side of Roanoke Sound.

"On the first day of June in 1586, Lane and twenty-five soldiers went to the village to see the chief, supposedly to ask for help with feeding his men. And with a cry of 'To Christ Our Victory' his men opened fire, killing eight Secotan warriors and wounding many others with pikes and swords. In the confusion, a wounded Pemisapan ran into the woods. He was caught by one of Lane's men who shot the chief and took his head. And from that day on, Lane and his men were in constant fear of attack by the other Indians who had allied with the Secotans.

"A week later, help arrived from the sea. Three months after Grenville and the re-supply ships were supposed to have returned to Roanoke, Francis Drake was on his return home from raiding the Spanish and burning the town of Saint Augustine in Florida. He wanted to visit the fledgling colony and brought his fleet to the Outer Banks. Assessing the desperate situation, he offered to re-supply Lane, which was readily accepted. But a great storm, lasting several days blew many of Drake's ships out to sea. He then offered Lane and his men passage back to England. And while some of them were reluctant, most were happy to be leaving. Skico, for his great service and friendship, was presented with many gifts and released to return to his father and the Chowanocs.

The Third Voyage to Roanoke: Re-supply, 1586

"Less than two weeks after Ralph Lane and his company of men departed Roanoke, the third voyage, with Richard Grenville and the re-supply ships, finally arrived. All they found was a deserted fort. But to ensure England's claim to the land, Grenville left fifteen men there with supplies for two years. Then he returned to England where plans would be made for a fourth voyage that would carry the Lost Colonists to Roanoke Island.

The Fourth Voyage to Roanoke: The Lost Colony, 1587

Roberta looked empathetically at Luther, who seemed to be withering through the history lesson. "Are you still with me, Luther?"

"Yes, but all this information you seem to have in your head, and recall so effortlessly... "

"You forget, Luther, this is part of my thesis. That's why I know it so well."

"Yes, I know. It's just a trait you seem to share with Carl, and Wesley Paskil and George Mackey."

"Thank you, Luther, now on to the Fourth Voyage. John White, who was an artist by trade and had been with Lane the previous year, was named as governor of the next colony. There were a total of 119 people: 91 men, 17 women, 9 children, and the two returning Indians, Manteo and Wanchese. Also, in the first month, two babies were born in the colony, Virginia Dare, and then another child with the last name of Harvie.

"They departed Plymouth on April 26th and arrived at Roanoke on July 22nd. And a very interesting footnote in history occurred on that day. You see, Luther, they were only supposed to stop at Roanoke Island to pick up the fifteen men left there a year earlier by Grenville. Then they were to continue up the coast to Chesapeake Bay, because the year before, Ralph Lane had determined the waters around Roanoke were much too shallow to offer any hope of a seaport. And during his explorations, Menatonan of the Chowanocs described to him a great bay just a few days journey to the North.

"Chesapeake Bay was supposed to be the destination of the fourth voyage in 1587. But for some unknown reason, Simon Ferdinando, Admiral of the small fleet, told Governor White and the men who had loaded into the pinnace to search for Grenville's men, they could not return to the ship. Only the long boat could return, for the purpose of unloading the other planters and supplies for the colony."

"Really," Luther exclaimed. "I may have heard that before, but I had forgotten. I wonder why he did that?"

"No one knows for sure, but some have speculated that it may have been a secret agreement between Ferdinando and Walter Raleigh. Or perhaps he just wanted to get back down into the Caribbean to try for a Spanish prize ship on the way home."

Luther nodded his head as if he understood. "But what about the fifteen men who were left the year before?"

"According to Manteo's people at Croatan, a group of Secotans, led by Wanchese, took revenge against the English who occupied the fort in July of 1586. Two were killed in the initial attack on the fort and the others fled by boat and were never heard from again. I guess you could say they were the original Lost Colonists. But remember, Grenville didn't know he was leaving them in a virtual hornets nest.

"And that same hostile environment is what John White and his planters settled into in late July of 1587. Less than a week after they arrived, as the colonists set about trying to repair the buildings of the previous year, John Howe, one of White's twelve assistants, went out alone crabbing. He was found the next day floating in a tidal pool with sixteen arrow wounds. His head had also been bashed by a war club, but there were no Indians to be found on Roanoke Island.

"On August 13th, Manteo, in a ceremony ordered by Raleigh and his investors, was declared Lord of Dasamonquepec and all the Indian lands there about. And on August 18th, Virginia Dare, the first English child born in the New World, was delivered. She was the daughter of Ananias Dare and Eleanor White, daughter of John White, governor of the colony.

"On August 21st, as Ferdinando and his ships were about to leave for their return voyage to England, there was a great debate among them as to who should return to request additional supplies needed by the colony. After some dissension, it was decided that Governor White should be the one to return. And he very reluctantly agreed.

"White told them that if for any reason they had to depart Roanoke, such as Indian attack or for want of supplies, to leave some sign indicating where they might go. And if in distress, they were to leave another sign, such as a cross. He left the colony on August 25th, 1587, never to see any of them again."

"But why didn't he return?"

"He tried, Luther, but Queen Elizabeth wouldn't let any ships leave English ports, fearing they would be needed to defend against an assault by the Spanish fleet being built to attack England."

"The Spanish Armada of 1588?" Luther asked.

"That's right, Luther, the ill fated Armada that never landed a single Spanish soldier on English soil. They suffered so much at sea from attack by the smaller English ships, and the many storms they encountered, that less than half the fleet made it home to Spain."

"But John White did eventually return to Roanoke. I mean, isn't he the one who found the word Croatan carved on a post?"

"White tried desperately to return, several times. Raleigh once put him to sea in a small ship that was captured by French corsairs, and White had to ransom himself back to England. Another time he took passage on a foreign trading vessel bound for the Caribbean, and they met with so much grave misfortune at sea, they had to return to England.

Fifth Voyage to Roanoke: The Colony Is Lost, 1590

"After the Spanish threat was over, White finally secured passage on a prize-taking mission to the Caribbean that had been paid a fee by Raleigh to return the governor to his colony at Roanoke. After a summer of cruising about the islands, taking a Spanish prize here and there, the small fleet sailed to Hattorask. On August 15, 1590, White saw a pillar of smoke rise from behind the sandy banks along the coast, in the area of Roanoke. He thought for certain it was a sign from the colonists that he should return to them.

"The next morning, two small boats went ashore with a landing party with the sound of cannons firing from the ships to alert the colonists of their coming, but they found no one on or near the inlet area. Next morning they set out again, planning to go on to Roanoke, but one of the boats overturned in the inlet and seven sailors drowned.

Only through sheer force of will could White inspire the men to continue, and by nightfall they made the North end of Roanoke Island where they saw a fire in the distance. They fired guns and sang songs, but no one came to greet them. So they stayed on their boats till morning and then went ashore.

"They found an abandoned fort with a palisade of trees around it, with everything overgrown and rusted from years of exposure to the elements. Near the entrance on the right, carved into a post, they discovered the word CROATAN, indicating where the colonists might have gone. With no cross, either above or below, to indicate distress, White believed the colonists were safe, with Manteo and his people, on the island of Croatoa. Or perhaps they had moved 'fifty miles unto the main,' as they had agreed upon before his departing in 1587, and left only a small group at Croatoa to show them the way to where the other colonists had gone.

"The small boats left Roanoke Island and returned to the ships. It was decided they would make for Croatoa the next day, but yet again the weather intervened. The ships were so beaten by the storm that, to the utter dismay of John White, the captains planned to go back to the Caribbean for the winter, take more Spanish prizes, and return in the spring to relieve the colonists at Croatoa. But even that was not to be, for on the way South, another great storm blew them westward, almost to the Azores, and they finally returned to England in October of 1590."

She stopped her narrative and looked into Luther's eyes, until his head shook slightly. "That's it?" he asked. "No one else ever went to look for them?"

"Not until 1609," Roberta answered. "It was after the Jamestown colony was settled and they had time to pursue stories told by the Pamunkey Indians about white people living among a large tribe on a great river to the southwest."

Luther thought for a moment. "The Roanoke?"

Then Roberta repeated carefully the same words Governor John White used in his narrative to Richard Hakluyt in 1593. "And it was agreed upon that for want of supply they should move fifty miles unto the main."

Luther shook his head, "Fifty miles north toward Chesapeake, or fifty miles inland to... " Then his eyes lit up. "Skico and the Chowanocs," he said with delight.

"That's right, what other Indians in the New World, besides Manteo's people, might offer assistance to the colonists?"

Luther sat back for a moment considering all that Roberta had told him. "I think I understand. Carl's theory was that the colonists had to leave Roanoke, either because of attacks by the Secotans or for need of supplies. But the Croatoans on the Outer Banks could not support all of them, and that some, perhaps most of them, left Croatoa and went to live with Skico and the Chowanocs. And the colonists left on the Outer Banks remained to tell the re-supply ships where the others had gone."

Then he paused. "But White never reached Croatoa, so he never knew about the colonists at Chowanoc." He thought for a moment. "But if they were living with Skico on the Chowan River in 1590, how did they get to Indian Wood, on the Roanoke, in 1712?"

"The Mangoaks," she replied.

Luther shook his head. "You mean the Tuscarora took them to Indian Wood?"

"Yes," she responded. "Let me explain."

"As part of its mission, the Jamestown Colony was to try and locate, or at least find out what happened to the Lost Colonists of Roanoke Island. John Smith wrote in 1608 that the Pamunkey Indians on the York River, largest of the 28 tribes united under the Powhatan Confederacy, told him there were people living on the Chowan River who dressed just as he did, like Englishmen. And in 1613, William Strachey, secretary of the colony, noted that Raleigh's colonists had moved inland to live among the Indians."

"If the colonists had moved fifty miles inland, they could have been living with the Chowanocs," Luther said with a slight smile on his face.

"That's right, and the Mangoaks often raided Chowanoc villages. Carl believed that years later the Mangoaks raided the village in which the colonists and their descendants were living. They took everyone captive, the women and children, and the male survivors. And along with the colonists came their surnames, which later became part of the Northern Tuscarora lineage."

"The Northern Tuscarora, the ones that did not fight against the English during the Tuscarora Wars."

"Very good, Luther. And now you have the Bowden Theory of how some of the descendants of the Lost Colonists came to be living at Indian Wood in 1712."

Luther smiled and shook his head. "Okay, let me see if I have all of this straight. On the Third Voyage to Roanoke, Ralph Lane took Skico as a captive, befriended him and generated enough good will with the Chowanocs that they may have taken in the colonists from Roanoke, until they could be rescued by the re-supply ships. But before they could be found, the Mangoaks raided the village where the colonists and their descendants were living and took them away to live in a village along the Roanoke River, but we don't know exactly when this happened."

"Carl believed it was within twenty years of their leaving Roanoke," she replied.

"And why do you say that?"

"Because in 1609, Michael Strathmore and two other men from Jamestown traveled southwest to try and locate any white people living among the Chowanocs. All they found was a burned out village with some evidence that Englishmen had once lived there. They discovered clay brick foundations, and nails fashioned from what metals could be found, heated and crudely shaped.

"The Chowanocs said the village had been raided by a large war party of Mangoaks, and that many had been captured and taken up the Moratoc or Roanoke River. So, Strathmore and his men decided to go there and find where any white people might be living. And they may have gotten close to the area of Indian Wood, but due to continuing threats from the Mangoaks, they feared for their own lives and turned back. They reported to the governor of Jamestown that they had found signs of English settlement, but no sign of the settlers.

"Carl believed that in May of 1712, the descendents of the Lost Colonists were living peacefully along the Roanoke River at a place called Indian Wood. They were there at the end of the first Tuscarora War, when they were swept up in the treacherous attack by Barnwell and his Yamassee Indian followers. Nearly 500 Northern Tuscarora Indians, among them the descendents of the Lost Colonists, were captured and carried south with the intention of their being sold to the slavers in the markets of Charleston, South Carolina."

Luther nodded his head in understanding. "And rather than be sold into slavery they rebelled on the Little Pee Dee River. And while many of them probably drowned, others escaped to go up Drowning Creek into the swamps of Robeson County."

Roberta paused in her lecture and looked carefully at Luther. "When you combine Carl's theory with Paskil's thesis, you can follow a reasonable migration pattern of the Lost Colonists from Roanoke to Croatoa, then to Chowanoc, on to Indian Wood, south to the Little Pee Dee River, then up Drowning Creek and into the swamps of Robeson County, where their descendants may still be living today.

"And with the DNA studies being collected by other organizations, we may one day be able to determine, once and for all, if there are any genetic markers connecting the Lost Colonists of Roanoke Island to the Lumbee Indians of Robeson County." She stopped, as if the story had ended, and her thoughts turned to Carl's last phone call.

"You should have heard him, Luther. He was so excited, and he got me so nervous and excited that I knew I couldn't sleep. So, I decided to return late Sunday night. I suspected that Carl might stay late at the library, and when I drove in to Greenville and reached Tenth Street, just after midnight, and saw all those lights and police cars." Then her voice trailed off into a whisper.

"I knew something had happened, but I had no idea that it involved Carl, until..." and her voice choked while her eyes brimmed. "I saw one of the janitorial staff that I recognized. He works on the 3rd floor in the North Carolina Collection, and he told me that a man had been killed up there, a history professor, and they wouldn't let anyone inside the library."

Roberta's hands rose to cover her face and her head slipped into her lap as she sobbed quietly. Luther thought to himself. 'Finally, something I can document that may work in her favor. I'll get Jimmy to verify the conversation with the janitor.'

She lifted her head, her eyes red and swollen. "I'm sorry, Luther. I cannot help myself. Every time I think about how I stood there in the darkness, all alone, realizing that I may have lost..." and her voice trailed off. "It just seems that my life has been plagued by a series of bitter disappointments. Were it not for Camron, I may not have found the will to keep going. And now," she whispered as her voice fell even quieter. "When will it end, Luther? When will the suffering end for me?"

The words hung in Luther's heart as he drove in the darkness back to Blount's Creek. 'Was she truly suffering or was she an incredible actress?' he asked himself over and over as he yearned for the comfort of his bed after such a long and tiring day.

'Well, I'll have another chance to find out tomorrow,' he thought as he recalled they would travel together to Manteo where he would get to meet her son, Camron. 'Wonder if he drives an old blue pick up truck?' he asked himself as his head finally hit the pillow, and he drifted quickly away into a deep and restful sleep.

Indian Wood

Part Five

Last Voyage to Roanoke

Eastern
North
Carolina

CAMRON OF THE LOST COLONY

The coffee maker began growling at six-thirty in the morning. Luther pried his eyes open, stared out the window into an overcast sky hanging low over Blount's Bay and thought to himself. 'Have to meet with Lucy at nine to go over the program for the memorial service.' Then he remembered the copy of Carl's will he retrieved from his safe deposit box. Years ago the two had exchanged legal documents, pledging to act as administrators in the event either one should expire before the other. They never seriously considered it might actually happen.

Carl's instructions were very simple. Sell all the personal property that his family, or Luther, did not want. Then sell his home in Greenville and the beach cottage at Nags Head, that had more than quadrupled in value since he purchased it in 1982. He was to cash out all other instruments of value such as life insurance and retirement accounts, and after funeral and estate expenses, donate everything to the university library, to increase the holdings of the North Carolina Collection.

It seemed odd that after 64 years, Carl's life should be reduced to a number, well over a million dollars thanks to the beachfront property. 'Wonder what my final number will be?' he asked himself as he kicked off the comforter and crawled out of bed.

The coffee gurgled gently as it poured into a large pottery cup, purchased only a few months before on the last trip Luther and Carl had taken to the coast. Carl was a board member of the fledgling Graveyard of the Atlantic Museum in Hatteras Village. He was invited to speak at the opening ceremony, and of course, wanted Luther with him to cover the event for the Washington paper. As the vanilla creamer turned the caffeine brew into a rich foamy brown, Luther smiled at the memories he had shared with his friend along the Outer Banks. He recalled searching for the old bones of shipwrecks, fishing for yellow-fin tuna from the deck of a restored wooden Chris Craft yacht, and sifting through sand with archaeology students behind Buxton for any trace of the Lost Colonists.

As Luther savored the first sip of coffee, he considered what needed to be done before he picked Roberta up and they drove out to Manteo to meet her son. 'I'll call Jimmy on the way in and give him an update; let him know where I'm headed, and thank him for having Detective Harris keep an eye on the apartment building while I was talking to Roberta.' Then he thought of the task he dreaded most, going by the funeral home to observe as Carl's body was moved into the crematorium, the gas furnace ignited, and his body and clothing reduced to an urn full of ash and bone fragments.

'Cremation,' he thought to himself. Carl wanted part of his ashes spread on the university campus, part at Fort Raleigh on Roanoke Island, and the rest poured from the bridge spanning Blount's Creek, next to Luther's home. All three were places Carl loved. Luther recalled one memorable New Year's Eve party when a guest suggested that at midnight everyone should jump from the bridge into the cold water below. And after a gentle shove in the back from Veronica, he and Carl were the only ones to actually do it.

"Any man with a friend like Carl Bowden is a rich man," Luther whispered to himself. And at that moment he was feeling poor and alone.

* * *

Even though the sun peeked in and out of gray buffeted clouds, the forecast was for occasional rain to sweep in from the west and cover most of the eastern part of the state by late afternoon. Luther promised Roberta that on the way to Manteo, they would stop for lunch at the old Cypress Grill in Jamesville that had been serving up small crispy fried herrings for over fifty years. The small fish were caught in river nets at the foot of the hill beside the restaurant, then cleaned, cooked and served piping hot to hungry customers who had been coming to the small eatery for decades.

"Bones and all?" she asked as she grasped one between her fingers.

"Everything but the head," Luther answered as he took a bite out of a hush puppy then chased it with slaw and a swallow of iced tea.

Thirty minutes later they were back on Hwy 64, exchanging stories of their good times with Carl, and he was amazed at how much his old friend had confided in her. 'He must have loved and trusted her to have shared so much,' he thought as they passed over the Scuppernong River and through the small town of Columbia.

Another hour passed and they crossed over the Croatan Sound on the new Virginia Dare Memorial Bridge then exited into the village of Manteo. As they drove through the downtown area Luther spied a 'Waterfront' sign and turned right on Sir Walter Raleigh Street. He wanted to show Roberta his favorite lodging and restaurant, where he and Veronica had shared many intimate weekends.

The Tranquil House Inn sat on the waterfront beside a small bridge leading over to the Roanoke Island Festival Park, with its replica of a 16th century sailing ship. The Elizabeth II was made from the plans of Elizabeth I, one of seven ships that carried Ralph Lane and his men on the Second Voyage to Roanoke in 1585.

Luther and Veronica always enjoyed the five o'clock wine tasting held on the upper deck of the inn, with its lovely view out into Shallowbag Bay. Then around eight in the evening they would skip downstairs to '1587,' a five-star restaurant on the first floor, named after the year the Lost Colonists arrived on Roanoke Island. The entrees were sumptuous, the desserts delightful, and the wine list as good as any in the state. Luther pointed at the steps leading into the Inn. "According to one of my former wives, this place embodies the three goods; 'friends, food, and wine.'"

"What was your favorite dessert?" Roberta asked with a smile.

"A dark chocolate raspberry tort," he replied with a sigh.

She glanced back toward the Inn. "Carl never mentioned this place to me."

"I'll bet he was saving it for a special occasion."

"Yes, that would have been nice," she whispered, as her smile faded and eyes clouded, realizing what would never be.

"Well," Luther said, changing the conversation. "Just a few miles and we'll arrive at Fort Raleigh and the Waterside Theater."

"Yes," she added wistfully. "I called Camron this morning and let him know to expect us around two o'clock."

They rode the last few minutes in silence as Luther considered what he would ask her son. Was he in Pembroke last Sunday night with his mother? Did he know of the phone call from Carl? Did he go to Greenville? Did he kill Carl? Did he do it for himself or for someone else? Did he do it for his mother?

Luther looked over at Roberta, still not sure how much she knew, or whether or not she was involved in what had happened to Carl. 'Lord, I hope not,' were his final thoughts as he pulled into the Fort Raleigh Historic Park entrance.

"Toward the back," she said. "Next to the long building at the end of the lot. That's where he said to park."

The sky was darkening and wind rising as they exited the car, precursors of rain that was sure to follow. They walked through a side entrance and onto a large concrete pad in front of the sets and buildings where the Lost Colony play was performed each summer evening. "Used to be a sand stage," Luther whispered to himself, and he looked out into the stadium seating area where rows upon rows of individual green molded chairs were neatly arranged into three main sections. "And those used to be wooden benches," he said with a smile, thinking of the comfort in which thousands of tourists now sat as they enjoyed Paul Green's famous play, a reenactment of the saga of *The Lost Colonists of Roanoke Island*.

Several men were scraping old paint from the iron bars of the aisle guides and metal posts that held the molded green plastic seats into the elevated concrete risers. With heavy wire brushes they scraped away the loose chips, preparing the metal surface for a new seasonal coat. And down near the front row was a tall strapping young man, with pale skin and reddish-brown hair pulled back into a bushy ponytail.

"Camron," his mother called as she stepped quickly off the stage and down the grassy slope toward her son.

He turned and ran toward her, lifting and swinging her around in a joyous circle. As Camron set her down, Roberta pointed over to where Luther was standing on the stage, and he watched as the grin on the young man's face slipped away and fell into a blank expression, as if uncertain whether Luther were friend or foe.

"Luther," she shouted. "This is my son, Camron."

Luther forced a smile as he walked down the grassy slope and extended a hand to the young man. "Very nice to meet you," and he studied the innocent features of Camron's face. 'He's almost as uncomfortable as I,' Luther thought to himself as they stood together and made small talk about his work in preparation for the summer season.

How did he like the work? Was it part-time or full-time? How about the people? How did he get the job? His cousin... did he work there, too?

"Yes, he's right over there," Camron said, pointing toward a short burly man who was scraping chairs further up the isle.

"His name is Henry," Roberta added, "Henry Berry. He's my Aunt Lydia's oldest son. And like Camron, he has a slight learning disability. But they are both sweet young men."

"And how did Henry come to get his job here, so far away from Pembroke?"

"A man named Mr. Bryant," Camron responded. "He's from Lumberton, and he knew someone here that hired Henry, and then me."

"Langdon Bryant, from the Lumberton Herald?" Luther asked in surprise.

"Yes," Roberta answered. "I thought you knew, Luther, or I would have mentioned it."

"No, but it sounds just like something Langdon would do," he said in a relaxed tone, trying to gloss over his surprise. Then he glanced over at Henry Berry, studying him from a distance.

"I'm going to speak to Henry," Roberta said, offering Luther an opportunity to talk with Camron in private. She waved at her cousin as she moved up the isle.

"Can we sit here and talk?" Luther asked.

"Okay," Camron said innocently and pointed at two seats on the front row.

Luther wasn't sure why, probably because he had just met the young man, but he felt more comfortable leaving one seat between them. As he started to ask his first question, he stared into the brown eyes and innocent face, thinking that if Camron were involved someone else must be influencing him. Then his mind went back to Roberta. 'If not her, then who?' and the first question tumbled out of his mouth.

"Do you know who I am?"

"Yes, mother told me."

"Do you know why I am here?"

"Yes." The answer was short, and he offered little else.

"Did your mother explain what happened in Greenville on Sunday night?"

"Yes, people were killed, and you are helping to find out who killed them."

'He seemed like a nice kid,' Luther thought to himself, 'just like Roberta said. Good manners, and no hint of a learning disability, at least not so far.' Then he asked another question, "Were you at your grandmother's home in Pembroke this past Sunday night?"

"Yes."

"Did you know that your mother received a phone call from a man in Greenville?"

"Yes."

"And how did you know that?"

"She told me. When she came back into the kitchen I asked who called and she said it was one of her professors from Greenville."

'So Roberta did tell someone,' Luther realized. "She didn't tell you anything about why the professor had called?"

"No," he said with an innocent expression. "And I didn't ask."

"Oh," Luther said to himself, almost in a whisper. "Did anyone else ask her about the phone call? Did she tell anyone there about why the professor called?"

"I don't think so. I never heard her mention it to anyone. She could have, but I didn't hear anything."

'Damn,' Luther thought to himself. 'This kid is good. Not a flinch, not a blink, not even a glance away to break eye contact.' "When did you leave Pembroke?"

"I had to be at work the next day, so I left early that evening, and drove here."

Luther thought for a moment, 'So he left earlier than Roberta and drove back to Manteo, and she drove to Greenville, but...' and he asked another question. "Did you drive straight back here, or did you go any place else?"

The pause was barely perceptible, but he thought he saw something in the young man's eyes as he responded, "No, I drove straight here."

"What kind of vehicle do you drive?"

"I was driving Henry's truck."

"A truck," Luther repeated, and alarm bells began ringing in his head. "What kind of truck?"

"A small one."

"A small truck," Luther repeated. "Not a large one?" And then he asked, "What color?"

"It's white, and it's right outside. Would you like to see it?"

Luther was thinking about the late model blue pickup that had run him off the road the night before, and if Henry's truck were white then it couldn't be the same one. But for some reason he wanted to see for himself.

'Yeah, I'd like to see it."

As they stood up Roberta came back over to them. "Going somewhere?"

"Mr. Surles wants to see Henry's truck, the one I was driving on Sunday."

She looked over at Luther, a curious expression on her face. "Okay," and the three of them walked out to the parking lot next to the side entrance.

It was a five-year old Dodge Dakota, not the truck that had run him off the road, and Luther was relieved.

"Mom," Camron said with some excitement. "Henry wants to sell his truck so he can get a new one. Said he would make me a good deal," and then his voice trailed off. "But I can't afford it, unless I get some help. Do you think grandma would help me?"

Roberta tucked her arm under his. "I think we may be able to find some help for you, Camron, but we'll have to talk about it later."

Luther thought to himself that this was not the conversation of a young man involved in a murder conspiracy. It spoke innocently of the future, of owning something, and making payments, not hiding from the law. He was feeling some relief, even admiring the small white truck and thinking that it would be a great vehicle for a young man to own when he looked up and something caught his eye across the parking lot.

A cold chill swept through his body as he realized it was the blue truck that had run him off the road the night before. And if that truck were in the parking lot, then the killer must be nearby. He turned toward the young man and his mother, a menacing tone in his voice. "Whose truck is that, Camron?" and he pointed across the lot. Luther's demeanor had hardened and it startled the young man.

Camron stared across at the old Ford F-150, a two-tone blue model that was at least ten years old. "I don't know, Mr. Surles. I've never seen it before."

'Damn, he's good,' Luther thought to himself. 'He's here, the truck's here and he acts like he's never seen it.'

Without hesitation Camron walked past Luther. "Let's take a look at it."

As her son started across the parking lot Roberta reached out and touched Luther's arm, "What's the significance of that truck?"

He stared hard into her blue eyes and whispered. "That's the truck that tried to run me off the road last night."

Her mouth fell open. "Luther, why didn't you tell me about that?"

"Could have been an accident, but now I'm not so sure," and the three of them walked across the lot to the truck.

Camron knelt down beside the right front quarter panel and saw a long scrape from behind the headlight to just above the tire well, and a faint line of green paint in the abraded surface. "What color is your car, Mr. Surles?"

Luther turned and pointed toward the Jaguar. Then Camron stood and studied the classic old car for a moment. "Reckon this truck scraped your vehicle?"

"Could be," Luther mumbled as he began walking around the pickup and thinking to himself. 'Camron knew we were coming. He could have easily hidden this truck if he wanted to, and besides, I don't remember seeing it when we drove in the parking lot.'

Then something alarming occurred to Luther. 'If the truck arrived after we got here, then someone may have followed them from Greenville to Roanoke Island. And if someone else were involved, it could mean that Camron and his mother may not be. But who then?' he asked himself as he wrote down the truck's license plate number.

THE WAY TO INDIAN WOOD

A rising breeze swept through the pines trees swaying over the parking lot of the Waterside Theatre. "Rain's comin'," Camron said to no one in particular, as he stared up into a darkening sky.

"I enjoy thunderstorms," Roberta added. "Especially when I'm tucked under an afghan in my favorite rocking chair."

"Passenger seat in a sports car will have to do for this afternoon," Luther said.

"You can stay for awhile, if you like Mr. Surles. We have a nice shed in back that'll keep you out of the rain till this blows over."

Luther glanced back toward the blue pickup truck sitting across the parking lot. "No, we'd better get moving," he said with some discomfort. "I want to get back to Greenville before too late," and he looked over at Roberta. "Why don't you take a few minutes to say goodbye to Camron, then we'll get on the road."

As she walked around to embrace her son, Luther slipped down into a custom leather bucket seat. He pulled his legs up, spun sideways and fit them into the cockpit of the Jag. Then he cranked the motor and listened to the finely tuned purr of its powerful engine.

Roberta tucked her forearm into Camron's side, grasping his arm as they walked away for a private moment. They were talking and smiling as her left hand slipped down into his right hand and she spun him around. Luther could not see what she was saying, but suddenly the young man's face grew serious, and his mouth fell open in denial. His head shook quickly side-to-side, then nodded forward as if to say he understood.

A cool shudder ran down Luther's back. 'Would Camron follow them in the blue truck? Surely not with his mother in the car,' he rationalized. 'But then again, some of the canals along the two lane portion of the highway were ten to fifteen feet deep, and if his Jaguar were to run into one of those black water drainage ditches they might never be found. He suddenly felt the urge to look back across the parking lot, and cold fear swept through his body. The blue truck was pulling slowly toward the exit.

'Who's driving?' he asked himself in a panic, and feeling an urge to overtake the pickup he pumped the gas pedal. The motor revved powerfully, but he was also pressing in the clutch with his left foot, and the jaguar remained still. 'What would it prove?' he asked himself. 'And I might put myself in more danger.'

He felt the passenger door swing open in a rush. "Luther, what's the matter?" Roberta was leaning down, staring at him, a frightened expression on her face.

Luther glanced toward the exit. "The truck, Roberta. The blue truck just left, and whoever's driving..." Then his voice trailed off as he felt the presence of someone bending down beside his window. It was Camron, knees bent sharply with his hand on the window ledge.

"You should be okay, Mr. Surles," he said in a calm voice. "As long as my mother is with you, you'll be fine." His brown eyes were focused and steady as if he knew what he was talking about.

Luther's palms were sweating as he gripped the leather steering wheel cover. 'Would he be safe as long as Roberta was with him? Like she protected Carl? Was she involved in this? Jesus,' he screamed silently. 'I'm not sure of anything anymore. Some damn good investigator I've turned out to be.' Then he realized he was still revving the engine.

"Luther, we can leave now if you like," Roberta whispered calmly as she eased herself down in the passenger seat.

"Yeah, let's get moving," he said in a dazed tone, confused even more by the trip to Roanoke. "Nice to meet you, Camron," he said as he rolled the window up, and the low profile of the Jaguar slipped out toward the exit. 'He would just have to rely on Camron's youthful optimism, or his inside information. As long as Roberta was with him,' and he looked over at her, smiling nervously. "Just knowing that truck was here, and that it's on the road ahead of us makes me nervous."

"I understand," she responded thoughtfully. And then added, "If the truck is in front of us, and whoever is driving thinks we'll go back across the new bridge, then why don't we take the old route over to Mann's Harbor?"

"Good idea," Luther said as he turned right out of the parking lot.' As he drove toward the northern bridge he considered that everything she said could have double meaning. 'What if that were the plan all along, for her to talk me into going back the old way, and I just fell right into it?' He shuddered uncomfortably at the paranoia creeping over him.

Roberta noticed his constant glancing up at the rear view mirror, but didn't know what to say to comfort him. She had an idea that talking about Carl might relieve his mind, and as they drove across the William B. Umstead Bridge through a shower of rain she said, "Carl always liked driving over this bridge. It reminded him of the fishing trips you took with him to Mann's Harbor, and how you used to troll for rockfish alongside the pilings."

A smile crept over Luther's face and the furrowed ridges of his brow relaxed as he recalled the times he and Carl had trolled along the bridge. As they reached the peak of the span he glanced back one more time, and seeing no one for a mile behind them he nodded. "Yeah, we used to spend an entire day out here trolling the channel and along the bridge. Then he laughed, "And one time on a cold foggy day, when we had fished for hours and hadn't caught a single striper, we did something we swore we would never do, and never did again."

"What was that?" she asked with a grin.

"We pulled up to a net and took a few stripers so we could go home and make up a nice fish stew. I'm not proud of that, and we both promised each other we would never do it again. But what was so bad, we not only took their fish, we had to cut the largest one out of the net."

"But, Luther, Carl always had fish in his freezer. Why did you have to take them from some poor fisherman's net?"

"You ever try to make a fish stew with frozen fish?" he asked her. "It's just not the same. The meat cooks to pieces, no big tasty chunks." Then he shook his head, "No way, if you're going to make a fish stew, you need fresh fish, and a couple of three to four pound stripers is just perfect for Carl's old cooking pot."

The conversation went on for half an hour as Luther discussed in detail the recipe he and Carl had used for years to prepare their famous Rock Fish Stew. "We always used a big ole' seasoned cast iron skillet over an open gas flame. First, we fried up about a pound of bacon and left the drippings in the bottom of the pan. Then we put the fish heads in the bottom, to keep from burning the layers of potatoes, onions and fish chunks we would add till the pot was full, and every layer seasoned to taste.

Then after an hour or so of stewing, when the potatoes were done, we added a half-dozen eggs on top. And when they had cooked up into a nice 'over easy' layer, we crumbled up the bacon and spread it all over the eggs. Then we added our secret ingredient, a bottle of Texas Pete hot sauce, all over the bacon and eggs. Damn, that was some good eating," he said, ending with a flourish.

Roberta sat quietly for a moment staring out the window into a drizzling rain. "He never cooked me a fish stew," she said with a touch of sadness. "But it sounds like something I would have enjoyed."

"Well, if he hadn't kept you such a secret, I would have fixed you a big ole' Rock Fish Stew. Sure would have," he added as his voice trailed off and he glanced once more into the rear view mirror.

"See anything?" she asked, staring ahead as the rain tapered off into a drizzle.

"No. Looks like we have the highway pretty much to ourselves."

The wipers tapped out a steady rhythm as they flapped back and forth across the windshield, and for a moment it was the only sound inside the car. Luther squirmed uncomfortably in his seat, pulled at the seat belt strap across his chest and glanced at Roberta. "I still don't understand why Carl was killed. What was it that he discovered about the Lost Colonists, and why was it so important that someone would want to kill him?"

"I'm not sure, Luther, but he called it the 'Tuscarora Connection.' It was a way to trace the migratory route of the Lost Colonists from Roanoke Island to Indian Wood, and from there to the swamps of Robeson County."

"But why did he have to die? I mean, what is the motive for killing him?"

She just shook her head gently from side to side, staring through the windshield, "I don't know, Luther, I just don't know."

He thought to himself, recapping what he knew against so much that he had not yet figured out. 'Roberta was involved, one-way or another, and her son, and maybe that guy, Henry, back at the theater, but how, and why? What were they trying to hide, and who stood to benefit if Carl's story of the Lost Colony were ever told, or not told?'

"Would you like to go there?" she asked, breaking his train of thought.

"Where?"

"Indian Wood. It's a little out of our way, but you might like to see it."

"It's just north of Williamston, off Hwy 17, right?" Luther asked as he glanced down at his watch then up at the sky. There were patches of late afternoon sunlight streaking through rapidly moving bluish- white clouds. The rain had nearly stopped, reduced to little more than an occasional drizzle. He looked at the sign ahead, straight into Plymouth, or the turn south on Hwy 32 toward Washington. If they were going to Indian Wood, he had to make a decision.

"Okay, let's go. But first I have to check in with Jimmy Bonner, give him a license plate number, and let him know about the change in plans."

* * *

Twenty miles later they reached the by-pass skirting Willamston, and Luther turned north on Hwy 17, heading toward the Roanoke River. As they approached the elevated bridge that would carry them across the great waterway, he glanced over at several old buildings on the waterfront, next to the public boat ramp. "Moratoc," he said with a grin.

Roberta responded as if it were a word game. "Algonquian Indian name for the Roanoke River."

"Really," Luther said in surprise. "I just thought it was the name of the park down there beside the boat ramp." And he glanced back at a concrete ramp that disappeared into the swift muddy water. "Just last year me and Carl were cited by two wildlife officers for having illegal rockfish," he said with mock disgust. "Damn those slot limits."

"I haven't got a clue," she responded. "What are slot limits?"

As they drove high above the river and began to descend into the Roanoke National Wildlife Refuge, Luther explained the intricacies of fishing regulations. "In order to increase the number of stripers, the Fishing Commission set a limit on the number and size that could be caught. The slot for keepers was 18" to 22", and each fisherman could keep two, but had to release anything over or under the limit. "

"Sounds a little confusing," she said.

Luther laughed. "Not really. It's just that in the excitement of finding a school of rockfish, you get in a hurry when you take them off the hook so you can begin casting again. You start culling by eye, how big you think they are, not how long they really are, and that's how we got in trouble."

"So you measured incorrectly?"

"One of us did," he said with a smile. "We went a few miles up river and tied off on a tree branch in the mouth of Coniott Creek. We stood at the back of the boat casting a couple of old crank baits and just caught the heck out of those stripers. I bet we hooked sixty or more before the school finally broke and went back out in the river. And all along we had been culling by sight, measuring only those we thought might make the slot. After each of us had two, we tossed everything else back in the water."

"You didn't check them again before you went back in?"

Luther shrugged his shoulders. "Should have, but didn't. And when we got back to the boat ramp the wildlife officers were waiting to greet us. They were nice enough, at first, but when they measured our fish and found that one was just under eighteen inches, and another just over the twenty-two inch limit, well, we were criminals then. We had broken the law, and they seemed to enjoy writing us both a citation. And to top it off, they took our fish. Didn't even leave us enough for a decent fish stew."

She laughed to herself at the sight of the two men, having their fish taken away from them and then asked. "Did you say Coniott Creek?"

"Yeah, about five miles up from the bridge we just crossed."

"Coniott was the main waterway leading from the river up to Indian Wood. And I'll bet while you were fishing, Carl was thinking about how the Tuscarora had taken the Lost Colonists up that creek and into their village." Then she leaned forward. "There it is, Luther, the sign for Indian Wood. We need to turn left."

THE BERRY STONE

Luther slowed to make the turn onto Saint Francis Road then tried to read the black letters on the grey marker mounted on top of a six-foot metal pole. "As many times as I've passed this way, I never stopped to read this sign," he confessed.

"I always read the historical markers," she said. "I think it's wonderful the way they site them to mark important places and events in our state's history."

Luther read slowly. "Indian Wood. Reservation established in 1717 for Tuscarora remaining in N.C. after wars of 1711-13. Sold in 1828. Five miles NW." Then he stopped and looked at Roberta. "Doesn't say anything about a massacre taking place."

"Of course not, Luther. It wouldn't have been politically correct in the 1950s for North Carolina to admit that our early colonial government may have been involved in a massacre of Tuscarora, and also a thriving Indian slave trade. And that is probably why Dr. Paskil's paper was suppressed at the time."

"Yeah, Paskill mentioned that, but was it ever really a reservation?"

"Yes, it became a reservation just after the two wars with the colonists. But prior to that it was one of the largest Northern Tuscarora villages. After the warring Southern Tuscarora were defeated in 1711, the remaining Tuscarora gathered at Indian Wood to receive the blankets and corn promised by Barnwell and the colonial government, and that's when the Yamassee Indians attacked. They killed over a hundred Tuscarora. And while hundreds more escaped into the forests, five hundred were taken captive, to be sold in the slave markets of Charleston. A few years later, in 1717, the remaining Tuscarora were granted the land near Quitsna for a reservation."

"Quitsna, where's that?"

Roberta peered through the windshield as they continued down the road. "See that turn to the left just ahead? That's Indian Wood Road. We'll be turning there, and about three miles further we will turn left on Quitsna Road."

"Okay," Luther said as he made the turn. "But back there, the sign said the land was sold in 1828."

"By 1750, there were no more Tuscarora living on the Indian Wood reservation, and the land reverted back to the North Carolina colony."

"Look at that," he said in surprise and slowed to read another historical marker in front of an old home to his left. It was Liberty Hall, former home of Civil War Captain Edward Outlaw, CSA. It was a large wooden Georgian design, with towering brick chimneys exiting through a silver aluminum roof. "Is it open to the pubic?"

"I wish it were," she replied, "but it's privately held. I've been told his descendants still live there."

"Very nice," he added as he drove slowly toward Quitsna. "So what happened to them, the surviving Tuscarora?"

"They were Iroquois, of the great Iroquois nation in New York State, and most of them migrated back to their ancestral homeland. Some probably stayed in Eastern North Carolina and assimilated with other Indians into the growing colonial culture. But by 1750, there was no longer a functioning Tuscarora tribe in North Carolina."

The afternoon sun was creeping low behind clusters of darkening clouds as he drove up to a small dirt and gravel lane to his left. There was a green sign on top of a pole that said Quitsna Road. And the rain that had stopped earlier now returned as a faint line of drizzle on the windshield.

"Turn here," Roberta whispered in a hushed voice. "And follow this road until you see it."

"See what?" Luther asked, glancing at Roberta.

"Two miles, then you cross a wooden bridge and you will see it," she said, staring through the windshield with glowing eyes, as if she were returning to a sacred place.

A few hundred yards from the main road, the gravel ran out and the road turned into what seemed like a dirt pathway. Trees rose high above them, nearly blotting out the last bit of light filtering through the dark clouds. The Jaguar bounced along the road, rutted in many places by rainwater that had crossed the path and carved small trenches in the loose soil.

"There's the bridge," she said with excitement. "There it is, Luther. Can you see it now?"

Luther pressed on the brake and stopped the car. Perfectly framed through the rails of the bridge and the trees rising on each side of the road, was a magnificent great oak standing alone in the middle of a huge field. "It's beautiful," he said as he continued across the small bridge, and out to a field, colored green with small soybean plants just emerging from the soil.

"Please, stop here," she said reverently, pointing to a shallow drainage ditch that ran through the middle of the field, and passed beside the great oak tree. "Do you mind walking a little? There is something beside the tree I need to show you, a marker that Carl discovered. And when I stood next to that stone... " Her voice quivered, then faded away. She quickly opened the door, and sprang from the Jaguar in such haste that she left her raincoat.

Luther peered through the windshield as she danced across a field of emerging green plants toward a small mound of earth beside the great oak tree. It had been skirted so often by tractors that it seemed slightly higher than the loamy soil around it. As he got out of the car, he felt an invisible mist touch his face. And mesmerized by her twilight performance he followed Roberta into the field, leaving his own jacket in the car.

She stood perfectly still in the middle of a small cluster of weeds at the base of the great oak tree. As he approached he could see that her eyes were closed. "This is the place, Luther. Look around," she said. "Imagine hundreds of Tuscarora huts, with the main lodge somewhere near this tree." Then her eyes opened and she scanned the tree line across the field.

"Carl said that if we were to cut down this tree and count the rings, we might find it was just a young sapling at the time of the massacre." Then she took a deep breath and exhaled. "It feels like I was here, Luther, in the days of Indian Wood before it was a reservation. I felt it the very first time Carl brought me to this place." Then she pointed to a large flat stone near the base of the tree, protruding slightly out into the drainage ditch. "It doesn't look like much, I know, just somehow out of place here in the middle of the field."

Luther studied the long flat rock that stuck out of the ground at one end and disappeared into the soil at the other. It was a sheet of grey-black stone nearly two feet wide and three feet long, with a varying thickness up to several inches along its length. "Looks like one of those slabs used for grave markers," he commented.

"It is a grave marker," she said quietly, and knelt down by the stone, running her hands gently over its rough surface. "Help me turn it over, there's something you have to see."

Mist was seeping through the tree limbs above and onto their clothing as the two of them pulled hard and lifted the side of the marker until it stood on edge. They let it go and it fell with a thump into the weeds, exposing an old chiseled inscription. Roberta pulled a small handkerchief from her pocket and began wiping away the soil embedded in the letters. "Read it, Luther."

He bent over the slab and studied the words that had been carved into the surface nearly three hundred years before. "Here lies Richard Berry of Devonshire and Oshanoa of Croatoa. Anno," and he stopped. "Can't seem to make out the year." Then he exclaimed, "Oshanoa, from Carl's story. She was a real person?"

"Yes, the maiden from Croata, the same island as Manteo," Roberta answered with a glow on her face. "You are reading from the grave marker of one of the Lost Colonists of Roanoke Island, the first one ever to be found."

"Richard Berry," he repeated. "He was one of the Lost Colonists?"

"Yes, Richard and his brother Henry were listed on the roster of colonists that arrived at Roanoke Island in 1587. And the surname Berry is also very prominent among the Lumbee Indians of Robeson County."

Luther stared at the inscription on the stone. "So Richard Berry married Oshanoa, a Croatan Indian woman, and they ended up here at Indian Wood?"

"That's right. According to Governor John White, he and his assistants had agreed that the colony needed to move *'fifty miles unto the main.'* And according to Carl's theory, many of them moved to Chowanoc, on the Chowan River, to live among Skico's people. Within twenty years, they were captured by the Tuscarora, taken up the Moratoc, or Roanoke River, and settled at Indian Wood, eventually assimilating into the Tuscarora culture.

"And, Luther, that would place their descendants here at Indian Wood in 1712, when the massacre took place. Barnwell and his Yamassee warriors captured and carried them south, intending to sell them in the slave markets of Charleston. But somehow, many of them escaped. They made their way up the Little Pee Dee River in South Carolina, to Drowning Creek in North Carolina, and into the swamps of Robeson County, where their descendants are still living today as Lumbee Indians."

"Carl's theory," Luther exclaimed.

"Look around you," she added with a tone of urgency. "This is Indian Wood, and if there is one Lost Colonist grave here, Carl believed there could be more. That's why he was trying to buy this land, all 500 acres, from the heirs that lease it to local farmers."

"But why didn't he tell me, or at least tell someone who could help him?"

"He wanted to tell you, Luther. He wanted your help, but can you imagine what the value of this land would be if the heirs thought they might have remains of the Lost Colonists buried on their property. He was offering them two thousand dollars an acre; a million dollars, but they were asking for twenty-five hundred an acre."

"But he could have come to me. I have some property I could have sold."

"But would you have been willing to donate everything to the university?"

Luther was shocked. "That's what he was going to do, buy all this property and donate it to East Carolina?"

"That's right. He wanted to buy this property to protect it, donate it to the university and maintain a life estate so that he could live here and coordinate the search for Lost Colonist remains. And of course preserve the integrity of any Indian remains and artifacts that might be found."

"But how would he know if they were colonist remains? How could he tell them from the Tuscarora?"

"Mostly by the artifacts in the graves, and also by the bone and teeth wear. The original colonists would have been easy to distinguish from the Indians. And when he was certain that he had English remains, such as those of Richard Berry, who may be buried right here, then he could have DNA studies conducted of the living Berrys in Robeson County. And hopefully, later discover some Berry family remains in England that could also be matched.

"Don't you see, Luther? The technology to accomplish this didn't exist until a few years ago, but now it could prove once and for all whether or not the Lumbees were descended from the Lost Colonists of Roanoke Island."

"But if Carl were so close to proving the Lumbee genealogy, then why was he murdered?"

Roberta was about to say that she did not know when they were interrupted by the sound of a vehicle rushing down Quitsna Road.

Luther stared through the dimming twilight and was instantly filled with the same fear that had overcome him in the parking lot of the Waterside Theater on Roanoke Island. The blue truck was crossing the bridge, and there were people inside.

"Hurry," she said. "Help me turn the stone back over," but Luther seemed frozen in place. "Please," she begged. "We have to protect Carl's theory."

Hearing Carl's name Luther turned toward her. "Okay, on three." He counted quickly and they lifted the stone up until it flipped over, face down, once more concealing the inscription.

They stood up and stared at the truck as two people got out and walked slowly toward them. "Oh my God!" Roberta groaned to herself as she recognized the woman and the man beside her. It was her cousin, Ramona Oxendine, whom she had grown up with, and she was walking with Langston Bryant, publisher of *The Lumberton Herald.*

"Oh, Jesus," Luther said. "Not Langston, but why in the hell would he be involved in this?"

Roberta stepped closer to Luther, clutching his right arm between her hands as Ramona and Langston approached and stopped only a few feet away. "Nice of you to bring Luther out to such an isolated place, Ms. Locklear. Makes our work a little easier, wouldn't you say, Ramona?"

"I'm so sorry, Roberta," her cousin said, her shoulders slumped and head sagging to one side. "None of this was ever supposed to have happened. It's all gotten so out of hand."

"Why, Langston?" Luther asked. "Why did you have to kill Carl?"

"Pardon me, Luther, but your friend, Carl, was about to mess up a very delicate financial transaction that has been years in the making. And for your information, I would never personally stoop to such a thing, killing people for money."

Then he waved his arm back toward the truck. "There are other people for that sort of thing." The passenger door of the truck opened and a tall young man stood there for a moment as if he didn't know what to do.

"Camron," Roberta wailed, as she suddenly realized that Langston had somehow influenced her son to kill the man she loved. She let go of Luther's arm and started to move toward her son as he walked across the field with a .38 caliber Smith and Wesson revolver in his hand. But Luther held her back.

"He's a simple minded boy, Roberta," Langston said. "He just wanted to protect his mother from a man who had done her harm."

"You told him that?" she screamed. "You told Camron that Carl was trying to hurt me?"

"And more," Langston replied with a smile. "And now he has to finish the job."

"What," she said in disbelief. "You want him to kill his own mother?"

"Not you, Roberta," and then he glanced toward Luther. "Him."

Roberta looked up at Luther, then over at Ramona who stood like a sad statue in the continuing drizzle, and then at her son who had walked up behind Langston. "No, Camron," she cried. "You cannot do this. They have not told you the truth. I loved, Carl. And Luther is my friend. He is trying to help me."

"No, Momma, that's not what Miss Ramona and Mr. Langston said. They told me that Carl forced you," and then his head fell down a bit, "to have sex with him; that he raped you like those men did before I was born, and that if I didn't take care of him, that he would do it again. I couldn't let him do that to you, Momma. I just couldn't."

"But Camron," Luther asked. "Why Dr. Worthington? Why did you kill poor Ludie?"

"Because Mr. Langston said she knew what I did. She was going to tell everyone and that I would go to jail, and Momma, too. I couldn't let that happen, Mr. Surles. You understand, don't you?"

'Langston was right,' Luther thought to himself. 'He's a simple-minded boy; kind, gentle, and easily influenced.'

"Camron, listen to me," Roberta pleaded. "Carl never raped me. That was a lie to get you to do something terrible that would help them."

"Help them do what, Momma?"

"That's a good question," Luther said, and all eyes turned toward Langston. "What's this about? What kind of financial deal was Carl about to mess up?"

"It's about money, Luther, lots of money. Not just for me, but for Lumberton and Robeson County, and especially Pembroke State University."

"What are you talking about, Langston?"

"It's about the Lumbees getting recognized as a Federal Indian tribe," he said with some pride. "Do you know what that means, Luther? Have you got any idea how much money could be involved?"

"No, but tell me. I need to know what it was worth to you to manipulate this young man to kill Carl."

Langston shuddered at the accusation then shrugged it off. "You know that North Carolina has recognized the Lumbees as a state Indian tribe, the Lumbee Indians of Robeson County. And the House of Representatives in Washington, D.C. approved a bill recognizing them as a Federal Indian tribe. All that's left is to have the senate vote to confirm the bill, then get the President's signature and it's done. To the Lumbees will accrue all the benefits of federally recognized Indian tribes. And you know what that means, don't you Luther?

"Sure you do," he said in a mocking tone. "I told you a few days ago when I showed you the property around the I-95 and Hwy 74 intersection. When the Lumbees gain federal recognition, they can designate the lands around Pembroke as their reservation, from that intersection all the way to Maxton. And you know what federal Indian tribes can do on their reservations?

"Gambling. This is about gambling casinos?"

"Yes, but first, those people who own the land around that intersection are going to get rich selling it to the Lumbees for their casinos."

"And do you own that land, Langston?"

"Some of it," he said with pride. "And my extended family has title to the rest. On paper, we look wealthy because we own the land. But none of us have any real money. After we sell it to the Lumbees, we'll be cash-mad millionaires."

"So that's it, you just want to be a rich man?"

"That's only part of it, Luther. Don't you remember me telling you about all the business opportunities that would be created because of those casinos; hotels, motels, restaurants, shops of all kinds, and unbelievable tax revenues from increasing land values."

"And that's not all of it. Pembroke State University stands to benefit from an endowment that could make it one of the flagship universities in the state, maybe even the nation. There would be new programs, new buildings, the best-paid faculty and staff, and all because of federal recognition and the gambling casinos. And as Director of the Foundation at the university, Ramona, here, would head the committee deciding how to invest and distribute the income of the endowment; a very important and well- paying position I might add.

"Can't you see the vast opportunities for Robeson County, Luther? And your friend Carl was about to screw it all up."

"But how?" Luther yelled, still confused. "How was he going to screw it up?"

Ramona suddenly spoke. "He wouldn't listen to reason, Roberta. He wouldn't delay his findings until after the senate vote on the bill to recognize the Lumbees?"

Roberta stared at her cousin in confusion. "You spoke with my Carl?"

Ramona confessed. "I was in the bedroom when Camron said you had a call from someone at ECU. I listened in to your phone call, and I heard what he told you, about finding the connection between the Lumbees and the Lost Colonists.

"I panicked, Roberta. Do you know what it could mean if the connection were made, that the Lumbees were actually descended from the Lost Colonists? It means that we may not have as much Indian blood as we claim, and that we are not entitled to federal recognition as an Indian tribe. And that would impact the senate vote, possibly ending forever our effort to gain recognition.

"It would be over, Roberta, something the Lumbees have been working toward since before the Civil War. But Carl was a purist. He said the research would reveal what it would reveal, and that he planned to announce his findings later in the week after he had confirmed everything with you. So I called Langston, and it was out of my hands."

"And I just had a little talk with Camron," Langston added " I convinced him that in order to protect his mother," and then he paused. "Well, you know the rest."

Luther finally understood why Carl had been killed; for money. And perhaps because his old friend could sometimes be stubborn, especially when it came to his research. But it didn't matter anymore. Luther was about to join Carl where-ever he now resided.

"It's time, Camron, time to finish the job," Langston said.

"No, Camron, you cannot do this," his mother pleaded. "They lied to you. They did not tell you the truth."

"Go ahead, Camron," Langston admonished. "You understand that if you don't finish the job, you and your mother will go to jail for a long, long time."

"Momma, I can't let you go to jail." And he raised the gun toward Luther.

"We won't go to jail," she shrieked as she stepped in front of Luther. "They will. They lied to you. Langston and Ramona are responsible for all this."

Camron wavered now that his mother stood between him and Luther. Then he turned back toward Langston. "My momma says you lied to me, Mr. Bryant." Then he let the gun slip down to his side.

"You stupid, bastard," Langston yelled as he moved toward Camron and reached for the gun. Camron held it tightly and raised it into the air, nearly out of Langston's reach.

"Give me the pistol, you son of a bitch, and I'll finish the job." Langston jumped up and grabbed the gun with both hands, pulling it down and trying to wrestle it from Camron's strong right hand. Then the gun fired.

The sound beat against their eardrums and echoed across the field as both men stopped struggling. And Camron wailed like a wounded animal. "Momma."

He struck Langston violently in the face with his free hand, causing him to let go of the pistol. Then he turned toward Luther, who was trying to hold Roberta upright.

Roberta's head fell forward and she could see her blouse turning crimson as blood oozed from a chest wound. The bullet had smashed into her breastbone, passed through her heart, and exited her back into Luther's left elbow.

He could barely hold Roberta up, and they slumped together onto the Berry Stone where he cradled her head in his lap. She looked up at him, whispering Camron's name as blood curled from her lips. She could say no more. Her heart had stopped and her lungs would no longer fill with air. Roberta Locklear was dying.

Camron knelt beside his mother, his anguished face in tears as he repeated over and over. "I'm so sorry, Momma. I'm so sorry. I didn't mean to hurt you."

Luther reached over with his right hand and pressed his left elbow, trying to staunch the flow of blood. He felt a slight bulge against the bone. It was the bullet, a wad cutter from the pistol, the same type of round that had killed Carl and was now ending Roberta's life. He could hear Ramona screaming in the background, even over the heart rending sobs of Camron, and then a swift movement caught his eye.

Langston realized he had no choice but to get hold of the gun and kill Camron, as well as Luther, or he and Ramona would be going to jail for the rest of their lives. He dove through the air reaching for the weapon, and grasped it firmly. The weight of his body knocked Camron over, but the young man would not let go of the pistol. They struggled in the soggy dirt, and then Camron pulled himself free. He rose up on one knee with the pistol pointing in Langston's face.

No one had heard the other car pull up behind the Jaguar. No one had seen the other man running across the field with a 9mm automatic pistol in his hand. But everyone heard the voice scream, "Drop the gun or I'll shoot." Detective Harris had been shadowing Luther since he left Greenville earlier that morning. He was now standing just behind Ramona, his pistol pointing directly at Camron.

"Not until this bastard's dead," Camron screamed. Two blasts from the pistol shattered Langdon's nose and forehead.

Harris crouched in firing position and fired twice. The first round passed harmlessly by, but the second smacked into the bicep of Camron's right arm, spinning him onto his back. The detective rose and took one step toward his prey, and was astonished when Camron rose up with both hands on his pistol.

As Harris raised his 9mm to fire, he saw the flash of light and heard the sound that sent a wad cutter into his chest. He stumbled backward several steps, nearly falling down, and Luther watched in horror as the old police detective reached up with his left hand, clutching himself as if he were in the midst of a fatal heart attack.

Harris fell to his knees then raised his pistol for one last shot at Camron, but as he squeezed the trigger he fell forward with his eyes closed. His grip on the pistol was firm, finger pressure on the trigger sufficient, and the 9mm automatic fired rapidly as it arced through the air.

Luther saw every one of the four flashes and watched in terror as Ramona toppled forward, two of the rounds striking her in the back. He waited for one of the errant bullets to find him and thought he heard it whistle by, when he heard Camron yell.

The young man fell on his back, holding his side where another 9mm round had entered. Twice wounded, Camron rolled over on his stomach and was struggling to get to his knees. Luther quickly surveyed the situation and realized he was the only one left who could walk out and summon help.

Langdon's head was torn open. Blood gurgled from Ramona's mouth with every dying breath, and Detective Harris lay still in the field. Roberta's hair was spread across his lap, a gentle smile upon her lips. She seemed as lovely in death as she had in life, and Luther realized, Roberta Locklear was finally at peace.

Camron groaned as he struggled to his knees. He raised himself up, waving the pistol at Luther who was trying to count the shots that had been fired. 'One for Roberta, two for Langdon, and one at Detective Harris; there's two more left, and he's going to shoot me.' But to his surprise the young man looked at him and said, "Go."

"Go now," Camron repeated as he struggled to breathe.

Luther was numb. He had faced certain death so many times in the last few moments that he didn't notice the drizzle had turned into rain. His left arm throbbed from shoulder to fingertips as he gently eased Roberta's head from his lap onto Richard Berry's grave marker. He rolled to his knees then used his right arm to push himself up. Slowly rising to his feet he looked over the bodies that littered the field.

"Tell them Momma was innocent. She didn't know."

Luther nodded, then staggered toward the Jaguar. He paused by the detective's body, wondering how he knew to come to Indian Wood. Then he remembered the phone call to Jimmy Bonner, telling of the change in plans. He bent low and whispered, "Thank you, Harris." Then he continued walking slowly toward his car.

The pistol fired again and Luther froze as the explosion echoed off the trees across the field. He spun around, looking back toward the great oak just as Camron's body fell over that of his mother. And they lay there together across the Berry Stone.

Luther stood for a long moment in the cold dark rain, thinking of a banner headline for the story he would have to write for his newspaper. But only one appeared on the front page in his mind... 'Another Massacre at Indian Wood.'

❖ ❖ ❖

A REQUIEM FOR QUITSNA

Luther sat on a small folding chair behind a waist high podium. It had been placed there, along with several others, under the great oak tree in the middle of the field. A single page of comments trembled slightly in his hands as he surveyed the gathering of dignitaries in the audience before him. They had come to acknowledge the legacy of Dr. Carl Lee Bowden, and to dedicate the newest state archaeological and historic site.

As administrator of Carl's estate, Luther had directed all the assets, along with significant contributions from himself and others, to purchase the five hundred acres near Quitsna known as Indian Wood. It had taken nearly two years to negotiate the sale and donate the property to the state. And it was his hope that after several more years of survey and excavation, that this historical property might one-day rival the pre-Columbian Pee Dee River Valley site of *Town Creek Indian Mound*.

As the warm spring sun climbed behind billowing cumulus clouds and their shadows danced across the field, Luther's thoughts drifted to a spot near the small bridge. He envisioned a paved area for visitors to park, and beside it a modest brick building where park rangers could offer a short video describing the site and its history. Afterwards, the Rangers would lead visitors on guided tours of a reconstructed Tuscarora Indian village, just as it may have appeared in 1712.

It was an ambitious plan, one that he and Veronica had conceived as a tribute to Carl. And it was their good fortune that her new husband's philanthropic family had generously endorsed the concept. They had also used their impressive social and political connections to ensure the idea would be well received in the state legislature.

Luther looked up and smiled at his former wife, sitting in the front row. It was a sad smile, and he wondered if she was truly happy, nestled in the bounty of all that Winston-Salem had to offer. She acknowledged him with a warm smile and gentle nod of her head. Then he heard the words from the Director of the North Carolina Museum of History that called him to the podium.

"And it is my great pleasure to introduce the man who has contributed so much of his time, energy and personal resources to the establishment of this, only the second site in North Carolina dedicated to our American Indian heritage... "